# FRANK McNAIR

# LIFE ON THE LINE

## Football, Rage and Redemption

Bagpiper Press™ – Winston Salem, North Carolina
Trade Paperbacks
*Worldwide*

2016 Bagpiper Press™ – Winston Salem, North Carolina
Copyright © 2016 by Frank McNair

Published in the United States of America by Bagpiper Press™ –
Winston-Salem, North Carolina
Bagpiper Press™ is trademark pending

Printed in the United States of America by Amazon Createspace
www.lifeonthelinebook.com

18   20   22   21   19   17

Book Design by Judy Jordan and Frank McNair

*Photo of football players © Richard Mabry*
*Author photograph © Tanya Odom*
*All other photographs © shutterstock*

*"Football is an honest game.
It's true to life.
It's a game about sharing.
Football is a team game.
So is life."*

Joe Namath
New York Jets


*"Football is the hardest and most beautiful of all
team sports. Where else do all eleven team members
have to execute their responsibilities perfectly,
and at the same time, to achieve a good outcome?*

Shaw Smith, Ph.D.
Davidson College

*When the going gets tough, the tough get going.*
*If you can't play hurt, you can't play at all.*
*Get up! You're killing the grass!*

Coaching Exhortations

*For my beloved Laura,*
*as always*

# 1 | Prelude

## Franklin

August in the South is a trial run in hell. It was hot as a firecracker in the classroom and sweat rolled down Franklin's back. He squirmed on the hard wooden seat. Mrs. McClellan was reviewing absence policies, PTA meetings, and such. Boring.

There was some new stuff now that he was in eighth grade and at a different school. All the eighth graders had been merged into a single junior high school, something about a space crunch. Changing classes, having more than one teacher, having your own locker, this was all new. And scary.

Franklin looked around the room to see how many kids he knew. Maybe half of them. There were a bunch from his old school, but also a lot he had never met. It was like starting over.

He checked out the girls. Some of them had bosoms pushing at the front of their blouses. A few of them had been fooling around with make-up. Franklin's friends were fascinated with bosoms. He didn't get it. Maybe that was just him.

"Psst, listen up!" The whisper was loud and urgent. Franklin half-turned in his desk, and Kenneth caught his eye. "You need to hear this." Kenneth whispered and nodded in the direction of Mrs. McClellan.

Franklin quickly realized why Kenneth was so persistent. The teacher was talking about sign-ups for the football team. He scrambled to pick up the thread of her announcement.

*...the informational meeting will be this afternoon at four o'clock at the*

*baseball field below Hillside Cemetery. The coaches will hand out release forms for parents to sign and a physical form for your doctor. Both forms must be completed before you can practice.*

*First practice, in shorts, t-shirts, and cleats, is next Monday. Coach McInnis invites anyone, experienced or not, to come out and join the team.*

Mrs. McClellan shuffled her papers and went on to an announcement about cheerleading.

Kenneth had introduced Franklin to football. The second week of third grade Kenneth asked Franklin if he wanted to play. They rode their bikes to practice at the scrubby field in front of the Presbyterian Church. It was the beginning of Franklin's football life. He was hooked from day one.

This was little league football, and there were only four teams. Franklin was a Blue Devil; Kenneth was a Golden Bear. Neither of them knew a damn thing about football, but Franklin owed Kenneth a debt for bringing him to the game. Kenneth quit football after fourth grade. He didn't have whatever madness drove Franklin through the agony of practice. But Franklin was captivated.

He wasn't even sure he *chose* football, it was more like football chose him. It was the only sport he had half a chance to be good at. He was too square and slow for basketball and lacked the hand-eye coordination for baseball. But football, at least on the offensive line, didn't require much. You had to be able to count to three for the snap count. You had to be willing to knock the snot out of someone. And you had to be willing to get the snot knocked out of you. That was it.

Franklin met all three requirements, but his greatest asset was his brain. He flashed back to the first time he realized he could *out-think* an opponent, could use his brain as a weapon. It was five years ago.

*He had never done this before, and he was scared. Sun baked the practice field, and sweat soaked his uniform. He felt the unfamiliar weight of shoulder pads drooping across his body and the heaviness of the helmet on his head. That all paled in comparison to his fear. Fear of being hit. Fear of being hurt. Fear of being embarrassed.*

*A line of six or so elementary-school-age boys snaked back from the site of what the coach called a "skills drill." The objective was to learn how offensive linemen block. As a fat, slow, clumsy kid, Franklin had been consigned to the offensive line from day one. It was the least desirable of all positions.*

*Because he was fifth in line, he had time to get a handle on what was going on before his turn came up. At the head of the line, facing the first player, was the coach. Coach Cooper they called him, though his first name was Clyde, and he ran a barbecue restaurant not far from the bank where Franklin's father worked.*

*Franklin studied what happened as the guys in front of him went forward. Each player would squat in his stance, then burst out of the stance when Coach blew the whistle. Each player tried to block Coach Cooper by slamming into the dummy positioned in front of them. And all of them were easily thwarted by the coach's counter-moves. Franklin was next.*

*He considered his options. It was not going to work to hit the dummy head on, he had four examples to prove it. What could he do differently? He chewed on the problem, then trembled as he squatted in the unfamiliar stance. His stomach was pressing on his lungs, and it was hard to breathe. Coach blew the whistle.*

*Franklin's squat legs exploded with all the power he could muster and he launched himself low and hard at Coach Cooper. It was an unexpected move and caught the coach completely off-guard. Franklin hit the coach just below the knees, flush on the shins, and the man grunted and toppled over. Franklin bulled on top of him in a damp pile, panting.*

*Waves of guilt swept over him. Had he hurt the coach? Franklin's breath got tight. He began to panic.*

*"Way to go!" Coach roared and leapt out from under Franklin. "You see that, guys? Sometimes you have to out-think your opponent. Franklin*

*did that. You see that? Way to go!" Coach slapped Franklin on the butt, and Franklin felt the adrenaline rush of redemption and approval.*

*There was nothing in his entire life that had ever felt like this. Franklin wanted to feel this way forever. He jogged back to the end of the line, grinning broadly, and determined to knock the next guy on his butt, too.*

Five years later, Franklin remembered this moment clearly, as if it had just happened.

Since that time, Franklin had played in dozens of football games. He had hit others, and he had been hit. He had won and lost and once busted his nose so bad it looked like the thing was going to come loose from his face. There was nothing in life like knocking the snot out of someone on the football field and having other people applaud. That didn't happen much in everyday life. At least not in Franklin's life.

He glanced around the room and wondered who else would be on the team this year. Harvey was sitting beside him; he would play. Franklin had played with him for several years in little league, though never on the same team. He was a decent quarterback.

Danny, across the room at the head of the first row, was a defensive end and running back. He'd surely play. Franklin envied Danny's athleticism. He was broad-shouldered and slim-waisted, with agility and speed and a feline quickness. Danny didn't say much, just flew to the ball and flattened the ball carrier or knocked down a pass intended for a stunned receiver.

Franklin scanned the rest of the students. It looked like there were only three football players in the room. He couldn't see the people directly behind him.

He swung his body slightly to the left and glanced over his shoulder. A girl with braces was sitting right behind him. He didn't know her. At the back of the row, behind her, was a guy who looked like he might be a football player. Franklin had seen him somewhere.

Franklin turned to face the teacher. Who *was* that dude? He looked older than everyone else, more like a high school student. Thick

4

shoulders. A face shed of baby fat. Franklin noticed his jaw line first thing. The guy had scowled, lowering his brow and tightening his lips. Franklin hoped the guy had not seen him stare. He'd have to sort it out later. It sounded like Mrs. McClellan was saying something important.

"All right, class, I know I have thrown a lot at you in the last half-hour. It is always boring trying to cover all the details at the beginning of the year; sometimes it bores *me*. Let's take a break and get to know each other since we're going to be together for the whole year. Why don't we start with this row?" Mrs. McClellan smiled and pointed at Franklin's row.

She picked up a piece of chalk and wrote as she talked. "I'd like each of you to introduce yourself and tell us three things. First, tell us your name and what you'd like us to call you. So, if your name is Susan, but your friends call you *Susie*, let us know."

"Second, I'd like you to tell us your favorite thing you did this summer." This went up on the board as the class groaned. "Finally, please tell us what you most want to get out of being in eighth grade." Mrs. McClellan wrote as the chalk squeaked, then she nodded at the girl sitting at the head of Franklin's row.

Bingo, Franklin thought. I will get to figure out who the guy at the back of my row is, and if I'm supposed to know him.

The girl at the head of the row went first. She was followed by some guy Franklin didn't know, wearing a damp and wrinkled blue shirt. When Franklin introduced himself, he gave his name and said something about Scout camp in answer to the second question. He said he hoped to make lots of new friends in answer to Mrs. McClellan's final question.

Franklin's answers were sincere when he gave them, but when they came out of his mouth he thought they sounded ridiculous. As he finished question three, he heard a half-stifled snort from the back of his row. It came from the guy whose name he couldn't remember.

The girl with braces went next, and Franklin couldn't wait for her to finish. Then a gravelly voice, it sounded like a man, came from the back of the row. Everyone turned to look, so Franklin felt free to turn around as well.

"My name is Bart Wagram and my friends, at least those who have any sense, call me 'Mister.' My favorite summer activity was lifting weights so I can kick some serious butt in football. I sure didn't go to any summer Scout camp. What I hope to get out of eighth grade this time around is to pass and go on to high school." Bart smirked, and the class giggled.

"Thank you, Bart," Mrs. McClellan said, ignoring the smirk. Then she added, "Class, please do not use words like 'butt' in my classroom. I'm sure you can find a word that serves you just as well, but is less offensive. I'd also ask you not to make fun of other people's answers; just give your answer."

She smiled at the class and continued, "Let's move to this row." She nodded toward the row where Danny was sitting, and Franklin turned to look at Danny. As he did, he again heard the half-stifled snort. It came from Bart Wagram.

That's it. Franklin had heard about Bart Wagram, they went to the same elementary school for a while. Bart was in third grade when Franklin was in first, so their paths rarely crossed. But Franklin knew all about him.

Bart was a terror in sports. And in life, too. He played all three major sports: baseball, basketball, and football and it was clear football was his favorite. Now that Bart had flunked eighth grade, he and Franklin would be on the same team. Franklin thought about Bart, maybe football is this guy's best subject in school. He chuckled to himself, careful not to laugh aloud.

The big clock on the wall ticked slowly toward three o'clock. Day one would soon be over. Only 179 days and Franklin would be in high school. The bell rang and there was a crush of folks trying to get out the door.

Franklin made a mental note to call his mother and let her know he'd be late because of football sign-ups. She would worry if he didn't call.

# 2 | The Corner Pocket

## *Bart*

"Coming through!" Bart shoved his way through the crowd blocking the classroom door and wedged himself into the hall. The other students looked lost, and Bart remembered that feeling. This year he wasn't lost; he was lonely. Repeating eighth grade meant Bart had been left behind by the friends he'd had since fourth grade. He was starting over.

His closest friends and football buddies had gone on to high school, where they were doing well. Murdock and Fairley were even going to play on the varsity team. They were skipping junior varsity altogether.

Bart knew he could play on the varsity if he ever got to high school. His father had been a badass football player. Bart was determined to be better.

His new classmates made Bart sick, especially that suck-up Franklin Gibson. *I went to Scout camp and I hope to make some new friends this year.* In his mind's ear Bart mimicked Franklin in a high-pitched, sing-song voice.

What was it about that kid? Bart put his mind up against the question. He didn't even know Franklin, though everyone knew *about* everyone else in a town as small as Laurinburg. In Bart's mind, everything came easy for Franklin. He didn't have a witch for a stepmother. His family had tons of money. Teachers loved him. Franklin was the opposite of Bart in every way. Bart was fit; Franklin was fat. Franklin had a regular family; Bart had a wreck of a family.

Bart stiffened his back, pulled himself up to his full height, and stood ramrod-straight like a Marine. He knew the ads: *The few. The proud. The Marines.* Sometimes life put you in a tough place and you had to man up. Kids like Franklin hadn't learned that. Hadn't had to learn it.

They would know something about tough places if they had to live with Doris Wagram. And Franklin Gibson was gonna find out about tough places if he came out for football.

Bart made his way down the hall and out into the mid-afternoon glare. The heat of the day hit him like he had run into a wall. He was glad practice didn't begin today. The football field would be flat and hard and scorched. He remembered early practice from last year, with heat shimmering off the field.

The field belonged to the Laurinburg recreation department, and it was close to the school. Bart could be there in fifteen minutes, ten if he hustled. He felt for the money in his jeans pocket, found it, and headed to the Corner Pocket.

The Corner Pocket was the only pool hall in town. It was a quarter-mile from school. Bart could see the crooked Budweiser sign the minute he got to the road. The sign was old and faded, like the place itself. It hung cock-eyed from a rusty pole that had once been painted silver. The parking lot was a rutted gravel and mud puddle affair, littered with empty cigarette packages and thousands of cigarette butts.

The pool hall served beer, so no one under twenty-one was supposed to go inside, but old Rufus didn't care. Bart, Fairley, and Murdock hung out in there last year, and no one said a thing. By the end of the school year, they could shoot a fair game of eight-ball. Bart was the ace by far.

There weren't many people who played pool in the middle of the afternoon. Bart figured he would know them all. He slipped around back so no one could see him and stepped into the cool, damp blackness.

It was so dark Bart was disoriented. He had forgotten how long it took for his eyes to adjust and had to wait for his pupils to dilate. He remembered a discussion in health class about rods and cones in the human eye, and wondered which of those helped him see in this dump.

There wasn't a window in the whole place. Except for lights above each pool table, and a few above the bar, there wasn't any artificial light either. Bart could make out the faint shape of the pool tables and the blue glow of a television perched above the bar. Someone stood under the television.

"Hey Bart, what's shaking?" Rufus spotted him.

"Rufus, is that you? I can't see a damn thing in here. It's bright outside."

"Hot, too, ain't it? Come on in. I'm over here at the bar." Bart's eyes began to adjust. "What you been up to this summer?"

"Not much. Working out for football, mostly. Making a little dough mowing grass. And trying to stay out of trouble with my stepmother. I'm on the way to football sign-ups and had a few minutes to kill. Want to play a quick game of eight-ball?"

"How come you ain't playing at the high school? Murdock was in here the other day talking about you and what fun y'all had playing ball last year."

Bart hated this. Who wants to be known as the guy who flunked two grades before he got to high school?

"I got a do-over on eighth grade." Making a joke out of it sometimes worked. "They didn't think I got it right the first time. Now what about that game of eight-ball?"

"Sure. Rack 'em up and break. How's the team going to be this year?"

"Don't know. All of 'em just moved up from the elementary school. Last year's team is all at the high school now. All except me."

"Tough break. How did you manage to flunk eighth grade? You're plenty smart enough. I know that from your hanging around here. What's the deal?"

"Lots of stuff going on at home, man. Now, are we gonna play pool or what?"

"I'm gonna whup you bad, is what I'm gonna do. Sorry it's tough at home. You deserve better. Want something to drink?"

"Yeah. You got a cold Sun Drop in the cooler?"

"Sure thing."

Bart racked the balls and broke them with a crisp shot. The balls spun wildly across the green felt, but none went in a pocket. He took the cold, wet bottle from Rufus and sucked down a long draw. The citrus sweet taste was a perfect antidote to the late summer day.

"Man, that's good," Bart said. "How much do I owe you?"

"The game's on me. The soft drink is a quarter." Rufus took his shot and the ball rolled slowly into a pocket. His next shot yielded nothing. Bart's turn also yielded nothing.

Bart caught Rufus's eye and flipped him a quarter for the Sun Drop. The quarter spun brightly though the air before Rufus reached out a big right hand and snatched it in mid-flight. He slapped it down on the top of his left hand and called out to Bart, "Call it. Double or nothing. You could be playing for free *and* drinking for free."

"Sure. Heads."

Rufus uncovered the coin. "Heads it is. Lucky dog." He flipped the quarter back to Bart and lined up his shot. The balls clicked together. One rolled into a pocket and Rufus moved for his second shot.

"Hey Rufus, you know a kid named Franklin Gibson?"

"Nope. What about him?"

"He's in my class. I remember him from elementary school. Sort of a chunky, goody-two-shoes kind of kid."

Rufus laughed. "Why do you think I'd know him? We don't get many kids like that in this place."

"Hell, Rufus, you know everybody. You've lived here almost forty years. Think, man. Do you know anyone named Gibson?"

Rufus stared into space. "Well, yeah, there was a kid in my class in elementary school named Gibson. Fact is, I think his first name was Frank. He didn't go to high school here, went to some fancy-smancy prep school up in Virginia."

"What happened to him?"

"How would I know? I ain't his mama. I think his old man worked at the bank. Maybe that's where he works, too. Why are you so interested in this guy?"

"Nothing. It's something about this kid. You look at him, and you just want to knock the shit out of him. You ever felt like that?"

"Nah, man. I'm a lover, not a fighter." Rufus lined up his second shot. He missed, then took a long look at Bart. "This Gibson kid do something to you?"

"No. Just sat there at his desk looking like some sort of candyass. You telling me you never wanted to kick a guy's tail just for how he looks, just to see if you could?"

"Well, maybe once in a while when I was younger. But not in a long time. I was running out of teeth." Rufus laughed and smiled an enormous gap-toothed grin. Bart never noticed how many teeth Rufus was missing. Almost all the front ones were gone, top and bottom.

"You really get all those knocked out fighting?" Bart was fascinated. Rufus had never talked about this.

"Yeah. You should have seen the other guy; he went to the hospital in a meat wagon. Now, you gonna play pool or you just gonna stand there and shoot the shit?"

Bart lined up his shot, he had to get the bridge to reach across the table, then tapped the cue ball gently. The target ball rolled slowly across the felt, paused at the pocket, then dropped in with a clunk.

"Lucky dog," Rufus said.

"Lucky and good ain't the same thing. Now watch this."

The balls had split in a way that Bart thought he could run the table. He lined up his next shot, took it, and heard another soft clunk. Again. Clunk.

"Some gratitude," Rufus said. "I give you a game and a soft drink, then you kick my ass. I'm glad there ain't nobody else in here to see it."

Bart ran the table, then glanced up at the yellowed clock above the bar. It was three-forty eight. He had twelve minutes to get to the team meeting, and he was going to have to hustle. "Thanks, man. I hate to run, but I got to get to sign-ups. You'll get me next time!"

"Fat chance," Rufus said. "You're on the way to being a world-class hustler. Good luck with football. Sorry to hear about the school thing."

"Thanks," Bart said. Then, more softly, "Me too."

"Oh, and Bart...?"

"Yeah?"

"Take it easy on the candyass, will ya?" Rufus winked at Bart, who shot him the bird.

Bart set out for the practice field at a slow jog, picking up the pace as he got closer to the field. It hadn't gotten any cooler, and sweat was pouring off of him by the time he reached the hill above the field. His stomach gurgled and he burped loudly. He wished he hadn't drunk the Sun Drop. It wasn't good the second time around.

He trotted down the hill to the field and scanned the group. There was Coach McInnis with some short, thick grown-up Bart didn't know. Maybe he was a coach, too. A bunch of kids milled around the coaches, talking nervously. Some of them looked like they might be able to play a little bit. He recognized Harvey and Danny from class with Mrs. McClellan. Bart remembered hearing about them when they played little league ball last year. Folks said that Harvey had an arm like a rocket; he could really air it out.

Bart wondered if the team was going to be any good. Maybe. Maybe not. Hard to tell at this point. Either way, he figured he was gonna have a heck of a good year. He had worked out all summer so he could jack some jaws big time.

"All right, men, listen up." It was Coach McInnis, and the group immediately stopped talking. "Head over to the bleachers so we can see and hear each other. I want to make some announcements and pass around a sign-up sheet. We'll use the first three rows over there, about ten guys to a row. Hustle up now, we've got a lot to cover."

Bart turned toward the bleachers and there was Franklin Gibson, sitting right in the middle of the bleachers like a teacher's pet. "Man," Bart thought, "there's something about that mama's boy I don't like at all."

Bart jogged toward the bleachers and took a seat on the fourth row up, right in the middle, overlooking the team and above the coach. He wanted to eyeball everyone.

# 3 | Sign-Ups

## *Franklin*

Franklin saw a knot of students at the front of the class, all trying to get out the door at once. Then Bart Wagram came busting through the group, pushing and shoving like it was fourth and goal. What was his hurry? There was an hour before sign-ups, and the field wasn't fifteen minutes from school. Bart seemed mad at the world. Franklin would bet anything that Bart didn't have to call home to report in.

But Franklin had to call *his* mother. She made him promise to do it, just like when he was a kid. Franklin read about mothers who practiced *smother*hood, not *mother*hood. They hovered over their kids so much that the kids never got to make an independent decision, a mistake, or a choice of their own.

That's my mom, Franklin thought. And if Bart had a mother like mine he wouldn't be cussing and bullying people and flunking grades in school.

Franklin wondered what his mama would think about him playing football with eighth-graders, especially Bart Wagram. Franklin knew his mom didn't get football. In fact, she didn't get *guys*. Maybe it was because she didn't have any brothers.

He had drawn the line when she wanted him to take an umbrella on a Scout camping trip. Even though it had rained like crazy and an umbrella would have been handy, he was not going to be the only guy with an umbrella on the camping trip. Next it would be fuzzy bunny slippers.

The knot of classmates was still hung up in the doorway. Franklin had plenty of time, so he walked over to chat with Mrs. McClellan. He reintroduced himself and asked her where she had taught the previous year. He told her how much he was looking forward to the year and how he had enjoyed the way she conducted class, especially the introductions. She seemed pleased and that made Franklin happy.

The room emptied. Franklin headed down the hall to the school office. There was no one else in line to use the phone, he couldn't believe it, and the secretary said he was welcome to use it as long as he was quick about it.

He called home and told his mother he was going to football sign-ups and would be home by six. Franklin figured it would actually be five-thirty, but he had to give himself a cushion. If he was late, she'd be all spun-up and worried.

"Be careful, honey," she said to him. And then, "Don't get hurt."

"Okay, Mom. See you in a little while." What did she think he was going to do, fall off the bleachers? Stick himself with a pencil? It was hard to get hurt at football *sign-ups*.

He thanked the school secretary for letting him use the phone, and she asked his name. "I'm Franklin Gibson," he said. Then he remembered his manners and added, "I'm sorry, I should have introduced myself when I first walked in."

"Don't worry about it. I thought I recognized you. We go to the same church as your family, and my husband Bob works with your father down at the bank. I'm Mrs. Robertson."

"Nice to meet you, Mrs. Robertson." Franklin stuck out his hand. He couldn't remember the rule about shaking hands with ladies.

"It's nice to meet you, too, Franklin." Mrs. Robertson took his hand. "You have excellent manners. I look forward to seeing you in school this year."

"Yes ma'am. Me, too."

Franklin left the office and stepped into the afternoon. The glare bouncing off the concrete driveway was so bright it hurt his eyes. He raised his hand to shield them. It was blazing hot.

Franklin had resolved not to be late for sign-ups, and so he headed to the field. It was only half a mile, and he wanted to get there early.

"Hey! Wait-up!" Someone shouted, and Franklin turned to see Harvey and Danny behind him. They jogged to catch up, then slowed to a walk. The three boys hugged the side of the road under the oak trees, walking from one puddle of shade to another.

"You guys excited about football?" Franklin asked.

"Yeah," Harvey answered. "I've been waiting for this day since the end of football season last year. What kind of team do you guys think we're gonna have?"

"Sounds like Bart Wagram is ready." Danny added. "I wonder if we're ready for him."

Franklin remembered Bart's snorts during introductions. And his sarcasm, *I sure didn't go to any summer Scout camp.* Bart made Franklin nervous. It wasn't that he didn't like Bart. He didn't even really know the guy. It was just something in the wind. Like Bart wanted to bust Franklin's mouth, or worse.

"You guys ever played with Bart before?" Franklin didn't want to appear scared.

"I've never played with him, but I've heard about him." It was Danny. "They say he's a headhunter. Just as soon crack your head as look at you. He runs wide-open all the time, and he don't take nothing from nobody. I heard he even attacked a custodian in elementary school."

"My brother was there when it happened," Harvey spoke up. "He was in Bart's class when they were both in fifth grade. The janitor, I think it was Old Man Thomas, told Bart to do something. Bart kicked him square in the shin. It was a big deal. They suspended Bart for a week, but Bart didn't care. He said he stayed home all day, watching TV and eating popcorn."

"What about that time when he was in seventh grade?" It was Danny again. "I thought they were going to toss him out for good after that fight."

The stories about Bart were legion, but this was the most famous of them all. In seventh grade Bart had gotten into an epic fight on the playground. Bart was the strongest guy in the school, and his opponent was the biggest. As the fight unfolded, one teacher said, "I'm not going to risk my life to break it up. They're both bigger than I am. Just let them work it out like two young stallions. Then we'll patch 'em up once they're finished."

They worked it out, all right. Bart and the other guy rolled across the playground, flailing each other while grunting and swearing and sweating. They wound up knocking over two huge trash cans and a bunch of benches, spilling garbage over most of the schoolyard.

No one ever knew what the fight was about, but the end result was clear. Bart pounded the other guy, leaving his nose bloody and both eyes black and blue. Other than getting dirty, Bart didn't seem any worse for the wear.

The maintenance man finally broke it up. He grabbed each of them by the collar and half-dragged them to the principal's office. Bart gloated even as he was horse-collared, turning to some wide-eyed younger kids watching the fight. "I really packed his lunch, didn't I?" The maintenance guy told him to shut up and then hustled off with both of them.

"I guess we should just be glad he's on our side," Harvey added. "Imagine having to play against the sumbitch."

"Let's hope he *is* on our side," Franklin added. "That guy seems mad at everybody. Did you see how he pushed through everyone to get out of the classroom?" Franklin waited for a reply, but the incident hadn't made much of an impression on Danny or Harvey.

"Someone told me Bart would have made the varsity team at the high school if he had passed eighth grade," Danny said. "I know Murdock and Fairley made it, and they played with him last year. He's better than either one of them. Think about that, we're gonna be playing with a guy who could be playing varsity football. That guy's a man, is what he is."

"He ought to be a man. He's flunked two grades. I bet he's sixteen years old if he's a day. Heck, maybe they'll let him drive the team bus." Harvey laughed at his joke and the others joined in.

They walked in silence for a bit, still trying to stay in the shade of the oak trees. The lone highway they had to cross was shimmering black asphalt with transfer trucks whizzing by. They waited a while, then dashed across, cleared a small rise, and saw the field come into view.

Franklin had never set foot on this field. It was way across town from where he lived. But he knew where it was, just down the hill from the cemetery where they buried his Grandmama in September of last year.

He pushed that memory down and checked his watch. Three fifty-two. He was not going to be late. He didn't have much control over how slow he was, bad genes and all. But he could be on time.

"Hey look, there's Coach McInnis. Hey, Coach!" Danny spoke up and waved. Coach turned and threw up a hand, but Franklin wasn't sure he knew who he was waving at.

Coach McInnis was standing in the middle of a crowd of twenty-five to thirty boys, all sweating and milling about. Franklin didn't know half these guys. They must have come from the other elementary schools, the newer one on the west side of town, or some of the ones out in the county.

A whistle broke the nervous buzz of conversation, and the whole group stopped its chatter. "All right men, listen up. Let's head over to the bleachers so we can all see and hear. I want to make some announcements and then pass around a sign-up sheet. We'll use the first three rows over there, about ten guys to a row. Hustle up. We've got a lot to cover." Coach McInnis turned and headed towards the bleachers.

The boys followed him, jogging, and Franklin took a seat in the middle of the second row. Danny and Harvey sat in front of him on the front row, scuffing their feet in the dirt and waiting. Some guys wore cleats; they made a tremendous racket when they clattered over the metal bleachers.

Coach McInnis thanked them for coming and introduced a short, muscular man as the assistant coach. He explained that Coach Wittenburg had been a small-college All American lineman at Lenoir Rhyne College.

Then he told them about the season: the number of games, some of their opponents, and so forth. They would play a few games at home, in the same stadium the high school team used. The balance of the games would be on the road. Franklin glanced around as the coach talked. He saw some familiar faces from his years playing little league football.

Coach began talking details and Franklin focused. "I need each of you to bring your release form and your proof-of-insurance on Monday. Show up at four o'clock sharp, in shorts, t-shirts, and football shoes. For those of you who don't have a jock strap, get one and wear it to our first practice. Don't forget to put it on right; the pouch goes in the front." Coach's eyes crinkled at the corners when he laughed.

"We'll do a light conditioning work-out on Monday, and then fit you for your equipment. We've got a lot to cover, so we're going to practice every weekday for the next three weeks. We'll be hitting by the end of the first week."

"When you're ready, we'll have our first game-type scrimmage with referees and the whole business. Then we head into the games and the season. That's all I've got. Does anyone have questions?" No one spoke.

"See you Monday, then. Four o'clock sharp." Coach McInnis's whistle shrilled loudly to dismiss them.

# 4 | Doubts

## *Franklin*

Franklin said goodbye to Harvey and Danny, then headed home. It wasn't even five o'clock. He would be home in plenty of time to placate his mom.

At the end of practice Coach had solicited questions, but no one had spoken.

Franklin had a million questions. *Am I gonna be good enough? Will I get to play? Will I get hurt? How many games will we win? Will I make any new friends? Will I ever have a girlfriend? Why does Bart Wagram have it in for me? Who else will hate me at this new school?*

These weren't questions a player would ask a coach, or even a friend. They were questions kids asked themselves, in silence, when no one was around. Then the kids lived their lives and got their answers as life revealed them.

Franklin wondered if other kids shared his questions.

*Am I good enough? Will I get to play?*

Franklin had played football – if you could call it that – last year. He couldn't make the weight limit for little league football, just like he couldn't make it in sixth grade, either. The weight limit thing made no sense to him; football rewarded size and speed, but he was rejected for being too big. You didn't see any fat guys getting kicked out of the NFL.

He recalled the stupid weight limit: a hundred and thirty pounds. In uniform. Franklin weighed every bit of a hundred and fifty last year, stark naked. He couldn't have gotten to one-thirty on a diet of celery

21

stalks and tap water. So he couldn't play on the team with his friends.

Instead, he played on a team way over on the east side of town. Many of the kids were from the adjacent mill village. They were bigger and meaner than Franklin, and they thrashed him from day one.

He didn't fit in. These guys were older than he was, not so much chronologically, though that was also true, but in life experience. They had black hairs sproinging out of their legs, and most of them smoked Marlboros. They made jokes he didn't understand. He tried, but it was like they were all inside jokes. And he seemed to be the butt of most of them.

Then his grandmother died in September, and he just didn't have a heart for football or much of anything else. He had never been the most agile guy, but he had usually been able to out think his opponents. Not last year. Last year he had been tired and sad and afraid.

Franklin remembered plodding the mile and a half to practice. He would hide in the brush on the border of the field and wait until the team finished warm-up exercises before he trotted up to join them. The coach made him run laps when he pulled this stunt, but it saved him from push-ups and leg lifts. It also pissed the coach off. Maybe that was one of the reasons he played so little. He would not make that mistake this year.

Coach McInnis seemed like a nice guy. And Franklin liked the fact that Coach Wittenburg was short and square. He might get the fat kid thing. Maybe it would all work out. Maybe he would get to play.

*Will I make any new friends?*

Franklin worried about the new school and was anxious about all the changes. He was like his mom this way. At his old school, seventh graders were king of the hill. He didn't feel like the king of anything at this new school.

There were twenty-one classrooms in the old school, and he had been a student in a third of them. He knew where every bathroom was, knew how to go down in the basement to find the custodian, and was one of the chosen few who operated the projector in the auditorium.

At the new school he was just another kid from across town who had to ask where the bathroom was. It was different, and lonely. It wasn't like he had lost any friends, exactly, but things were changing too fast. Some of his friends had real jobs now, and others were into rock bands and thinking about cars or girls. Franklin still felt like a little kid inside, though he also was thinking about girls.

*Will I ever have a girlfriend?*

There were some nice looking girls in his homeroom. Not that it mattered. No girl his age would ever be interested in him. Because he had a younger sister, little kids, boys *and* girls, liked Franklin. He'd even made a couple of bucks babysitting, though he didn't brag about that to the guys.

Ladies over the age of thirty loved him, too. But girls his own age always told him they thought of him as a brother. He already had a sister. He didn't need any more.

He would probably never have a date in his whole life. Maybe that was okay. What would he do on a date with a girl? He couldn't drive a car. And whatever in the world would you talk about for a whole evening? Franklin could see why all the high school kids went to the movies on their dates. It would fill up half the time, and you wouldn't have to think up stuff to talk about. Still, it might be nice to have a girlfriend.

*Why does Bart Wagram have it in for me?*

Franklin chewed on this question. It was clear that he chapped Bart's ass. Franklin didn't know what to make of this, but he knew he was afraid of Bart. Bart was one mean motor scooter. Franklin knew that in his heart. And in his heart, he also knew he was chicken.

He glanced up and was almost home, like he had walked home in a daze.

When he stepped into the house, Franklin carried his books in his right hand, his release forms in his pocket, and his questions in his head. The questions were the heaviest of all.

# 5 | Bullied

## *Franklin*

Franklin was running late so he picked up his pace. They had been practicing in full uniforms for five days, and he was sore and stiff.

When he got to the field, Coach McInnis was unloading dummies and balls from the trunk of his car. Half the team stood by, joshing with each other in the run-up to practice. They'd be running laps before you knew it, and Franklin had to pee some kind of bad.

He ducked into the woods and unlaced his football pants, groping urgently through the layers. He was about to explode and was startled by an unexpected rustling behind him. He glanced over his shoulder just as he heard the question. "Hey short dick, how's your hammer hanging?" It was Bart.

Bart unlaced his pants and sneered at Franklin. "This, my friend, is a dick. What you got there is a wee wee." Franklin hurriedly finished peeing, laced his pants, and ran from the woods. Bart laughed after him, "What's the matter? Ain't you ever seen a dick before?" Franklin's face flushed as he raced to join the team.

"All right boys, circle up!" Coach McInnis shouted into the crowd. "Let's do a couple of quick laps and then some warm-up calisthenics. We've got a lot to do, so get hot. Take off!" They were off. Some guys sprinted ahead as Franklin lumbered to keep up. Bart slipped into the main group of runners just as it passed him coming out of the woods. "Hey, short dick!" he hissed at Franklin. Just like him, Franklin thought. He dodged half a lap of running and still found time to torment me.

25

Bart ran so much faster than Franklin that they were soon out of earshot of each other, which brought a temporary end to the torment. After the laps, the boys formed a series of irregular rows and prepared for calisthenics. Coach McInnis watched, scowling. "Listen up, guys," he shouted, "you look like crap! These rows look like snakes, all squirmy and squiggly. Square it up! How you practice is how you play!"

The boys now measured the space between themselves and their surrounding team members, eyeing Coach McInnis as they did it. They were soon arrayed in perfectly straight lines and rows. "That's more like it!" he bellowed. They began the warm-up exercises.

Franklin had quickly learned that this was an entirely different level of football than he had ever played. It was both more violent and more beautiful. The defensive backs were graceful as they leapt to knock down passes intended for the wide receivers. It was like a vicious, savage dance.

He loved watching the punter boom tight spirals high into the clear blue sky. This football was much more like what you saw on television, not like the scrum of twenty-two noisy little kids who ran into each other and fell down immediately. This was the game of warriors in the trenches. As a lineman, Franklin embraced the gladiator model.

The hitting was violent. The team hadn't had a full-out scrimmage, but a couple of folks were already nursing bad sprains. Everyone was nicked-up in some way or the other. One teammate had a half-dozen stitches in his hand when he was trampled by someone whose shoe was missing a cleat. The screw that held the missing cleat gouged a jagged rip in the flesh on the top of the hand. Franklin could see white bone glistening through the skin just before the kid was whisked off to the emergency room.

The guy leading calisthenics called for them to bridge on their necks, and Franklin groaned to himself. He lay on his back, grabbed his face-mask with both hands, and pushed hard with his feet. The sky rotated in his facemask as his back arched and he was bridged only on the top of his helmet and the heels of his feet.

The whole world appeared upside down from this vantage point: trees where sky should be, and below the line of trees nothing but blue sky and blazing sun. The exercise was designed to strengthen neck muscles, but it made Franklin disoriented and seasick. He was glad when it was over and everything went back to right-side-up.

The team finished warm-ups and began stretching. These didn't feel like work, but Coach said they were important to prevent cramps and muscle pulls. Franklin sat on the ground with his left leg extended in front of him and his right leg bent at the knee. He grabbed his left foot and felt the stretch in the back of his left calf and thigh. He breathed into the stretch, leaned forward as far as he could, and the muscles in his lower back began to lengthen. It was a great way to end warm-ups; he felt limber and supple, like he had been good to his body. It was a paradoxical beginning before moving on to practice, where his body was a weapon.

After the laps, the warm-ups, and the stretching, the team broke into groups for what the coaches called "position work." Coach Wittenburg took the linemen, while Coach McInnis took the backs and linebackers.

Franklin had no idea what drills the backs did; he had been consigned to the line from day one of third-grade football practice. But he knew exactly what the linemen did: they practiced knocking the crap out of each other.

They blasted out of their stances low and hard and tried to bulldoze over each other. They practiced getting knocked down and jumping up immediately. They ran into each other at full speed. They got dirt and spit and sweat and snot all over each other. They bled and they swore and they occasionally fought, sometimes out of real anger, sometimes out of frustration and exhaustion.

Practice for a lineman was bereft of glory. It was all fingers in the eye, rolled ankles, banged up knuckles, and a mouth full of dirt. This is why the linemen considered the receivers, running crisp routes down the field with little contact from the defenders, prima donnas.

Football teams always have tension. There's the natural tension between those who want to star and those who are stars. There's the tension between the offense and the defense, especially when one unit markedly outperforms the other. And there's the tension between the linemen and the glory boys in the backfield. It's not always in the forefront. But it's always there, waiting to pop up when something hooks it.

After the linemen had bashed themselves bloody, Coach Wittenburg gave them a break. "Take off your bonnets, boys, and grab some water. We'll fire this mother back up in ten minutes."

Franklin and his comrades gathered in the shade of the trees bordering the field and gulped water from the battered dipper in the galvanized bucket. "Hey man, take it easy!" one teammate hollered as someone greedily poured the whole dipper of water into his mouth. Rivulets of water ran down either side of his chin. "That water's got to last for all of us, man. Don't waste it!" Coach McInnis gave the backs a break, too, and soon the whole team was gathered around the water bucket, teasing and making fun of each other. This was Franklin's favorite part of practice.

After the water break, it was back to work. This time Coach McInnis took the entire offense to install some plays. Coach Wittenburg gathered the defensive players for some controlled hitting.

Franklin trotted off with the offense to learn the plays, while Bart, as a middle linebacker, headed over with the defense. Coach promised everyone they would meet for a few full-speed plays at the end of practice.

The drills were uneventful. There were four plays, and the team worked until everyone understood them. It was really only two new plays, a trap off tackle and a sweep around the end of the line. But, since you could run each play either to the right or to the left, it wound up being four unique plays.

This was the part of football Franklin found the easiest, the thinking part. It had taken him years to will himself past his clumsiness, so he could succeed in the physical parts of football. But the thinking part was a snap. It puzzled Franklin that his teammates couldn't see the plays were mirror images of each other. Coach had to approach each play like he was starting from scratch, like the guys had never seen a football.

Franklin looked at his teammates. Maybe it wasn't a handicap having people on the team who weren't all that quick mentally. He should give them a break. He wasn't all that quick physically, and they didn't seem to judge him.

He could hear the defense practicing across the field; an occasional shrieked profanity let him know Bart was still there. Once there was a sharp whistle, and he heard Coach Wittenburg screaming. Franklin couldn't make out what the Coach was saying, but he saw Bart take off on a lap, head down and running fast. Franklin smiled. This was payback for the lap Bart ducked when they were pissing in the woods.

The offense finally ran through all four plays at half-speed with no mistakes and Franklin was relieved to get one more shot at the water bucket. The defense got a breather, too, and everyone was excited about the opportunity for some live-action practice.

Franklin sniffed around a bit and discovered why Bart had to take the lap. Coach Wittenburg was pretty cool about swearing; he did a fair amount of it himself. But Bart, in a fury during a drill, called a teammate "cocksucker" and earned himself a lap. Some things even Bart couldn't get away with.

Coach McInnis whistled the team together and talked about what would happen as the offense and defense met for a few live-action plays. There would be no kick-offs and no punts, just a controlled practice where the offense got the ball on the twenty-yard line and tried to move it down the field. Coach McInnis would command the offense and Coach Wittenburg would direct the defense.

He stressed that everyone was to stop hitting as soon as the play was whistled dead. The objective was to determine if the team was making any progress, not to kill each other. As a final point, Coach emphasized that no one was to hit the quarterback at any time. It was important to keep him in one piece, at least until the first game.

Coach McInnis split the team into offensive and defensive squads and called the first play. It was the off-tackle trap play they had just learned. The offense broke from the huddle and headed to the line. Bart, anchoring the defense from his middle-linebacker slot, loomed over Franklin. "Hey short-dick," he whispered, "I'm gonna smash your head in." At just that moment the play erupted, and Bart dashed through the off-tackle hole, only to be flattened by the trapping tackle's block. The play worked far better than anyone expected, and the back dashed through the hole for a fifteen-yard gain.

Bart was lying on the ground, stunned. Franklin took a few steps and stood over him. "How's your hammer hanging now, peckerhead?" The words sprang from Franklin's mouth like they had a life of their own. He was astonished he'd actually *said* it.

Bart leapt to his feet and shoved Franklin in the chest, but the coaches pulled them apart before things could escalate. Franklin suspected he would regret his remark.

Bart was enraged now. He was running up and down the defensive line, slapping people on the butt. Franklin could hear the shouted exhortations. Clearly, Bart was the quarterback of the defense.

The next play was a screen pass in the right flat. As the offense approached the line of scrimmage, Bart was wild with energy. Franklin anticipated the worst as he snapped the ball. Bart rushed directly at Franklin, reading the play all the time. He saw the screen develop, screamed "screen pass" to alert his teammates, and then flew to his left towards the screen and the receiver. He split the blockers and arrived at the same time the ball landed in the hands of the back. Bart destroyed the receiver.

Franklin didn't see the hit, as much as he *heard* it. When he looked back, he saw the ball squirt in one direction and the receiver's helmet roll in another. Someone screamed "fumble," and a defender covered the ball just as the coach whistled the play dead.

Bart bounced up from the pile before the coach could arrive to check on the receiver who lost his bonnet. No one was hurt. Bart brushed past

Franklin on the way back to the defensive side of the ball. "Your ass is mine," he rasped.

The balance of the practice was uneventful. Sometimes the offensive plays were flawless, with blockers opening wide lanes and backs sprinting through the holes for big yardage. The passing game looked good, too. Harvey could sling pinpoint spirals forty yards, right on the money. A few of the receivers had fingers like Spiderman and could web the ball in. Franklin was encouraged.

The defense was just as stout. There were times when Franklin was amazed by what he saw: defenders shedding blocks to get to the ball-carrier, and vicious open-field tackles that stopped sure-fire touchdowns. It was a good, sharp practice, especially for folks who had only been at it a few days.

Coach McInnis called them all together to talk about what he had seen. His enthusiasm was obvious. Then he made them an offer they couldn't refuse. Practice always closed with wind sprints, a dozen of them, fifty yards each. Franklin hated this part. Twelve wind sprints at fifty yards was a third of a mile. Franklin was an endomorph, built for comfort, not for speed, and he hated to run unless it was purposeful.

Coach's offer was this: run five plays, run them all out, and practice is done. No sprints. A cheer went up from the team, and then the offense and defense clustered around their respective coaches.

The ferocity level inched up a notch. The energy in the huddle was electric, and the passion coming from the defense was unmistakable. The first couple of plays were pretty much a draw, everyone was so jacked-up and tight that neither side dominated. Then Coach McInnis huddled the offense around him and suggested a quarterback draw. The quarterback would drop back as if to pass, freezing the defensive backs for fear of giving up a completion. The offensive line would block their opponents out towards the sidelines, opening a seam right up the gut for the quarterback to scoot through the defense.

While Coach McInnis was directing the offense, Coach Wittenburg gathered the defense around him. He wasn't trying to embarrass the offense; he knew you couldn't win games without a well-balanced team. On the other hand, the defense belonged to him, and he wanted them to be all they could be. So he took a chance.

All afternoon he had wanted to blitz a linebacker, but had held back so his team could master the fundamentals of their defensive scheme. Now he decided to go for it. He reminded them that no one was to hit the quarterback. Then he outlined the defensive assignments for the blitz package, and told Bart to blitz right up the middle of the offense. Bart's eyes lit up in anticipation.

The offense broke the huddle, and Franklin trotted to the line. Bart was there to greet him, standing directly over the ball. Bart was showing blitz; Franklin wondered if it was for real. Each play was like a chess match, all about appearance versus reality, deception and misdirection. Franklin bent over the ball and tried to read the tendons in Bart's calves and feet. Sometimes you could tell, just by the way a player positioned his feet, whether he was really going to come at you. Franklin couldn't tell.

The quarterback stepped into position and Franklin felt hands under his rump. Bart was jumping up and back on the line of scrimmage like a maniac. Harvey shouted the signals and Franklin snapped the ball. Bart hadn't been faking; he bull-rushed into Franklin low and hard, standing him upright with the force of the impact. Franklin fought back, churning his legs to force Bart into an outside lane. Fully extended, Franklin was at his most vulnerable. He was having success driving Bart to the outside when Bart brought his right fist up hard and fast into Franklin's groin.

The world went bright white, then red, then deep black; Franklin crumpled to his knees. He heard the play going on around him, even as he fell to the ground in agony.

The distant sound of the whistle let him know the play was over, and it was then that Franklin's teammates noticed him in a fetal position. "Hey, over here! Franklin got hit in the family jewels."

Franklin's eyes were closed and he wasn't breathing. He wasn't even sure he could breathe, but he *could* open his eyes. He chanced a glance. The coaches were there, along with several teammates. He tried breathing. Nothing. Coach McInnis spoke. "What happened, man? You get hit in the 'nads?"

"Yeah," he gasped. It was all he could say. He wouldn't tell on Bart. This was between the two of them. It had nothing to do with the coaches. "Yeah, I got hit in the balls."

Coach Wittenburg rolled Franklin over on his back and grabbed the waistband of his pants. He slowly lifted Franklin's midsection up and down a couple of times. The pain moderated. Coach encouraged Franklin to draw his knees up to his chest, and the pain faded a bit more.

Franklin rolled over on his knees, his chest tucked down on his thighs, his head close to the ground. He looked like a supplicant to the gods of rage and violence. He decided he wasn't going to throw up, rose slowly from the ground, and shuffled a few steps.

Coach McInnis whistled the team together around the spot where Franklin was standing. "Great practice, guys. You gave it all you've got today. I'm proud of you, and this is a good time to quit. You still owe me two plays, though, don't forget that. No sprints today, I'm keeping that promise. See you tomorrow at 3:30 sharp!"

Franklin bent over to get his breath, and thought about the long walk home. The coaches recruited several players to load gear into the cars. The rest of the team began to disperse, some on bikes, some with rides waiting, and a few, like Franklin, who walked home.

A couple of guys passed by to check on him. He grunted thanks. Then he saw Bart, twenty yards away, walking straight towards him. Bart saw Franklin looking at him and he smirked. Franklin broke eye contact.

Bart kept coming, he was ten yards away, then five, and then he spoke. "How's your hammer hanging now, short dick?" It was all he said; he didn't even stop as he walked by.

Franklin turned and stepped gingerly towards home.

# 6 | Math Misery

## *Franklin*

Fried chicken was the best thing the cafeteria ladies knew how to cook. That and pineapple upside-down cake. They were serving both for lunch today. It was the one-two punch of drowsiness. As he ate the cake, Franklin knew staying awake in class this afternoon would be a struggle.

The guys at his table were talking about a show on television. Franklin didn't watch much TV during the week. By the time he finished practice, he was whipped. And he still had to shower, eat supper, and do homework. The homework wasn't too hard for him, at least not yet. He could knock most of it out in an hour. By that time all he wanted to do was get his aching body in the rack. He was the only eighth-grader he knew who was in bed by 9:30.

Conversation at the lunch table shifted to who was the cutest girl in the class. Franklin sighed and pushed his chair back into the aisle. He never had much to add to these conversations. It wasn't that he wasn't interested in girls; he was surprised how interested he was. It was just that the guys always seemed to be focused on bosoms. That didn't seem polite to Franklin. Maybe there was something wrong with him.

"Out of the way, asshole. You're blocking the aisle." It was Bart, holding a lunch tray and looming over Franklin. "Come on, move it." Bart kicked the leg of Franklin's chair, and Franklin slid the chair forward. Bart grunted and moved down the aisle.

"Isn't he on the football team with you?" Irwin asked. Irwin was a goofy-looking kid with thick glasses and bad acne, the kind of kid you would immediately assume to be smart. You would be right. He also had a keen insight into people.

"Yeah," Franklin responded then looked away. This was not a conversation he wanted to have. All of a sudden he was ashamed to be associated with Bart.

"Is he as mean on the field as he is in the lunchroom?"

"He's even worse."

"I'll bet you this. You guys are gonna spend the whole season wishing he wasn't on the team. Anyone that mean to a teammate ought to be in juvenile detention, not on the football team."

"Man, he's a damn good linebacker. What are you talking about?" Franklin agreed with Irwin, but he felt compelled to stick up for Bart.

"If he's that mean, he's gonna cost you at least one game. You wait and see. It will be unsportsmanlike conduct, a flagrant foul, something. He'll cost you a game."

"I don't know. He's good." Franklin wished Irwin would give it a rest.

"He ought to be good. The son-of-a-bitch is fifteen. If he didn't have shit for brains, he'd be in tenth grade."

"I'll tell Bart you said so. I'm sure he would be happy to hear your viewpoint."

"Having Bart play on the eighth grade team is like having someone from UNC come down and play on the high school team. It's not fair."

"Irwin, would you give it a rest? He's on the team. I'm glad he's on the team. He's the best player on the team. Just shut up." Franklin said this with more heat than he intended.

"I'll tell you what. I'll bet you a dollar he costs you at least one game. Are you willing to put up so I will shut up?"

"You're on, Irwin. Now put a sock in it." They shook hands on the deal just as the bell sounded to send them to class.

Franklin puzzled over his relationship with Bart while he made his way to math class. What had that whole conversation with Irwin been about? Franklin didn't even *like* Bart. And he was afraid of him. Still, Bart was a teammate. And teammates stuck together.

Irwin was right about one thing, Bart was older and more mature than the rest of the guys. It's a long way from thirteen to fifteen. Bart was damn near a man. Franklin wondered what Bart knew that he didn't.

The bell sounded for the beginning of class, and the last of the stragglers hustled in to take their seats. The desks had a writing surface attached to a seat by a large pole running down beside your right knee. Franklin didn't like them. The kind with separate chairs and tables were more comfortable since you had room to stretch out. He *did* like that there was a good place to store your books under your desk seat, and he leaned over to stack his books there.

"Out of my way, peckerhead." It was Bart, in a whisper so loud Franklin figured they would both soon be in the principal's office. Franklin moved aside slightly as the surrounding kids sniggered. Bart shoved by roughly, making sure to give Franklin's desk a good kick.

Class began, and the Indian summer sunlight stabbed through the windows and warmed Franklin's back. He was full and drowsy, and the arithmetic problems on the page danced in and out of focus. He couldn't pay attention anyhow. They were in the middle of early practice, and football was the main thing on his mind. Miss Kate carried on in front of the class, and Franklin half-listened. He hadn't had any trouble understanding the lesson, plus he had done all the homework. A piece of chalk whizzed by Franklin's head and smacked Bart squarely beside his right ear. "Bart! Wake up!" Miss Kate barked. Startled, Bart sat up and looked around sheepishly.

Miss Kate was a piece of work. At least that's what Franklin's father said. She had taught his dad in eighth grade, just like she was teaching Franklin. She had even been a classmate of his grandfather in elementary school. She was a force of nature. There was a legend about a time when Miss Kate taught at the high school. Someone went to sleep in geometry class, and Miss Kate, sharp-eyed as always, noticed.

She put a finger to her lips to shush the class, and then tiptoed to the sleeping student's desk. Miss Kate, a substantial woman, lifted the guy, still sitting in his desk, a full six inches off the ground. Then she dropped him abruptly to the floor.

The way the story went, the guy wet his pants. Franklin didn't believe that part, but the rest of the story had the ring of truth. Miss Kate was a tough one.

Now that she had Bart's attention, Miss Kate bore down. "Perhaps we should work some problems at the board. Bart, you and Gretchen and Susan and Harvey come up here. I'd like each of you to work a problem from page 87 in your book."

Now Franklin was paying attention. The others filed up to the board. As Bart walked by, Franklin noticed he was limping slightly. And he had the faint shadow of a black eye on the left side of his face. Franklin hadn't seen anything to cause that at yesterday's practice. Miss Kate doled out the problems, and everyone went to work. No one struggled except Bart. The others explained their problems and sat down pretty much without incident.

Only Bart was left at the board. Miss Kate tried to help him as he struggled. "Did you do your homework, Bart?"

He shifted from foot to foot. "No ma'am," he replied. Bart may have been a bully, but he was no liar.

He continued to answer Miss Kate's questions as she tried to help him untangle the problem, but he never could get it. Bart's neck got pink, and sweat began to run down the side of his face. Miss Kate finished the problem for Bart, and he walked back to his desk, head down. Moments later, Franklin heard an unusual sniffling. He looked in Bart's direction and saw Bart's head resting on his folded arms. Franklin stared, trying to figure out what was going on. As he was about to turn to face the front of the class, Bart lifted his head. His eyes were bloodshot and swimmy-looking. He shot Franklin the bird and mouthed, "Up yours."

Franklin turned his attention back to math class and tried to concentrate. The wall clock above Miss Kate's desk didn't seem to be moving. It showed just twenty minutes left in class, though, so it had to be working. He picked up his pencil and wrote backwards from twenty to zero. He'd mark off the remaining minutes as they ticked away. Maybe that would help him stay awake.

Franklin thought about the upcoming game, then ran down the list of new plays and his responsibilities on each play. He knew what to do. Now if he could only will his body to do it successfully. He wished he was a gifted athlete, but you get what you get. Their most gifted athlete was Bart, hands down. But Irwin had a point. It's not hard to dominate when you are almost a man, playing against people who are mostly in late boyhood.

The clock crawled. Seventeen minutes until class ended. Franklin crossed off the numbers twenty, nineteen, and eighteen on his countdown list. Miss Kate's voice seemed louder, and Franklin wondered what was going on. He gave a mental shake and noticed that she was introducing new material. The board was covered with a problem he had never seen. Funny, if you looked at the board in a certain way, it looked like that strange writing from ancient Egypt. What was the word for that? He couldn't remember. Franklin looked closely at the problem on the board. She had worked it in a series of steps, showing her work as she insisted they do. He was good down to the third step, but then he was confused. The class had gotten ahead of him while he rehearsed his football assignments.

Franklin looked down at his book and scanned the page in front of him, then turned another page and continued scanning. He hated to leave class in a fog. Okay, okay. Here it was. Here was the problem she was working. He could see it on the page and on the board. He compared the two. Miss Kate made it clearer than the book did. All right. Now he had it. He could do it himself.

The clock showed four minutes left in class. Franklin grabbed his pencil and crossed out all the numbers from seventeen to four. The pace of class had picked up here at the end. He copied the homework assignment down in his notebook.

Hieroglyphics! Yes, that was it. That's what the Egyptians called their writing, and that was what the math problem looked like when he didn't have a clue.

The bell sounded, and he quickly crossed off his countdown numbers from four to zero, then closed his notebook.

Thirty kids clambered from their desks and headed out the door. The usual jam of students was in front of Franklin, so he had to wait. He stopped and felt a sharp jab in his lower left side. It was so hard he almost yelped. Bart.

"Keep your mouth shut about what you saw a while ago. Understand?" Franklin nodded. "Say one word, and I'll pound your sorry ass." Franklin nodded again.

"All right, now. I mean it."

They headed out of the room.

# 7 | Happy Days

## *Bart*

Bart flopped on his bed and stared at the ceiling. Life was hard. He tried to breathe deeply, but couldn't do it. A shot to the ribs during practice had seen to that. The minute he got off the ground, he knew he was in trouble. He could stand upright. Or he could breathe. He couldn't do both.

The doctor checked him out, but there was nothing he could do. Bart's ribs were either bruised or cracked, and there was no treatment either way. Doc said it was up to Bart to decide how much pain he could stand. The good thing was that there was no likelihood he was going to hurt himself any worse. He could take aspirin, suck it up, and play. Or he could take a break.

"Then fix me up," Bart replied, "because I'm playing." He had been through worse pain before. But never from football.

They taped his ribs tightly, and gave him additional pads to protect the injury. Bart couldn't tell if either helped. Just made it harder to breathe. The aspirin helped, though he noticed a weird, constant ringing in his ears. He didn't tell anyone. The aspirin was the only thing getting him through. All in all, Bart's body was ideal for football. He was thick and well-muscled, with powerful thighs and solid biceps. But the rib thing hurt awful bad, and it was pissing him off.

Bart turned onto his good side and stared out the window at the tree tops. He should be feeling fine. It was Saturday. He was going to tonight's dance at the Ruritan Club. But he still felt like shit. When had life gotten so hard? When Bart's dad married Doris, life had gone downhill quickly. They had been drowning in misery since Stephanie was born. Bart pretended his life was a movie and tried to wind it back to a happy scene. It was a long time ago. Bart was fifteen now, and his Dad had been married to Doris for ten years. No happy memories there.

His eyelids drooped, and it was dark in the theater of his mind. The film whirred in rewind and finished with a snap, the end of the film whipping around wildly like when he rewound films in the school auditorium.

Bart mentally threaded the first few inches of his life-movie into the projector and started from the beginning. The big numbers counted down like on the films at school: three, then two, then one.

A black and white image flickered and flashed onto the screen. He couldn't make it out at first. The picture was faded and a little fuzzy. There it was, a smiling young woman squinted into the sunlight. Her hair was poufy and the medium-dark dress fell just below her knees. Her head was cocked to one side, and her left foot was rolled slightly inward. She held a small white bundle close to her chest. It must have been 1950.

The young woman was Bart's mother, he realized this as he watched the movie unspool. She wasn't much older then than he was now. He figured she was nineteen when he was born.

Bart stared hard at his mother's face. She was squinting into the sun as the camera lens took it all in. This was a picture he had actually seen, probably at Poppa Fitzhugh's house.

He studied his mother's smile. She was smiling a *real* smile, not a fake *say cheese* smile because someone was taking a picture. Maybe she was smiling at the photographer. Bart guessed that his dad had taken the picture, or perhaps Poppa Fitzhugh. Bart couldn't remember the picture being taken, of course. He probably wasn't even awake. The baby in his mom's arms didn't look a day over six weeks old. Still, the picture radiated happiness.

When else had he been happy? The happy times seemed to come before his mom left. He ran the movie forward and locked onto another scene. He was in a wading pool. He must have been about two years old. The pool was blue with big pictures of orange and green fish on the bottom. It seemed so deep when he was little. Probably wasn't but four inches, maybe six. He remembered splashing the cold water.

A new image emerged, this time with a sound track. Bart was in the pool now. He could see his red bathing suit and the bright yellow bucket he was using to scoop water. He was in the pool, and his mom was sitting by the pool in a folding chair, reading a magazine. Bart wanted her attention. He did not want her to look at the magazine.

"Mama! Mama play me!" He hollered at her. She looked up and smiled, then spoke to him in a language he understood.

"Me play Bart!" She grinned, rose from the chair, and dropped the magazine to the ground. She had on bermuda shorts and a blouse, but that didn't stop her. She took two short steps, kicked off her sandals, and stepped over the edge of the pool to sit down right in front of Bart. He squealed with delight and splashed her. She splashed him back and squealed herself.

Bart dipped his yellow bucket deep into the pool and filled it, then tried to lift it and pour water on his mom. The bucket was so heavy that he toppled face-first into the pool. He panicked and shrieked before she quickly scooped him up and hugged him to her. Bart snuffled on her shoulder for a moment, then she showed him how to scoop just a little water and pour it from the bucket. He squealed, filled the bucket, and poured it on her hair.

She grinned back at him, took the bucket, and dumped water squarely on his head. They giggled and splashed, and there was nothing but laughter and happiness and love and the sweet smell of his mom.

Bart jerked back to the present as a lump formed in his throat. Dammit, he thought, I'm fifteen years old. I can't cry about something that's long gone. It didn't work out. It's nobody's fault. They just couldn't live together. His ribs still hurt. Now his heart hurt too.

He turned once more to the movie, afraid he had lost the moment.

The screen flashed, and his life rolled forward. Now he was watching his fifth birthday party. The sun was bright, and you could tell it was early fall because of the angle as the light shot through the trees.

There must have been fifteen kids at the party. Bart couldn't immediately find himself, but the other kids had on those ridiculous pointy birthday hats. They were all lined up for something. What was it? Oh yeah, the pony rides! This was the year that Grandmama and Poppa Fitzhugh had the petting zoo come to his birthday party, and they had pony rides. Everybody was in line to ride the pony.

Bart sought himself in the picture. He remembered what to look for. There he was, cowboy hat perched on one side of his head and pistols at each side. He was a cowboy for sure! The pony rides were the best part of the best birthday he ever had. And the petting zoo wasn't bad.

He remembered when the baby lamb peed on Florence's foot. That was funny, not just the peeing, but how Florence responded. She shook her leg like crazy, pulled off her shoe, and raced off-balance around the yard, shrieking hysterically. The boys laughed so hard they almost peed on themselves, and the girls giggled and pointed.

There was something else that happened that birthday. What was it? It wasn't the cake, good as that was. Something had been really special about that birthday. Bart tried to play the day back scene by scene. Maybe if he began with the first thing that happened, he could remember.

He had been so excited about his birthday party that it had been hard for him to go to sleep the night before. Over and over at supper they discussed the details of the next day. Who was coming, what time the party started, the petting zoo and the pony rides. Bart was about to explode with anticipation, and his mother was equally excited. They were feeding off each other. When it came time to go to bed, Bart was so revved up he couldn't settle down, so his parents made him a deal. He remembered it clearly.

Bart sat in his mom's lap, with his daddy on the footstool right in front of him. Mary Catherine looked at his dad and said, "Ricky, will you get Bart's present out of your closet, the big one wrapped in the cowboy wrapping paper? I'll talk to Bart while you go and get it."

While his dad headed to retrieve the gift, Bart leaned into his mom's shoulder and she snugged her grip on his waist. "Bart," she said, and she said it so softly he had to lean into her to hear it, "you've got a big birthday in front of you tomorrow, and it's important that you get a good night's sleep so you can enjoy the day. Here's what we're gonna do…"

"This is the one, isn't it?" His dad was back with an enormous gift. The wrapping paper was covered with cowboys, cattle, and covered wagons.

"Yes, that's the one. I was just making a deal with Bart about tonight and tomorrow morning." She quietly picked up her speech again. "So here's what we're gonna do. To give you a reason to go to sleep tonight, we're gonna let you open this present first thing tomorrow morning. Even before you get out of bed. The first thing you'll get to do on the morning of your fifth birthday is to open this present, and it's something you really, really want. How does that sound?"

"Oh, Mom, can I open it now?" Bart was so excited he was trembling. She wondered if she had made a mistake with her ploy.

"No, not just yet. Today's not your birthday. But the sooner you go to bed and go to sleep, the sooner morning will be here and you can open it. And, this was the icing on the cake of her offer, "I'll make you pancakes for breakfast. As many as you want. Because I am so glad you were born, and I am so glad you are my little boy!"

Bart went right to bed and lay there staring at the ceiling. He wondered about the box and looked forward to the cake and the pony rides and all that was to come. He knew he'd never go to sleep. He kept thinking about that enormous box with the cowboys on it. Then he pulled his teddy bear closer and tucked it under his chin.

In the morning, Bart's parents crept into his room while he slept. The smell of breakfast filled the air. Ricky looked at Mary Catherine:

"It's gonna be a long, wild day. Are you sure you're ready for this?"

"No," she said. "I've always thought you should let them sleep when that's what they're doing. But we promised, and it's getting late. We've got a lot to do." She leaned forward and shook Bart gently. "Bart. Bart, wake up. It's your birthday and we've got something for you."

Bart remembered the rest. His eyes opened slowly, then flashed wide as he sat up in bed. He looked at the box his dad held, and shivered with anticipation. "Can I open it? Can I open it now?"

"Sure," Ricky said, and handed him the box. Bart flipped the box, grabbed the seam on the paper, and ripped the package wide open. He turned the box over to reveal the front, and his eyes grew wide. "Fanner-50's! Oh, this is the best present ever!"

Bart tore into the box and pulled out two pistols and the soft leather holster set. Some of the older boys in his neighborhood had Fanner-50's, and he had longed to have his own. He shoved one pistol into each of the holsters, wrapped the belt around his waist, and buckled it carefully.

He was a pajama-clad desperado ready to shoot anyone who got in his way. "How do I look?" he asked. Before his dad and mom could reply, the holstered guns and the belt slumped around his ankles. Bart's face fell with the belt.

"Don't worry," his daddy said, "we can adjust that belt so it fits you just right."

Bart stepped out of the puddle of belt and pistols and looked up at his mom and dad. "This is the best birthday present ever!" He hugged them both.

"Hand me the belt, Bart, and let's see if I can adjust it. Then look in the box to see if there is anything else in there, maybe some caps or bullets or both."

"While you boys are working on that, I'll go rustle up some pancakes from the old chuck wagon." Bart's mom laughed and headed for the kitchen.

"Oh, Mama, I forgot about the pancakes. I can't wait!"

"You won't have to wait long. They should be ready in seven minutes."

Bart retrieved the box from his bed and rummaged around in the packaging material. He pulled out four boxes of green caps, perfectly sized for the pistols, and a bunch of cartridges that would fit into the cylinders of each pistol. There were even enough cartridges for the loops on the back of the holster belt.

"Here you go, Pardner, try this on for size." Ricky handed Bart the belt, and he fastened it around his waist. This time it was perfect, riding low and easy across his hips.

"Hey, Dad, how do you do this?" Bart was struggling with the roll of caps.

Ricky showed him how to load the coil of caps into the chamber, and then feed them up through the mechanism and in front of the hammer. "You have to watch what you are doing, or you'll smash your finger. It really hurts. I know, because I've done it." Ricky smiled up at Bart, finished with the first pistol, and handed it to him. "Try it and see what happens."

Bart pulled the trigger. The hammer came back away from the gun, then returned with a tremendous crack. A flash of fire spit out, and a puff of smoke coiled around the gun. A broad grin creased Bart's face. "Man, that was loud," he said and then, "watch this!"

Bart had seen older kids "fan" their guns by rapidly clicking the hammer on top of the gun with the palm of their hand. It was quicker than pulling the trigger, a handy thing when you were surrounded by bad guys. The hammer was even shaped for fanning, wider and not as pointed as the hammer on Bart's other pistols.

Bart extended his right hand, pointing it in the direction he wanted to fire, then fanned the hammer just like he had seen other kids do. Pow! Pow! Pow! The room filled with flashes and noise and smoke.

"Okay, Buddy, don't use 'em all at once. Let's load the caps in the other gun while you put the extra cartridges on the belt." Ricky went to work on the second gun, while Bart carefully inserted six bullets into the cylinder of the first revolver. He set aside six for the second gun, then studiously pushed the rest of the bullets into the loops on the back of the belt.

"Hey, guys! Pancakes are ready!"

"We're on our way!" Ricky handed Bart the second pistol, and Bart fired it once to see if it would work. Pow! Smoke and flash and noise, it worked great. He shoved the pistol into the holster and swaggered down the hall next to his dad. Bart reached up and gave Ricky's big hand a squeeze just before they got to the kitchen.

Those were some good times, just me and Mama and Daddy. No Doris. No Stephanie. No school, either. Bart shifted positions on the bed, and pain shot through his chest from his ribs. With this, the memory movie jerked to a stop. He took a quick look around to get reoriented.

Happy memories. Not many of those anymore. Bart turned over and managed to do it without setting off any of the white flashes that came when the pain was the worst.

He sat up gingerly and started thinking about what to wear to the dance.

# 8 | First Scrimmage

## *Bart*

"What do you think, big man? You ready to tee it up and rip some-one's lips off?"

Bart's teammates chattered like monkeys at feeding time. It drove him crazy. They were more talk than action. Bart let his actions do the talking.

He *was* ready to kick some ass; he felt the tension in his body. He didn't need to talk about it. What he needed was to see the shock on an opponent's face when he drove them into the ground. He thought about Doris, his witch of a stepmother. He wished she were a lineman in this scrimmage. He'd stuff her head up her butt and get celebrated for his efforts. Coach might even stencil a bright red star on his helmet, like he did when someone delivered an especially vicious hit.

Thinking about Doris made him a better player. He remembered her screaming this morning. She threw things and raged at his dad last night. The woman was a nut job. What ever did his dad see in her? A whistle shrilled, and everyone gathered around Coach McInnis. Bart trotted over and shoved his way past the smaller players. He needed to be directly in Coach's line of sight. You had to keep your face in plain view. They wouldn't put you in if they didn't remember you. And Bart intended to be memorable. Coach gave them the ground rules for the scrimmage. There would be real officials like a regular game. The first team offense would run twenty plays against the first team defense, and then the second units would run twenty plays at each other. Special teams would practice kick-offs, punting, kick returns, and extra points at the end of the scrimmage. The first series of plays would begin on the twenty-yard line with the first unit offense pitted against the first unit defense.

Coach reminded the team that they were all in this together. "This scrimmage is to make us better," he said, "and to see where we need to improve. We're not here to hurt each other. Quarterbacks will wear red jerseys and, if you hit the quarterback for any reason, your ass is grass."

What sissies, Bart thought. If they don't want to get hit, they should go out for the damn swim team. Hitting is what makes this game work. Coach meant what he said, though. That much was clear.

Coach McInnis was coaching the defense for this scrimmage, while Coach Wittenburg led the offense. The team split into two groups and clustered on opposite sides of the field. Bart's heart rate picked up, and his breath caught in his throat. He played every major sport and liked them all. But nothing compared to laying someone out in football. There was something cleansing about destroying another human being, just wiping them completely off the field.

Coach gave last-minute assignments, and Bart lined up in his middle linebacker slot. He was right over the center, about four yards back from the line of scrimmage. The offense broke the huddle, and Franklin Gibson trotted up to the line. Bart glared at Franklin and resolved to jack his jaws just to get in the swing of things.

Harvey shouted the signals, and Franklin snapped the ball. Bart blitzed through the line with token resistance. He bore down on the quarterback like a locomotive, thinking all the time what a chicken shit Franklin was for missing the block. Too late he heard someone shout "Screen pass, screen pass!" and realized he'd been suckered. Harvey lobbed a quick pass over Bart's head just before Bart plowed into him and drove him headfirst into the ground.

Bart could tell things were going badly by the noisy pandemonium that broke out all around him. The offense roared as a wall of blockers formed on the left side of the field and the receiver sprinted for the end zone. Even worse, whistles blew and red flags flew as officials rushed to check on the quarterback.

"Dammit, Bart! Take a lap!" It was Coach McInnis, and he was screaming mad.

"What did I tell you about hitting the quarterback? You idiot! Take two laps. And when you get back, take a seat on the bench. Let's get somebody else in here, somebody who can listen!" Bart dropped his head and started running. The practice field was in the middle of a complex of sports fields, and the laps would take a while. He took off at a near-sprint so he could get back before the first unit finished scrimmaging.

Bart watched the scrimmage as he ran. The offense was working the defense over, especially now that he wasn't at middle linebacker. The guy who played behind him was a nice kid, but it was his first year playing football and he couldn't find his butt with both hands. In addition to the touchdown on the screen pass, the offense scored twice more before Bart finished his laps. He sidled up to Coach McInnis on the sidelines, trying to catch the Coach's eye. He regretted it when it finally happened.

"Didn't I tell you to sit on the bench when you finished? Sit!" Coach's eyes flashed as he pointed Bart to the bench.

Bart slunk to the bench and sat next to the water bucket. He grabbed the dipper and took a gulp, feeling the cool wetness roll down his chin and into the t-shirt beneath his shoulder pads. Damn, he thought, this ain't going so well.

He focused on the scrimmage and, disregarding the fact that he wasn't in the game, liked what he saw. The line was blowing the defense back; every play was a gain of four to six yards. Franklin was the best lineman by far. Who would have guessed it?

The whole thing would have scared some people, since the defense sucked on every play. But Bart knew the defense wasn't half bad. There were some stud horses on the defense. Maybe we've got a chance, he thought. Maybe we can do something special this year.

The two sides took a blow after the first twenty plays, and Coach McInnis called them together. "Way to go, guys. You looked really good out there. I like your hustle and your passion. We've got some stuff to work on, sure, but you look great for just three weeks of practice. And except for one play," he leveled a withering gaze at Bart, "you guys really kept your heads on straight and kept it clean. Take ten and then the second units will go after each other."

"Bart, line up at middle linebacker with the second team. Let's see if you can remember not to hit the quarterback." Bart's face went red inside his helmet, and he resolved to redeem himself.

On the first play Bart tipped a pass, bobbled and then intercepted it, and raced twenty-eight yards for a touchdown. He ran over, through, or around six of the eleven players who tried to tackle him. That was just the beginning.

Bart shed blocks like a waxed canvas coat sheds rain. He punished blockers, throwing them aside, then flattening the runners they were protecting. Even in the moment, Bart knew what he was doing. Second team? Watch this, Coach. I'm a one-man highlight film.

He ran up and down the defensive line, slapping his teammates on the back and exhorting them to crush someone. He vaulted the second-unit center and swatted a short pass back into the quarterback's face. He thwarted an end-sweep by tackling the running back and both blockers in one crunching pile. After eight plays, Coach McInnis had seen enough. Someone was going to get hurt. And it wasn't going to be Bart.

Coach called time out and beckoned Bart to the sidelines. "You're playing great, Bart, you really are. I'm gonna take you out before you hurt someone. You're clearly my first team middle linebacker and the leader of the defense. But dammit, don't hit the quarterback fifteen seconds after I tell you not to. Understand?" Bart nodded and trotted back to the water bucket.

The balance of the scrimmage went well. With Bart on the bench, the second unit offense and defense were evenly matched, and it was fun to watch. The offense scored twice, once on a long pass when two defenders collided and a second time on a trick play that Coach Wittenburg pulled out of his backside. It was a Statue of Liberty play, with a shovel pass thrown in for good measure.

The defense had its moments, too.

Bart's replacement was emboldened by his time with the first unit and played like a man with his hair on fire. He knocked down passes, blew past the second unit center, even picked up a fumble and returned it for an alleged touchdown. *Alleged* since you can't advance a fumble, and he knew it. Still, it was a heck of a performance.

When Coach whistled the whole thing dead and brought them together, you could see pride in his eyes. Coaches aren't much on compliments. They specialize in harangues intended to produce maximum performance. But this was an exception.

"Guys, I am really pleased with how you have come together. This was one of the best first scrimmages I have ever seen. We've got a lot to work on, but we have come a long way in a short time, and I am proud of you. Let's work on special teams and call it a day."

Special teams are hard to practice, since you need the best athletes on each special unit, and there isn't much left to put on the opposing team. Coach Wittenburg called out the kick-off return team, and Bart was surprised to hear Franklin's name in the first line of blockers. Bart was placed at shallow receiver, where he expected to be. He wouldn't get to catch many kicks, they would go over his head, but he would get to knock the shit out of people. And that was more fun anyhow.

Bart and Franklin trotted to their places, joined by nine teammates. Coach Wittenburg arrayed the receiving team across the field and gave last-minute instructions about the kick-off return they were practicing. Coach McInnis took the best of the rest of the players to fashion a kick-off squad. When everybody was set, the officials whistled the game into play, and the kicker's foot met the ball with a solid *thud*. The ball soared through the late-afternoon sky and tumbled into the hands of the deepest kick-returner.

Bart looked up to see eleven defenders converging on the ball carrier. He targeted one and bore down on him, only to have a blur streak by and knock the opponent completely out of the play. Bart found another defender and destroyed him. The kick returner gained forty yards and was finally knocked out of bounds by the kicker.

Whistles sounded, and Bart picked himself up. Who blew by him on that play? Bart looked around for the defender he had targeted and finally found him, underneath Franklin Gibson. Franklin had obliterated the guy. Who knew Franklin could move so fast? Bart chuckled. There's more to that boy than he would have guessed.

Coach didn't let kick-off practice run long; there were too many chances to get hurt in the high-speed collisions. The kid Franklin had hit on the first kick-off had to be helped off the field, and several other players got dinged up in the first few repetitions. Coach scaled back all the kick-off sessions to walk-throughs.

Punting and extra point practice was also done at half-speed. Bart was happy to see that the kicker's punts were high and true, with a tight spiral. And the extra-point kicks were high and hard to block. They also had some distance. Bart wouldn't be surprised if this team could kick a short field goal, which was rare for a bunch of eighth-graders.

Coach McInnis whistled practice to a close and rewarded the team for their good work: no wind sprints. Bart was disappointed. He excelled at wind sprints, and would like one more chance to make-up for his stupid hit at the beginning of the scrimmage.

Never mind. The rest of the team was probably exhausted. Bart had been in only eight plays in the scrimmage, so he still had plenty of gas in the tank. Coach thanked the team, told them to take the weekend off, and to be back at four o'clock sharp on Monday afternoon. Bart turned to go, and Franklin was standing right behind him.

"Hey, Peckerhead, good job. You had some nice licks out there."

Franklin's eyes telegraphed shock. "Thanks," he mumbled. "You, too," he added and then quickly walked away.

Bart headed home. He walked tall and straight, like the warrior he was. And he wondered what the weekend would hold.

# 9 | War

## *Bart*

Bart thanked God that his daddy would be home tonight. His step-mother would be nicer, and the whole house wouldn't feel so much like a war zone.

Earlier in the day Bart and Doris had clashed. Again. This time she had snapped at him when he didn't place the dishes in the drying rack correctly. When she snapped at him, he snapped back. Enough was enough. She was an emotional time bomb, and could go off for any reason or for no reason at all. They had not spoken since.

Supper was cooking. Doris never cooked anything decent when it was just Bart and Stephanie. Mostly it was frozen fish sticks or fried bologna or canned spaghetti.

Tonight she was putting on the dog. Bart could smell biscuits baking and apple pie too. Meatloaf was in the air. His mouth watered. A man could drown smelling that good stuff.

It was Friday night, the only night when he had half a chance of catching a meal with his daddy. Wednesdays and Sundays were out of the question because of prayer meetings. And there was something important going on at the church most other nights, too.

"Your Daddy ought to get a cot and sleep up there at the stupid church," Doris once said. "He has damn near moved in up there anyhow."

Grandmama Fitzhugh once told Bart "a lady never swears." Doris hadn't gotten the word.

Bart felt soreness in his shoulders and tightness in his neck. He squeezed hard on the base of his neck, trying to knead away a knot that ached between his shoulders.

School was easier this year. It was the same material from last year, and classes hadn't been in session long enough for him to get behind. Still, he was already struggling in math. And he had to sit in a hard wooden desk all day, in rooms without air conditioning.

Then there was practice. Bart's teammates thought it was easy for him because he was bigger and older than everyone else. And parts of it were easier. But you had to do the drills. You had to run full speed for two hours. You had to hit and be hit. And the coaches were watching every move, just waiting for you to screw up so they could make you run laps.

Bart picked idly at the dried blood scabbed atop the gash on his right forearm. There was a bruise under the gash, and his arm throbbed.

His mama would give a damn about the gash, but he didn't even mention it to Doris. She was so busy with her own stuff that she didn't have time for him or his gash.

Muffin barked sharply, that happy, welcoming bark that Bart loved. He loved that dog, loved that bark, and loved what it meant tonight. His dad was home. Bart headed to the kitchen to greet him.

Ricky Wagram swept in like a rock star. Bart envied his ability to make an entrance. He did it at church, at home, and everywhere he went. Ricky scooped up Stephanie, gave Doris a peck on the cheek, and greeted Bart with a grin and a light hug, all in less time than it takes to tell it.

Ricky still had on the suit, tie, and shiny black shoes of a minister. He looked important. Bart hoped God didn't call *him* to be a preacher, there had been two in a row in his family, and folks were already asking him if he was going to continue the tradition. He'd hate the dressing up part, especially the tie.

The God part wouldn't be too bad. Bart loved Bible stories and didn't mind the preaching, but singing was his favorite thing. He had thought about joining the chorus at school, but wasn't sure he could stand it. It was mostly girls and a few nerdy guys. They sang all this strange madrigal stuff from England, but Bart liked hymns and gospel songs. He had already picked out the songs he wanted folks to sing at his funeral. He wanted the final one to be "I'll Fly Away." He often wished he *could* fly away.

"So, what's for supper, sweetheart?" Ricky caught Doris's eye with a look Bart couldn't quite read.

"We're having some of your favorites, honey."

Bart wanted to puke. Doris was never nice unless his daddy was home. Not even to Stephanie.

"We're having homemade meatloaf, hot biscuits, and apple pie. I wanted it to be a special meal for you. We don't eat together nearly enough."

"You're right, honey, and I'm sorry. It just seems I spend all my time up at the church. There's so much to do serving God in the church."

"Of course there is, honey." Bart wondered if she'd lash out. He had overheard this fight more than once. She let it go.

"Supper will be ready in a minute; you got here right on time. Now go wash up."

Bart looked at the table. It was set with stainless silverware, four placemats and four napkins. He saw butter on the table for biscuits, and serving bowls for all the vegetables. The iced tea was even in the glasses.

It was humid in the kitchen, and condensate ran down the side of each glass. There were normal-sized glasses for Doris and Stephanie, and two super-sized glasses for Bart and his daddy. His daddy said the big glasses saved wear and tear on your feet, less going back and forth for refills. Bart liked them because they were a thing he and his daddy shared.

Doris began to put the food into serving bowls and place them on the table. She and Bart still had not spoken since their incident earlier in the day. She refused to even look at him.

When she finished, they all sat down to eat. Everyone except Ricky, who had slipped out to wash his hands. Doris shot Bart a hard look, and hissed, "If you weren't doing something you are ashamed of, you wouldn't be so hard to get along with."

Where in the hell did that come from, Bart wondered? It always came from left field. And when you least expected it. Then, in a motion so spontaneous and fluid that even he was surprised, Bart reached over, grabbed his iced tea, and dumped it squarely on Doris's head.

Doris screamed. The ice cubes bounced off her teased and lacquered hair, while tea streamed down either side of her face. The whole thing was every bit as satisfying as destroying an opponent on the football field.

"What in the hell is going on in here?" Bart had not seen Ricky enter the room. And he had never heard him curse. "What is going on in here?" Ricky demanded again. He surveyed the room. Doris was dripping tea and tears. Stephanie was cowering. And Bart, hackles up like a wolf, looked ready to rip someone apart. Ricky began to bark orders.

"Bart, go to your room."

Bart didn't move.

"Now!" his father shouted.

Bart got up to leave, and Stephanie began to shriek like she always did when she was afraid. He never knew how much that girl was picking up, but she was dead-on this time.

"I can't live with this boy! See what he's done!" Doris was standing in a growing puddle of tea. Bart didn't even acknowledge her, just made his way behind his sister's chair, and headed toward his bedroom. His Daddy grabbed him roughly on the upper arm.

"What were you thinking!" Ricky screamed it, his eyes big and the tendons in his neck bulging. Bart had never heard him scream.

"Ask that witch what she said..."

Bart didn't have time to finish before a huge right hand crashed into his sternum. He was stunned. Damn, that hurt. The son-of-a-bitch hit me with a closed fist. He couldn't breathe or speak.

"I'm calling the sheriff's office right now!" Doris shrieked. She was hysterical.

"Hang up that phone! I mean it! Bart, you go upstairs. I'll deal with you later."

Bart headed up the stairs. Even in the moment, with his sternum throbbing and his sister wailing and Doris weeping and shouting, he felt sorry for his old man. All this shit going on and no one to help him. Bart reached the second floor, turned into his room, and wondered what would happen next.

Doris' accusation hung in the air. *If you weren't doing something you are ashamed of, you wouldn't be so hard to get along with.*

If there were referees in home life, Doris would have been whistled for unsportsmanlike conduct. Even in his pain, Bart's mouth crinkled into a grin as he heard the ref make the call: *The stepbitch has been ejected from the game. Fifteen yards for unmomlike behavior. First and ten.*

The worst of it was that he wasn't doing anything he was ashamed of. He was a little sheepish about how little he was doing. His shame and sin occurred only in his fantasies.

Bart's door swung open, and his Daddy strode in. "Sit down and tell me what the hell just happened down there!" Ricky was swearing again. Had the whole world lost its mind?

"I am not sitting down. You hit me once already, and I'm not giving you an unfair advantage." His hand instinctively went to his sternum. It was tender and getting worse.

Bart looked hard at his daddy. What did he see in the old man's eyes? Was it fear? Resignation? Ricky seemed calmer now. Perhaps he was back in control.

"I leave for thirty seconds, and when I come back the shit is all in the fan. What happened?"

"Did you hear what she said to me?" Bart decided to meet his daddy like a man. He had already told him "no" about sitting down. He was going to be straight with him and see what happened. "Did you hear what that witch said?"

"No. I was out of the room. What did she say?"

"She said, '*If you weren't doing something you are ashamed of, you wouldn't be so hard to get along with.*' So, I snapped. Adults don't talk to each other like that. The woman has got snakes in her head. She's crazy. I can't take living with her, and you're never here."

"What is it with you and your mom, "

"*Step*mom!" Bart corrected him. "I tried that 'Mom' stuff because you asked me to, but I'm done. That shit is over."

"I just don't get it." Ricky ignored the swearing and noted the correction. He wouldn't jam "Mom" down Bart's throat anymore. "Why can't you two get along?"

"You will never understand this, Dad." Bart said it sharply, his words clipped. "I know your mom. She's many things, but she's not a bitch."

Ricky's eyes flashed and Bart stepped back. He prepared to deflect another blow. None came. Ricky dropped his head, and turned away. Bart heard his father inhale deeply, and then begin to sob.

Bart stepped toward his dad, but Ricky pulled away and slowly shuffled toward the stairs. He stopped halfway down to compose himself, and was gone.

Bart listened closely. Stephanie was still shrieking. Bart hated that sound. Crying was one thing, but shrieking made his blood pressure spike. She did it every time she was scared. Guess that's what happens when you can't really talk. Muffled words of comfort filtered up the steps. The shrieking softened to sobbing, and then silence settled in the hall.

Bart heard adult voices; there was some back-and-forth he couldn't make out. He heard his dad say, "What in the world brought that on?" There was silence once again. Then he heard his dad, this time with more heat, "Well, if he's not invited back to the table, I'm not eating, either." More silence.

Bart rummaged around in the top drawer of his dresser. Doris often sent him up without supper, so he was prepared. His stock was a little low, a jar of peanut butter, a box of graham crackers, half a dozen Slim Jims, but he could manage.

He waited to see what would happen. Bart hated to miss out on the feast laid out downstairs. He lay down on the bed, breathed in as deeply as possible given the ache in his sternum, and closed his eyes.

A single sharp word broke through the fog. "Bart!" It was his dad, and the call was loud and urgent.

"Yes, sir!" He checked the clock. Only ten minutes had passed since he lay down. He must have dozed.

"Haven't you heard me calling you? Come on down and eat!"

"Coming!" Bart hustled down the stairs and back to the table. The puddle of tea was gone from under his stepmother's chair. Stephanie seemed to be back to normal, whatever that was for her.

His stepmom had on a different dress, and her hair was damp and flat-looking where the ice cubes and tea had landed. His Daddy looked pretty much the same. You couldn't even tell he had been crying.

They ate supper more or less in silence. The meatloaf was great, it stayed warm through the whole drama. The biscuits weren't bad, though they had chilled enough that Bart had to work to get the butter to melt completely. And the pie was delicious. Doris could cook, but you'd never know it unless his daddy was home to eat the meal.

Bart wondered why they weren't talking about what was really on their minds. It was all "How was your day today?" and "Hasn't the weather been fine?" His daddy did ask him about the upcoming game with Hope Mills. "So, how do you think you guys will do against the Yellow Jackets?"

"I don't know, Dad. I'm fired up about the game. I'm sick of hitting the same guys every day."

"I know what you mean. I have felt that way myself. It gets monotonous. How's the team look?"

"The defense is probably better than the offense, at least so far. We're decent. The coaches have worked us half to death, so we're in good shape. We'll just have to wait and see how we do when it's for real. You can't tell until you strap it on for a game, at least that's what the coaches say."

"The coaches are right. I've been on many teams, some surprised me and some disappointed me. You can't tell what you've got until show time."

Bart chanced the question that was most on his mind: "Are you gonna be there for the game, Daddy?"

"I hope so. It just depends on how things go at the church."

# 10 | Game Time

## *Franklin*

"Hurry, Mom! My stuff is in the car, and we've got to go!"

Coach told them to be there at three, and Franklin didn't want to be late. He had seen what happened when others broke this rule: running laps, getting benched, even being left behind. That didn't appeal to him.

Betsy Gibson gathered her keys and called for Franklin's sister. "Hurry up, Julie. Your brother is about to have a stroke."

Next she turned to Franklin, "Honestly, honey, take a deep breath. You remind me of myself." Nothing irritated him more than when she said that. They were not alike. He didn't take the bait. He was saving his frustration for the game.

Julie slow-poked her way into the kitchen with her lip stuck out. "Do I have to go?" she whined. "I hate stupid football. We already ruined my last birthday with a dumb football game."

"No, Julie, you don't have to go. You are spending the night with Mary Anna, remember? You just have to go with me to take Franklin to the bus. Now get in the car." Julie stuck her tongue out at Franklin, and he thought about telling on her. That seemed like a little kid thing to do, so he squelched the impulse.

All week long Coach Wittenburg ragged him about this game. Tuesday Coach asked a peculiar question: "Franklin, what color roses does your mama like?"

Franklin had no idea. "I don't know, Coach. Why?"

"Because that nose tackle from Hope Mills, his name is Rock

Wilkins, is an animal, and he's gonna kill you. That sumbitch is only in eighth grade and he already shaves twice a day. I just wanted to know what kind of flowers to send to your funeral." The ploy worked. Franklin had never been so jacked-up in his life.

They wheeled into the parking lot with thirty seconds to spare, and Franklin struggled to get out of the car. His shoulder pads caught on the door jamb, but he jerked free, grabbed his duffle, and dashed for the bus. He glanced over his shoulder and shouted, "Thanks for the ride, Mom! I'll see you after the game." He had a fleeting desire to hug her, but ignored it. Some things you just don't do in front of the guys.

Coach McInnis checked his watch as Franklin climbed onto the bus, but he didn't say anything. Bart wasn't as reticent. "Damn, peckerhead, I hoped we would get to leave you. You cut it close." Franklin ignored him.

The ride was quick enough, since Hope Mills was only thirty miles from Laurinburg. Franklin moved to the back of the bus and took a seat alone. He liked to sit by himself. It gave him room to think.

In Franklin's mind, football players followed in the great tradition of warriors through the ages: gladiators, knights and the native peoples who roamed the land before the white settlers brought firearms, small-pox and venereal disease. What was it like for them before battle? Were they quiet and reflective, like he was? Or did they work themselves into a frenzy like most of his teammates?

Dying in battle, now that would be a great way to go. There was something so real, so *elemental* about physical conflict. To flatten someone (or even to be flattened) was the *realest* thing Franklin had ever experienced. He committed to being very *real* against Hope Mills. Franklin visualized himself smacking the shit out of Rock Wilkins and smiled.

The crowd at the stadium was tremendous. Eighth grade football was not a big deal in Laurinburg, but it must be the only game in town for these folks. He could smell the hotdogs and popcorn from the concession stand and was strangely hungry. It would have to wait.

The ref signaled for the game to begin, and Hope Mills' kicker met the ball with a solid thwomp. Franklin sprinted straight towards the player he was supposed to take out. They locked eyes for an instant, and then the opponent planted a forearm squarely across Franklin's facemask. His head snapped back violently, and he was dazed as they crashed to the ground. He jumped up just as the ball carrier was tackled on the thirty-one yard line.

Franklin trotted back to the line of scrimmage, a familiar metallic taste in his mouth. A quick spit confirmed it, he was bleeding. He had never felt more alive in his life. He spit into his hands and wiped the bloody spit on his pants. A little blood might intimidate his opponent.

The first play was a dive play, designed to gain three or four yards. It was right over Franklin's position. He bent over the ball and glanced up at Rock Wilkins. Damn, he was huge. And he looked old. He was missing all his upper front teeth. Didn't even have a mouthpiece in his mouth.

Franklin reached out and grabbed the ball. A couple of drops of blood dripped from his mouth onto the white laces. Rock Wilkins growled: "I'm gonna kill your ass."

The play exploded around them, and Franklin obliterated Rock Wilkins. Flattened him and lay on top of him while the halfback burst through a seam in the line and headed for the goal. The screaming of the cheerleaders, and the groans from the Hope Mills fans, let Franklin know the play went well. But even he was surprised to see the referee's raised arms signal a touchdown.

Take that, Coach Wittenburg. Send the flowers to Rock Wilkins' mom.

That opening play set the tone for the entire game. Franklin was invincible, bulletproof, incendiary. He burst off the line with enormous power. Rock Wilkins spent the first half of the game flat on his back and the second half sitting on the bench. Everything Franklin touched turned to gold. Even when he was whistled for unsportsmanlike conduct, Coach Wittenburg told him to shake it off and slapped him on the butt in encouragement.

Franklin's passion ignited the entire team. Bart tackled with a ferocity that was rare, even for him. On a particularly vicious lick, he sent his opponent limp and unconscious to the ground. The crowd grew hushed and even the Fighting Scot players quieted. The body lying motionless on the field tempered Franklin's adrenaline rush.

He saw the concern on the faces of the medics as they wheeled the stretcher from the ambulance. He overheard bits of their conversation. *Stabilize the neck...easy, easy...pupils dilated...heart rate elevated...* Franklin felt a lump rise in his throat and tears form in the corners of his eyes. He wanted to knock the shit out of people as bad as anyone, but this was serious. Sounded like the guy might really be in danger. He didn't want to actually *kill* anyone.

Then he heard Bart. "Tough shit for the guy. If he didn't want to get hit he should have joined the damn chess club. Now let's line up and play ball. I'm getting cold and stiff out here."

Stunning. Franklin would never understand Bart.

The ambulance pulled slowly out of the stadium and roared into the night. Franklin took a blindside hit on the next offensive series. Suddenly he was back in the zone, flying to the ball, crushing oncoming defenders, screaming in the faces of opponents he had just destroyed. Blood streamed from the split at the corner of his mouth. His uniform looked tie-dyed. Splotches of bright red new blood alternated with rust-colored older blood. Looking down at his own blood, he felt electric.

Late in the third quarter, Franklin picked up his second unsportsmanlike conduct penalty, this one for a clip. It was a questionable call, since the guy turned at the last minute. Franklin hit him anyhow, folding him in half and sending him flying out of bounds at Coach Wittenburg's feet. He could hear the coach yelling before he got up, but couldn't make out his words.

Coach raced to Franklin, grabbed him by the shoulder pads and lifted him completely off the ground. He was a thick man, and he was screaming, eyes big and mouth wide. "That's what I'm talking about, son! Kill his ass!

You are playing out of your mind! Keep it up! Great hit!"

Franklin wished the night could last forever.

The rest of the game was more of the same. The starters spent the fourth quarter on the bench, and the subs did a great job. They even scored a touchdown with four minutes left. Franklin was glad to see it, since those guys busted their butts every day at practice. They deserved to have some fun.

The final score was 42–7. And it could have been 77–0 except that Coach McInnis was a good sport and stopped passing the ball. The second unit scored their lone touchdown on eleven straight running plays, right up the gut of Hope Mills' defense.

As the game wound to a close, Franklin felt his adrenaline rush fade. His mouth hurt where his lip was split. A huge knot was rising on the back of his right hand where he smashed it into someone's face mask. His left calf had a small rivulet of blood running down the backside. He hadn't noticed either injury when it happened. You miss a lot when you are in the zone.

The gun sounded to end the game. Franklin felt himself lifted completely off the ground. He was swung around so violently that his feet flew out from under him. "Way to go man! You are a beast! I never saw you play like that before! What an animal!" It was Bart. Franklin was astonished.

Bart came to himself and dropped Franklin awkwardly. "Really man, great game! You were amazing. I got jacked up just watching you!"

"Thanks, Bart. You were awesome, too." Franklin had recovered enough to speak. "We demolished 'em, didn't we?"

Bart and Franklin made their way to midfield for the handshaking routine. Franklin heard the Hope Mills coach thank Coach McInnis for not running up the score. Coach Wittenburg inquired about the injured player; it sounded like he was going to be fine.

Old Rock Wilkins was nowhere to be seen. Maybe he was off shaving somewhere. Franklin hoped his mother would like the roses.

# 11 | Franklin Eavesdrops

## *Franklin*

Franklin turned onto the walkway leading to his house. It had been eight weeks since practice began. The football team was better than he had dared dream. They had played five games and won them all. Now it was the middle of the season.

After the open date this week, they had five games left. Having no practice today was sweet relief because Franklin's neck and shoulders were tight. He was glad to get a breather.

The weekend stretched before him like an island of rest in a sea of activity. He wanted to do nothing. His mother probably had other ideas for his time, like picking up pecans from the five big trees that ringed the house, cleaning his room, or some other task. She was a tornado of activity and often sucked him into her vortex.

The door slammed behind him as he made his way to the kitchen. "Mom, I'm home!" There was no answer. He dropped his books on the table, reached his right hand up to massage his shoulders, and again called out, "Mom, I'm home!" Still no answer. Franklin leaned over the sink and searched for his mom's car in the driveway. It was in its usual spot, so she was around somewhere.

He tugged open the refrigerator and stared inside. Shuffling the items, he found the fried chicken from supper two nights ago. All the good pieces were gone.

He grabbed a chicken leg off the plate and stuck it all the way into his mouth like a giant lollipop. With his teeth clamped firmly around

71

the leg, he pulled the bone slowly from his mouth. It came out clean as a whistle. Franklin tossed the bone in the trash and struggled to chew the cold chicken. Not bad at all. Maybe he would start reaching for a leg, rather than letting it be his piece of last resort. They seemed to have more taste than the breast meat he usually preferred.

The newspaper was sitting on the breakfast table so Franklin glanced at the sports section. Baseball was heading into the playoffs, and the Yankees hadn't been above .500 since August. Nothing to celebrate there.

Franklin didn't much care for baseball, if for no other reason than he couldn't do a damn thing the game required. He couldn't throw or catch. He couldn't hit or run. Still, he had always been a Yankees fan. Maybe it was The Babe. You can be sure that, steeped as he was in small town Southern culture, Franklin had no use for anything else associated with the word *Yankee*.

The ACC football standings showed that his Tar Heels weren't doing any better than the Yankees. They'd win one, then lose one, then maybe win another. No momentum. No gathering of confidence like Franklin had seen the Scots experience this year.

Sports were strange, Franklin was learning that. Though plenty of it was physical, Franklin was convinced the biggest game going on was between the players' ears. Victory seemed to be as much mental as anything. Maybe that was what was wrong with the high school team. Maybe the players didn't think they could win.

Coach McInnis and Coach Wittenburg had damn sure convinced Franklin and his teammates that *they* could win. It was the first time he had ever played on a team that won consistently. He liked it.

He tossed the newspaper back on the table and headed to the fridge. The chicken was making him thirsty. Nothing in there but milk, Franklin hated milk, and orange juice.

Wait! There were some Cokes, way in the back of the fridge. These were the itty bitty ones. The kind his mother served to the ladies in her bridge club. If there were more than four he was in business. He counted four, exactly. Darn. He knew the penalty if you drank the Bridge Club Cokes.

He was only seven when he had learned this lesson. His mother had three cases of Coca-Colas down in the basement, the short green bottles in the yellow wooden crates with red writing. She put them there to keep them cool and out of the way, and probably to get them out of Franklin's sight.

But he found them. And he found his own artful way to open them. Franklin used his father's largest phillips-head screwdriver and a medium-sized claw hammer to punch a hole in the top of a bottle cap any time he was thirsty.

It took him less than three weeks to drink all seventy-two of them. The dark, syrupy-sweet liquid burned as Franklin sucked it out of the hole in the bottle cap. It was lukewarm from the basement and especially fizzy. But it didn't burn nearly as bad as his backside once his parents discovered his little caper.

The whole thing seemed funny now. He wondered if his momma thought it was funny. Probably not. She didn't find much funny.

He grabbed the orange juice and glanced over his shoulder to make sure the coast was clear. Then he threw his head back and lifted the cool glass bottle to his lips. The sweet-sour juice washed across his mouth, and he could feel the chill run down his throat all the way to his gut. He wiped his mouth with the back of his hand and screwed the top on the bottle.

Franklin was tired. He headed out of the kitchen and towards the stairs. Maybe he could get a quick nap before his mom knew he was home. When he passed the den, he realized where she had been all along. The den door was mostly shut, and she was talking on the phone.

He swung the door open and waved at her. She waved back. "Just a moment, Ethel." She covered the phone's mouthpiece with her right hand and smiled up at Franklin.

"Hi, honey, how was your day?"

"Okay I guess, but I'm beat."

"I'm talking to Ethel McIntyre, but I'll only be a few more minutes. Why don't you run upstairs and rest for a bit? Julie is playing at a friend's house, so it will be quiet."

She sounded like a mother talking to a three-year-old, but the nap appealed to him. It was what he had in mind when he headed out of the kitchen.

"Good idea," he said, and headed up the stairs.

"See you in a bit." His mom was going back to her conversation with Ethel when she called out, "Franklin, would you please pull the door shut."

"Sure, Mom," he was already halfway up the stairs. Why did the door need to be shut? Franklin came down the steps and pulled the door mostly closed, though he was careful not to shut it completely. He could hear his mom talking more softly than usual.

Then he bounded heavily up the stairs, grabbed his room door, and, still standing in the hall, pulled it firmly shut. It closed with the satisfying click a latch makes when it engages the strike plate on the door jamb.

Franklin crept to the top of the staircase and slowly down the stairs until he was once again right outside the den door. His mother was talking so softly that he had to strain to hear what was going on. He sat down gently on the carpeted steps and leaned closer.

"You know, that poor Bart Wagram has had a tough go of it from the beginning. I feel sorry for the child, bless his heart. But I worry about him, too. He ought to be in tenth grade by now. He's almost a man. And he's playing football with the eighth graders. Somebody could get hurt. Plus I've heard he's a bully, and mothers always worry about someone picking on their child. I don't know what I'd do if he took after Franklin."

*Please, God,* Franklin thought, *don't let Mom be running interference for me up at the school.* Bart would have a field day if he found out Franklin's mother was sticking up for him.

"You know, Ethel, Mary Catherine never wanted a baby in the first

74

place. They were way too young! Oh, they tried to make it work, I'll give them that. They even got married and played house for a few years. But everybody knew it wouldn't work. Who in the whole town believed the mayor's daughter could stand the life of a holy-roller preacher's wife?"

Betsy Gibson paused, and Franklin wondered what a holy-roller preacher was. He had mostly been to the Methodist Church, with a little Presbyterian and Baptist thrown in when he visited his grandparents or went to church with a friend. There wasn't any rolling at any of these churches, holy or otherwise.

Ethel must be talking now, because his mom was silent for a while. Ethel eventually took a breath, and his mom broke in. "You're right. I don't understand that, either. They should have used protection. It's no secret where babies come from. I certainly knew when I was their age. Mistakes do happen in the heat of the moment, we've got Julie to show for that, but still. That boy cost Ricky Wagram the chance to get a really good education up there in Cambridge. I wonder if he would even be a preacher if he had gotten a chance to finish his college degree."

There was more silence as Ethel talked. Then Betsy spoke: "I know, Ethel, it's awful. I couldn't believe she left them like that, with Bart just a little boy. I don't know what they would have done if Ricky's mom hadn't pitched in. She really carried them through those first months. She stayed there the whole time, looking after Bart and trying to patch Ricky together so he could keep his job at the church. I heard there were so many women swarming around Ricky that they were like bees to honey, each trying to snag him before the next one got there."

His mom sighed, and Franklin could tell from the rustling that she was shifting positions. He stiffened as a chill shot through him. What if he got caught eavesdropping?

He rose to a semi-crouch in case she moved towards the door. The muscles in the top of his right thigh ached from being kneed during last week's game. It was odd, you almost never knew it when you got banged-up. It was only after the game, when the adrenaline wore off, that you realized how sore you were. He remembered the shower washing sweat down his body and across dozens of scrapes and scratches on his forearms, hands and calves. It felt like a thousand stinging nettles.

Franklin heard his mother sit down and he silently did the same. His thigh burned from the awkward crouch.

Betsy Gibson began to speak. It was strange hearing a conversation this way, having to piece together Mrs. McIntyre's comments from his mother's responses. Franklin wished he was a spy because he would have some super-secret listening device and could also hear what Mrs. McIntyre was saying.

His mom coughed and then spoke: "I heard Mary Catherine told someone that Ricky was abusive, but I don't believe it. He's a preacher after all. Now I'm not saying he never raised his voice, but I don't believe he would…" His mama stopped short. Ethel must have cut her off. It wasn't long before she picked up the thread again.

"You are so right, Ethel. Of course you never know what goes on behind closed doors. Folks told me that Mary Catherine always thought Ricky's family was beneath hers anyhow. The whole deal was just one of those hormone things, we all know how that is. They were a hot couple back in the day. Him with that shock of jet black hair and that chiseled face.

"I've got to say he was easy to look at, even though he did run with a fast crowd. I'm sure she wasn't his first. More like his twenty-first. Maybe chastity is not such a big deal in his denomination." His mother chuckled and Franklin felt his face flush. That didn't sound like his mom.

Ethel was speaking again. There was an extended silence before Betsy Gibson spoke.

"You're right. I forgot all about that. She was hot, too. I admit to being a little jealous. She had those long legs and high cheekbones and full lips. I remember her shaking her ass as a cheerleader. She made good grades, too. Some people have all the luck."

Franklin couldn't believe it. His mother just said *ass*. He would have been grounded for a month. He couldn't even get away with *butt*.

"That's true. That second wife is a mean one. She looks like she was suckled on a lemon and weaned on a persimmon. I wouldn't be surprised if she hits those kids, even the poor girl with all the problems."

Mrs. McIntyre responded and there was a long pause. All Franklin could hear was the hum of the refrigerator and the ticking of the clock on the living room mantel. He was about to leave. The times when his mother was silent were clearly the times he was most likely to be discovered. Finally his mother spoke up, and he was glad he had hung around.

"I agree, Ethel. Life would have been so different for Ricky if he had been able to finish his degree at Harvard. He got in on his brains, of course, but he was playing football, too. You know, he was the first person from Laurinburg to ever to go to one of those fancy Ivy League schools. I kind of hoped he'd become a big deal just so I could say *I knew him when*. Isn't that shallow? I wouldn't admit that to anyone else. Please keep my secret.

"Even if he had decided to be a preacher, you know he would have gone to one of those good seminaries up north. Why he might even be an Episcopalian or something. It's a shame, it really is."

Franklin's mom stopped talking, and he realized his nap time was slipping away. He promised himself he'd leave when the subject changed. His mother jumped back in.

"I didn't know that. I always wondered what the problem was. You mean she has seizures in addition to all of her physical issues? That must be a tough burden on Ricky and Doris, even if Doris is hateful. Do they think the child will ever outgrow it?

"That's a shame, it really is. I feel sorry for the poor thing. What's her name? Stephanie? And I feel sorry for Bart, too. You know all this turmoil hasn't done him any good. They say he has a hard time in school and I can see why.

"It's got to be tough on Ricky. He has to know that tongues are wagging about the whole situation. What you've said gives me some compassion for Doris, though. Ricky's always up there at the church, so you know she does most of the child-rearing by herself. Bart or Stephanie would be a handful all by themselves, much less the two of them together.

"Well, Ethel, I've taken a lot of your time, and what I really called to talk about was book club. Have you got another minute?"

Franklin rose from his perch outside the den door and crept up the steps, then down the hall to his room. He gently turned the door knob and entered the room without a sound. He was fully in the room with the door shut before he drew a breath.

Franklin's head reeled from all he had heard. He pulled off his shoes, swung his legs up onto the bed, and pulled a worn teddy bear over to him. No one, not even Kenneth, knew Franklin still slept with a teddy bear. The bear's name was *Doctor Brown*, and Franklin had gotten him as a gift the year his tonsils were removed. His mom helped him name the bear: *Doctor* because he came when Franklin was in the hospital and *Brown* because that was his color.

Franklin cuddled Dr. Brown and closed his eyes. His mind was awash in premarital sex, accidental children, and handicapped kids. It was swept by seizures and Harvard and the prospect of Bart being beaten by Mrs. Wagram. His heart was thumping in his chest, and he wondered if he would be able to fall asleep. Those thoughts soon faded, and Franklin was asleep before he could sort out everything he had heard.

# 12 | Memories

## *Mary Catherine Fitzhugh Wagram (Bart's Mother)*

Even after the marriage came crashing down, Mary Catherine loved many things about the life she once had with Ricky Wagram. It hadn't been easy. They were so young. She was fifteen when they began to date; he was just sixteen. She wondered if it might have turned out differently if they had been older.

Her first conversation with Ricky had been a brief one. The cheerleaders were wrapping up practice as the football team came in from the field. It was early October, and there was a hint of cool in the air. A light breeze swept her hair out of her face and over her ears. She was hot despite the breeze. Her blouse stuck to her back and sweat clung to her forehead.

Suddenly he was there, tall and dark and dirty. His hair was plastered to his forehead, and dirt was smudged across his face. There was a gash on the bridge of his nose, and dried blood sketched a jagged line down his cheek. He smelled like dirt and seawater, a salt air smell that was new to her.

"Hi," he said. I'm Ricky Wagram. I, "

"For heaven's sake, I know who you are." She cut him off. "I've been cheering for you all season."

He was flustered, and his face grew pink beneath the blood and dirt. "I wondered if you would go to the Homecoming Dance with me after the game next week. I could pick you up after I take a quick shower. It might be kind of late. Would you think about...?"

"I'd love to." She answered before he finished.

She didn't need to think about it. She had already thought about it.

What would her parents think? Would they let her have a later curfew for homecoming weekend? Would they worry that Ricky was too old for her? Would they give her the old song and dance about his family background? She guessed *yes* was the answer for all three questions.

"Great," he said. "I'll call you later."

He was gone as quickly as he appeared. She marveled that it had happened at all. He could have had his pick of any girl in the school. Why her?

She had no answer, but even then the electricity between them was palpable. Ricky Wagram was not the first boy to kiss her, but he was the first boy she ever kissed back. Rich, deep, luscious, open-mouthed kisses. She could see what all the excitement was about now, why the older girls spoke in hushed tones about making out with their boyfriends.

When you got him cleaned up, Ricky Wagram was a good-looking boy. He had a head of black hair and a craggy face with high cheekbones. Ricky looked like he might be part Indian, perhaps Lumbee or Cherokee. Mary Catherine never asked and she didn't care. Even after all the pain of the divorce, she could still look at him in profile all day long.

In the years after that first awkward date request, she and Ricky made a great couple. He was tall, dark and rangy; she was leggy, blonde and blue-eyed. They danced their way through high school. There were parties after every home game, plus the Valentine's Dance and the Prom. His senior year she even got elected Homecoming Queen, riding on his football prowess, her good grades and general perkiness, and their mutual good looks.

The whole thing had been like a fairy tale. He was the charming prince, the knight-in-shining armor. She was the blonde-haired princess in the long, powder-blue dress. Of all Mary Catherine's memories, being on stage with Ricky before the homecoming election was one of her favorites, along with the day they married, and the day, not long afterwards, when Bart was born.

But if the whole thing had been a magic carpet ride, there had been plenty of in-air turbulence. Like the first time Mary Catherine's mother sat down with her to talk about Ricky and his family.

## "Ricky's People Aren't Like Us"

Mary Catherine was right about all three of her questions. Her parents did let her have a late curfew for the Homecoming Dance, but her mother worried incessantly about Ricky's age and his family background. The result was one of those exasperating mother-daughter conversations that drove Mary Catherine crazy.

In small southern towns everyone knows everyone's business. Each successive generation carries the sins of its forebears. People credit you with the successes of your ancestors and damn you for their sins. And you don't deserve either.

Mary Catherine was treated to the whole history of Ricky's family. *Ricky's people aren't like us*, her mother said earnestly. Whatever that meant. Her mama could be oblique. And a bit of a snob.

Ricky's great-grandfather had come down to Laurinburg from "somewhere up North" right after the Civil War. Mary Catherine's mom was pretty sure he was a carpetbagger. Whether Ricky's people were well-intentioned in the beginning, no one knew. That was lost in the tales about what happened when Reconstruction began.

The Wagrams were seen as oppressors, along with everyone who came south after the war. And once voters wrested control of state and local government from Reconstruction officials, the family became social pariahs. They were pretty much stuck on the margins of Laurinburg society. But they made out all right.

As her mama related it, the first couple of generations made a good living farming way up in the northern part of the county. That and making moonshine. Nobody much lived up in that end of the county anyhow, and making liquor was considered a man's right. Plus, they were good at it.

Even though people bore a grudge about Reconstruction, they admired a man who was good at what he did. Ricky's forebears made the best corn liquor around. People traveled miles over the rutted roads just to buy their 'shine from the Wagrams. They first came on horseback and in wagons, and then later in horseless carriages.

When prohibition was enacted, the Wagrams got downright wealthy in the corn liquor business. Everybody knew what they were up to, but nobody cared enough to stop them. Even in the Bible Belt, a man had to have a drink after a hard day in the field or at the cotton mill.

The Wagram's white lighting had a bead on it that told you it was good even before the first sip. It was smooth all the way down, clear and crisp and perfect. No one went blind drinking it either, because the Wagrams didn't cut corners like some fools who ran the 'shine using a car radiator as a condenser. Some said the Wagrams were like the Kennedys up in Massachusetts, except the Wagrams made their own liquor.

All that changed when Ricky's Daddy got religion and, as Mary Catherine's Mama told her, *the whole gravy train jumped the track.*


# Richard Wagram
# (Ricky Wagram's Daddy, Bart's Grandfather)

A traveling Pentecostal preacher came to town the summer Richard Wagram, Ricky's daddy, was sixteen. The preacher set up a big white tent on the edge of town, and preached for a solid week. There was a band, and every night people "fell out" in the power of the Holy Ghost.

Ricky's old man started going to the revival for entertainment. It was a blazing hot summer, and going to the preaching was a great way to get out of the house. The open field surrounding the tent was big enough to catch the nighttime breeze. And the tent had huge vents near the peak, so there was always a bit of a draft. That kept a breath of air running through the thing, though it could still get hot as the dickens when the tent filled up with people and the whole place started buzzing with the Spirit.

Getting out of the house wasn't the only reason to go to a revival meeting. There wasn't much else happening in Laurinburg on a summer evening, which meant that most of the cute girls in town were at the revival, along with all of Richard Wagram's friends.

Mary Catherine had heard Ricky's daddy tell the story on himself, how he'd sneak a half-pint of moonshine into the tent, and he and his buddies would sip it quietly while they watched the show. It was more entertaining than anything else that happened in the summer, except maybe the Fourth of July parade. But the parade only lasted an hour, while tent meeting went on for an entire week.

Ricky's daddy told the story with an expression Mary Catherine couldn't quite figure out. Was it bemusement, amazement, awe? He talked about the revival like it had two distinct movements: a *before* and an *after.*

*Before* was the time when Richard Wagram was sitting in the tent just taking it all in. Folks were waving their arms in the air and swooning in the Spirit. The band was up on the stage rocking out, especially the drummer. And Richard and his friends were sitting toward the back, passing the flask and laughing and elbowing each other when the show got good.

That was the *before* part, when it was simply entertainment. They'd take care to sit on the end of the row, in case they got an urge to pee or needed to hightail it out of the tent before the final act. They had learned that lesson well.

On their first visit to a tent meeting, the boys made the mistake of sitting dead in the middle of the row, right in the center of all the hard metal folding chairs. It seemed like the perfect place, like a seat on the fifty-yard line at a football game, to catch all the action. And it *was* perfect for watching. But it had major shortcomings.

In the first place, the boys quickly realized they were way too conspicuous to do much flask-passing. But that wasn't the worst of it. They got trapped. That was the worst of it.

Not long after they selected their seats and just as the band was cranking up, Ethel Roebuck and her four sisters plopped down beside them on the right. Now Ethel Roebuck was a *large* lady. You could have cut her in half, and each half would have outweighed Richard by a good fifty pounds. And Ethel was the smallest of her sisters. You could smell them when they came in, freshly powdered and all.

The boys were blocked on the right end of the row by five enormous ladies, pocketbooks in their laps, chubby knees pressed squarely against the seatback of the chair in front of them. These women were a full load, and there'd be no getting out once the revival got rolling. The boys weren't too worried. They could still make their escape from the left if necessary. But not for long.

Not everything that happened at revival time was impelled by the power of the Holy Ghost. Richard Wagram and his buddies were proof of that. It was the biggest week-long gathering of people in the county, except for the county fair. And since it was the biggest gathering of people in the county, some folks came to settle scores, to collect debts, or just, as the sheriff said, "looking for trouble."

The sheriff and his deputies kept a high profile at revivals. On this night, they chose the left end of Richard Wagram's row to park their considerable bulk.

Richard Wagram said it reminded him of *The Charge of the Light Brigade*, only instead of cannons to the right of them and cannons to the left of them, there were Roebucks to the right of them and deputies to the left of them.

So there Richard and his buddies sat. Through hymns and swooning and the movement of the Holy Ghost, they sat. Through a sermon so long that Richard almost learned how to say the alphabet backwards, they sat. Through three collections and six altar calls, they sat. And they didn't have a drop to drink, though Richard had the flask tucked snug in his hip pocket.

The sheriff was one of his Daddy's customers, so drinking wasn't the problem. But Richard knew the sheriff would consider passing a flask during the middle of a revival to be "looking for trouble."

The boys learned this lesson quickly. But they kept coming back. It was a damn good show, and the time after the tent meeting was the best time of all.

Something just gets in the air at revivals. All that heat and passion and Spirit moving across the crowd. Folks would be milling around, talking and laughing and carrying on. The sheriff and his deputies would be making sure nobody came looking for trouble. There would be people selling ice cream, plus Bibles, tracts, and records.

You could find a cute girl and buy her an ice cream cone. Maybe walk down the road just a piece to get out of the circle of light around the tent. Then, if you were lucky, you could sometimes sneak a kiss or two and get the girl back to the tent before her parents knew she was missing. When he told it, you could always tell that The Reverend Wagram considered all this part of his *before* story of going to tent meetings.

Reverend Wagram would talk about all the good times, and then he'd say: "All that was well and good and lots of fun. I wouldn't take nothing for it. But nobody was more surprised than me when the Holy Ghost was waiting for me one Wednesday night."

And then he'd tell *the rest of the story*.

# 13 | Conversion

## *Bart's Grandfather Gets Religion*

Even after all the years, Richard Wagram's eyes sparkled and danced when he told his story. The tent meeting had already been in town for three nights, it always started on Sunday, the Wednesday he and his buddies slid in at the last minute and settled on the folding chairs near the back of the tent.

So far they had been disappointed. This preacher wasn't the same guy from last year, and he didn't put on as good a show. You could tell it by the crowds. Attendance was good on Sunday but had been trailing off ever since. Tonight looked like a full house, probably because the Baptist churches had canceled Wednesday Prayer Meeting and sent their flocks to the revival.

Richard and his buddies made sure to sit directly behind a row of blue-haired ladies. That would shield them from the watchful eyes of the sheriff when they got to passing the flask. And they darn sure sat on the *end* of the row. They didn't need to repeat that lesson.

The service began like all the rest. The boys passed the flask and each of them took a little nip. The band cranked up with some singing. This new preacher had a good music leader, and she had the blackest hair and the reddest lips the boys had ever seen. She was dressed modestly enough, but the boys noticed she had no trouble filling out her dress, both in the hips and across the chest.

The music leader sang a couple of songs alone, then asked everyone to stand and join her. The little paper hymnbooks looked tired, and many of them were dog-eared, or missing covers. The crowd sang three hymns, finishing with a rousing version of *Are You Washed in the Blood?* Then the leader rose to welcome everyone.

The preacher was working his way through a series of seven sermons. Most people didn't attend the revival every night, so the first thing he had to do was catch people up on what had happened so far. Ricky's Daddy and his buddies had been there every night, and they knew the story. So they passed the flask and waited to see what would happen.

Once the preacher finished catching everybody up, he got real quiet. He looked out on the audience, and spoke all serious-like: "Now what I'm about to tell you is not part of the sermon I've prepared. But I don't feel like I have any choice but to preach it. I was praying in the bus before I came up here tonight, and the Lord put a burden on my heart. So I've got to preach it. I've got to preach the burden the Lord has given me."

Nobody said a word.

Richard Wagram and his buddies exchanged puzzled glances and took another nip. The preacher looked out at the folks gathered under the white canvas, the crowd appeared bigger than it had been the last two nights, and asked, "Can I get an 'Amen'?"

"Amen," came back from the crowd, but it was weak and their heart wasn't in it.

"I can't hear you," he countered. His eyes flashed as he jabbed a finger at them.

"Amen!" they shouted, and this time Richard and his buddies screamed at the top of their lungs, laughing while they did.

"All right then. I was praying tonight in my bus, and the Lord told me there's someone in this tent who needs to hear a special message. Someone here is called of the Lord to preach, to minister in the temple, just like the boy Samuel ministered with Eli in the Old Testament. I don't know who it is, and you don't know who it is, but God knows who it is! Amen?"

"Amen!" they shouted, and their hearts were in it. The sound bounced off the stage and the band's drumheads and the folding chairs, and reverberated out into the still night air.

"So, this part of the message is for the person God is calling tonight. Amen?"

"Amen!" It was thunderous.

"I'm talking to you out there, brother or sister. You may have known the Lord all of your life, or you may be new in your faith. God don't care. When God chooses you, God will equip you. Think of David, the little Israelite boy chosen to slay the giant Goliath. God equipped him, didn't he?

"You may be young or you may be old. God don't care. God chose the small boy Samuel to serve in the temple with Eli, and God choose the woman Sarai to bear the child Isaac when she was well past the age of childbearing. Age is no barrier to God. Can I get another 'Amen'?"

"Amen!" rang through the crowd. Richard and his friends weren't bored now. They were leaning forward, transfixed. No elbows, no side-long glances, not even a nip from the flask. It had gotten good.

"I don't know who God is calling, because the Spirit didn't tell me. What the Spirit did tell me is that God is calling someone in this tent, someone right here and right now, to respond in a powerful way. It might be a woman. God has worked mighty things through women like Rebekah and Leah and Naomi and Ruth, not to mention Mary, the Mother of God. It might be a woman.

"Or it might be a man, a man of God like Abraham or Moses or Solomon. Or a fisher of men, like some of the disciples who followed Christ. Or even a tax collector. God don't care what you've *been* doing, because God knows what you're *gonna* do!

"I don't know who it is, but God knows who it is." The preacher said "God" real funny and loud, then he eyeballed the audience one more time. "Can I get an 'Amen'?"

"Amen!" they roared.

"So we're gonna go to the Lord in prayer, and we're gonna ask the

Lord to speak to his servant in a special way. Brother," he turned to the piano player, "give us some praying music."

Richard and his buddies could barely hear the song coming from the piano as the drummer faintly joined in. It was an old song. No one was singing; there was just music, but they all knew the words. *Softly and tenderly Jesus is calling, calling to you and to me…*

The band got all the way through the first verse, and then the preacher started to pray. He started softly, too, just like the music.

"Oh Lord," he said, "We come to you as sinful people. We are all sinners, and we know it. But we also know that our sin is no barrier to your grace and mercy. No sir," he was picking up speed and volume now, "no sir, you are a good and powerful God. You are a God who loves, a God who comes, a God who saves. You are a God who calls us out of darkness into light, out of sin into goodness, out of death into life. Amen!"

The preacher was shouting now, and giving his own *Amen's* like he didn't need the crowd at all. Like this whole dialogue was just between him and God. Like the rest of us were just eavesdropping.

That's what Richard Wagram always said when he got to this part. He said it felt like he was eavesdropping on a conversation between the tent preacher and God, and he was embarrassed to be doing it.

"So, God," the tent preacher was on a roll now, "we ask you to speak to your servant here tonight as you spoke to me on the bus. Whisper in your servant's ear, O Lord. Call him as you called me and so many before me. By the power of your Holy Ghost move across the waters of your servant's life and convict him of your love and mercy.

"Listen, people!" Suddenly the preacher was talking to the crowd again. "Listen, people. Pay attention to the Lord. The Holy Ghost is moving in this place. I can feel it. The Holy Ghost is moving, and God is calling someone to serve. Attend to your heart. Attend to the Lord! Be obedient, even unto death, the death of your old self and the birth of a new creation in Jesus Christ. Listen to the Lord!

"Oh, Lord," the preacher was again talking to God, "I call on you to anoint your servant. Fill them with the Holy Ghost. Cast out all demons and bind Satan from them. Fill your servant with the joy of the Lord and have them, like your servant David, dance before you."

Even after he became *The Reverend* Wagram, Richard Wagram laughed at this point. "I knew that verse," he'd say. "I knew David danced *naked* before the Lord. I thought about poking one of my buddies, but decided against it. And that's all I remember."

He had no need to fear. The rest of the town would fill in the gaps in his story. What happened next was not in dispute.

Richard rose from the rusty metal chair on the end of the row and raised his arms above his head. He began swaying back and forth, moaning softly deep in his throat.

Most people didn't notice. They were far enough away that they couldn't hear him, and they should have had their eyes closed and heads bowed in prayer anyhow. But Richard's friends noticed, their eyes wide and their mouths gaping open. They laughed at first, thinking he was just putting them on. But soon they could tell that this was *for real.* God, or something, had a hold of Richard.

Richard swayed and moaned, and the moaning got louder. Then he began to talk, and the words didn't sound like a language anyone in Laurinburg knew how to speak. The boys looked from Richard to the stage, but the preacher wasn't up to speed on what was going on. He kept leaning on the beat-up pulpit, right there in front of the brown wooden cross.

"O Lord," he prayed, "grab a hold of your servant." The boys guessed the Lord had already answered that part of the prayer. "Grab hold of your servant and convict him of your goodness. Grab hold of your servant and don't turn loose till you get a 'yes' to your call to preach the Good News. Amen!"

"Yes Lord!"

The shout was so loud the boys jumped. "Yes, Lord, yes!!" It was coming from Richard, and now everybody was in on what was happening. The boys' eyes were big as saucers.

Richard was out in the aisle now, eyes shut tight, head thrown back, arms waving wildly from side to side. He was still saying those nonsense words, punctuated every so often with "Yes! Yes! O Lord, yes!"

The preacher was paying attention now. The boys saw him peek out from nearly-shut eyes, then go bug-eyed when he got a load of Richard. Richard seemed to be dancing now. At first it was like he was running in place. Then he slowly picked up a little shuffle, and he was dancing across the wheat straw laid in the aisle to keep the dust down. He moved toward the stage at the front of the tent.

The preacher grabbed the microphone from the stand and headed down a short flight of steps that led to an open area in front of the stage. He preached as he went.

"O Lord, your servant has heard your call. Amen. We thank you, Lord. We thank you for this young man whose heart has been touched by your call. Amen, Lord."

The preacher walked down the steps, and Richard danced on down the aisle. They arrived in front of the stage at the same moment. Something had changed in Richard. At first he was gently waving his arms in the air, sort of like a springtime breeze. Next he took to moving his arms frantically from side to side, like someone trying to flag down a train.

Finally, just as he arrived there in front of the preacher, Richard went to jumping and twitching like someone who had got hold of the wrong end of an electric wire. The boys didn't know what to think. It didn't seem to faze the preacher. He had seen it all before.

He kept preaching and motioned for a couple of stout men on the front row to come up and help him.

All the while, Richard is hollering "Yes, Lord! Yes!" and a bunch of words no one can make out and jerking around like someone having a fit. And the band is still playing, nobody had noticed it because they were focused on other things, *Softly and tenderly Jesus is calling...*over and over again. You would have thought they'd get worn out with it after a while, but you couldn't tell it if they did.

The preacher was wrapping up on thanking the Lord when Richard gave out with a mighty "Yes!" then went limp and slumped to the ground. Quick as a wink, the two big fellows from the first row grabbed Richard and laid him out right there in front of the stage. He went down so fast everyone was startled, like somebody had shot him or something. But the boys could see his chest heaving as he lay there, so they figured he was all right.

All of a sudden it was real quiet. No hollering and no preaching and no dancing down the aisle. After all that excitement, it was dead still. The band was playing, but they were playing so softly you could hear the bugs buzzing around the electric lights strung from pole to pole in the tent.

The preacher knew what to do. He motioned to the band to soften the volume and then knelt over Richard. "Let's close our eyes and go to the Lord in prayer one more time.

"O Lord, we thank you for sending your Spirit on this young man's soul. Be with him now as he rests in you, slain in the Spirit by your amazing love. Equip him for your ministry. Drive far away from him all devices and snares of the enemy and draw him close in your loving embrace.

"We thank you Lord that you are a Lord who calls your children to you, a Lord who loves us holy and wholly, always and in all ways. Help us to hear your call on our own lives, and to respond in faith and hope, with love and courage. Amen." He said the Amen quietly, like a man whose prayers had been truly answered.

When the boys opened their eyes, Richard was still laid out in the front of the stage, as peaceful as could be. The preacher spoke to the crowd. "Brothers and sisters, we are going to take a short break now while we minister to this young man. Please pray for him as you enjoy the cool night air. We'll flash the lights in a few minutes and begin our meeting with some more singing. While you are praying, please thank the Lord for His goodness and His steadfast love."

Ricky's daddy always told this story with a mix of awe and

bemusement. He had gone to a revival looking for entertainment and maybe a chance to steal a kiss, but he had come home called to preach. He'd always say, "That's just like the Lord. If you want to make God laugh, tell Him your plans!"

## "The Wagrams are not Our Kind of People"

"I'll give him this, though," Mary Catherine's mama made a rare concession, "he tried to live what he believed. And it cost him nearly everything he had."

See, the Wagrams had made some of their *money* off of farming, but they had made all of their *living* off of corn liquor. After that revival, Richard Wagram wouldn't have anything to do with making liquor. He poured out his flask right there at the front of the tent, with the whole world watching. Almost drove his buddies crazy. Not to mention the sheriff.

"Why didn't you just give it to me, dammit?" one of his buddies hollered later. "There wasn't no need to pour that stuff out. I woulda took it off your hands, no problem. You woulda been straight with the Lord, and I woulda had me a little nip to wet my whistle."

Richard wouldn't hear of it. And he wouldn't discuss it, either. "If it's wrong, it's wrong," he'd say. "You'll understand better when you get to talk to the Lord face-to-face."

Richard had a bad falling-out with his family. He stayed around the house just long enough to finish high school. He wouldn't help with the still anymore, and it made his daddy mad. "You ain't got to drink the stuff," his old man said. "Just help me make it."

The old man was getting on up in years, and Richard was far and away the best 'shiner of his generation. But he wouldn't do it. Told his old man the same thing he told his buddies: "If it's wrong, it's wrong. You'll understand better when you get to talk to the Lord face-to-face."

His daddy let him stay to work on the farm because Richard was a first-rate farm hand, but things were never the same. When he got out of high school, Richard took a job in the cotton mill and started preaching on the side. He got himself a little part-time church, then preached it up to a pretty good size. Got married along the way, and Ricky was born a couple of years later.

"So you see," Mary Catherine's mama was wrapping up, "the Wagrams are not really our kind of people. Carpetbaggers and moonshiners and tent preachers just aren't like us."

## Mary Catherine Fitzhugh Wagram

Mary Catherine wouldn't listen. Her family was boring, sitting in that stuffy Methodist Church, going to work every day in a suit and a tie. She had checked out her whole extended family, men and women, girls and boys, and not a one of them was as good-looking, as athletic, or as smart as Ricky Wagram.

Maybe it's time to get some new blood into this family, she thought. And I'm just the one to do it.

# 14 | Game Plan

## *Coach McInnis*

Bill McInnis arrived at the restaurant early and sat in the last booth against the wall. The sun streamed through the window, warming the tabletop. Phyllis came over to take his order, "Hey, Honey. What you having?"

"I'll start with some iced tea. I'm meeting Larry Wittenburg. He ought to be here in a minute. I'll order when he gets here."

"Sure thing. I'll get your tea. You reckon he's gonna drink tea, too? He usually does, don't he?"

"Yeah, bring him a glass."

Bill chuckled. Larry could drink enough tea to float a battleship. "You might as well put the pitcher on the table. It'll save wear and tear on your feet."

"Gotcha," Phyllis shot him a wink and was off to the kitchen.

Bill stared out the window. Fall was his favorite season. It was hard to beat late October in Laurinburg. The trees were beautiful, the suffocating heat was fading, and mornings were crisp and clear. The afternoons were perfect for football.

Bill had been fooling around with football most of his life. He had played little league as a kid and starred at Laurinburg High. His senior year he was a co-captain and first-team All Conference. He walked-on the football team at Carolina, but it didn't take him long to figure out he wasn't good enough to play for the Heels. He didn't care. He became a manager and then a student trainer. And he discovered he liked that part of the game every bit as much as playing.

The coaches at Carolina were surprised when he asked for a playbook and they initially declined. But his constant cajoling convinced them to relent, and he often sat in on chalk talks and film sessions. By his senior year Bill was an ad hoc student coach.

He considered a career in coaching, but his childhood dream had been to be a doctor. So he gave up the idea of coaching for the steady paycheck and more normal work week of a small town family doctor.

But Bill did *love* football. He was a student of the game in every sense of the word. He'd even found a way to work as an assistant high school coach when he was in med school at Duke.

Larry Wittenburg, on the other hand, was less a student of the game than a practitioner of the fine art of the motivational speech. It stood to reason. Undersized and underweight, he had willed himself onto the small college All-American team as an offensive lineman at Lenoir Rhyne. The team won the National Small College Championship his senior year.

Larry was smart enough, but his real gifts were determination, tenacity, and motivation. If Larry Wittenburg told you he was going to build a rocket and launch it from his backyard, you'd be a fool to bet against him.

Larry was from somewhere in Ohio, Bill couldn't remember where, but wound up in Laurinburg when his wife came to town to nurse her dying mother. After the mother-in-law died, Larry and his wife decided to stick around. The weather was more agreeable, they liked the sweet tea, and the only traffic jam was in the parking lot of the Honey Cone Drive-In.

It bothered Larry that the folks in Laurinburg were still fighting the Civil War, but he kept his mouth shut and enjoyed their company. Small town life had a lot to recommend it.

Bill glanced up to see Larry rushing towards him with a sheaf of papers in one hand and a wide grin on his face. "Hey man, I just left the Firestone store, and they're all talking about our football team. I don't know how those guys get anything done. They know more about sports than they do about tires.

"They've given up on the high school team. Said the team had already lost a bunch of games they should have won. I wouldn't be surprised if some of them show up for our game with Richmond." Larry slid into the seat just as Phyllis arrived with the tea.

"Here you go, hon." She placed the tea in front of Bill, then set a glass and a pitcher down in front of Larry. "I figured you'd want some, too. You guys need a menu?"

"Nah. I know what I'm gonna have. How about you, Larry?"

"You start. I'll be ready by the time you finish."

Bill ordered country style steak with mashed potatoes. Fried okra and steamed squash rounded out the plate, along with a basket of cornbread muffins. Larry went for breakfast: cheddar cheese and bacon omelet with grits, hash browns, sliced tomatoes, and biscuits.

Phyllis got it all down and nodded, "Eating light, I see." She headed to put their order in.

Larry spread his papers on the table and began to talk about ideas for the defense. He had designed a new defensive alignment that would take advantage of Bart Wagram's head hunting at middle linebacker.

The defensive plan sounded good, and Larry was deeply committed to it. Bill had long ago learned that an eighty percent plan with a hundred percent commitment would beat the brains out of a hundred percent plan with less commitment. They agreed on the new alignment, then began to kick around the season in general.

Larry looked up from his diagrams, "When the season started, did you have any idea we'd be where we are today?"

Bill rubbed his face with the palms of his hands. "I thought we'd be pretty good. I knew Bart was going to dominate on defense from day one. But no, I didn't think we'd be this good. I had no idea we'd be undefeated."

"Neither did I. The offense has come along better than I thought it would. The defense carried us the first couple of games, but the offense is catching up. I've been surprised by that Gibson kid. He's got a lot of fight in him."

"Yeah, and he's making Bart better, too. I watch them every time we scrimmage. They really go after each other."

"Is there bad blood between those two? Sometimes it's vicious between them."

"I don't know about bad blood," Bill responded. "I do know that Bart has it tough at home. His daddy divorced and remarried, and they have a little girl with all kinds of problems. I've never met Bart's stepmother, but he once called her a bitch when he didn't know I was listening. Something has got a burr up that boy's butt. He will rip an opponent's head off when a simple tackle would do the job."

Phyllis appeared with lunch and the men broke their conversation to thank her. "You boys need anything else?" Both men shook their heads no and she headed to the kitchen.

Larry sliced into his omelet and returned to their earlier conversation. "Remember that time when Bart punched Franklin in the balls?"

"Yeah, you know that had to hurt."

"Worst hurt I ever had. You reckon Bart did that on purpose?"

"I always figured he did. It looked like he slugged Franklin just because he could. That's the reason I called off practice. I didn't want it to get out of hand. I let it alone so they could work it out. Thought it might be good for Franklin. He seemed sort of soft when the season began. I wanted to see what he was made out of."

"He'll surprise you. He's a pretty tough kid. His brain is his best tool, but his body is catching up. What's his story?"

Bill answered, "His daddy runs the bank. He's not much of an athlete, more of a pillar-of-the-community type. His mom's named Betsy. She's cute, we went to school together, although she was a couple of years ahead of me. She's a little uptight, but a good girl. She taught math at the high school before they got married.

"Franklin has played football for several years, starting out in little league. Last year he weighed too much for little league so he played on the mill village team. I talked to the coach, who said Franklin was intimidated. Most of the mill village kids were older and bigger than him. They kicked his butt. A year makes a lot of difference at his age."

"No kidding. But, I'm still surprised how he manhandled Rock Wilkins. That guy was a beast, and Franklin beat him like a drum."

"Yeah, that was your doing, and you know it," Bill chuckled. "You worked him over with that 'roses for your mother' routine. He was so fired up he could have played for the high school team."

"It was fun to watch. I didn't even mind the penalties; he was a wild man. I wish I could get them all that fired up."

"Can't do it. Might not even want to. Some kids just don't respond to that stuff. I'm actually surprised it works with Franklin, smart as he is."

"You're right," Larry paused briefly. "It doesn't work with all of 'em. It doesn't work with Bart in exactly the same way. Bart has this enormous rage trapped barely beneath the surface. Tap into his rage, and you're in business. Franklin wants to prove himself, that's his deal. And Franklin's a lot smarter than Bart."

"No kidding. He hasn't flunked any grades."

"I'm not talking about flunking grades. You ever seen that thing he does with his fingers?"

"What thing?"

"Have you ever wondered why our opponents get called offside so often? It's Franklin. I've seen him. He bends over the ball, everyone is revved up just waiting for the snap count, and then he'll move one finger, ever so slightly. Someone always jumps offside. And now it's first and five instead of first and ten. And the opponent is crazy-mad because he feels screwed."

"I'll be damned," a wry smile creased Bill McInnis' face. "How come you never said anything about it?"

"I figured the less said the better. Plus I didn't want to spook him or the rest of the offense. Maybe Harvey is in on it; he's never said. I know Franklin only does it on plays when there is a long snap count. It's the easiest five yards we ever get."

"I'll watch for it. Can't believe you never told me."

"Some things you don't need to know." Larry grinned at Bill.

"Let's talk about the game against Richmond," Bill shifted in his seat. We really need to beat these guys."

"What is the deal with them anyhow? They've beaten us every year I've lived here."

"I have asked myself that question ten thousand times. Really, how can they be that much better? They're just like us, a mix of small town kids and farm boys. Thing is, they expect to win. And they do. We never beat them once in my whole time as a player. It's something of a joke."

"Well, it's ain't a joke to me. I don't have all that history. We're gonna beat 'em this time. Watch and see."

Bill and Larry bent to their game plan. They sketched fresh diagrams on napkins and the back of Larry's new defensive schemes. They assessed relative strengths and weaknesses versus Richmond, and talked about psychology. Both were convinced that this game was more about mindset than talent. No team is better than another for thirty years straight.

Phyllis returned with another pitcher of iced tea for Larry.

"What are you guys doing?" she asked. "I've never seen so many diagrams. You've been here all afternoon. I'm gonna have to charge you booth rent if this keeps up." She winked, this time at both of them.

"We're trying to figure out how to beat Richmond this week," Bill spoke first. "You got any ideas?"

"Just forfeit the game and save yourself the aggravation. We haven't beaten those guys in forever."

"Thanks for that vote of confidence," Bill said. "I'll be sure and tell the team how much faith you have in them."

"I'm not knocking your players. I'm just telling you the truth. How long has it been since we last beat them?"

"Bill tells me it's been at least thirty years."

"My point exactly," replied Phyllis. "So why do you two think this team is gonna be any different?"

"Because this is our team, and this is our year, and we're gonna find a way!" Larry Wittenburg was half out of the booth now, constrained only by the table top creasing his thick thighs. He wasn't shouting. Yet. But he was fired up. Phyllis stepped back a half-step.

This was one thing Bill loved about Larry; now Larry was pissed. He had been challenged, and he was motivating himself to motivate the team to do this thing that looked impossible.

"All right then, sweetheart," Phyllis recovered her familiar tone. "We're on the same side here. You're new around here; I was just giving you the history. Y'all whip 'em dead. I want you to win as much as you want to win." She headed back to the kitchen.

"Nobody wants us to win as bad as *I* want us to win!" Larry rasped.

"I believe that," Bill said.

In the end, the coaches couldn't figure out anything different to do. They had won all of their games. Everything they were doing worked.

Winning this game came down to three factors: execution, motivation, and confidence. The coaches knew the team could execute because they had executed all year. Motivation wasn't an issue either. No team from Laurinburg had beaten the Pirates in thirty years, so there was plenty of reason to be motivated. Confidence was the pivotal element. The team had to believe they could win.

The coaches divided responsibility for the key factors. They would both handle execution, Bill for the offense and Larry for the defense. Larry would take care of motivation. It was his strength anyway. Bill would think about ways to build the team's confidence, to convince the team that they not only had a chance to win, they had a *right* to win. That was the plan. It was nothing fancy, but fancy often gets teams in trouble.

It was 2:38 when they wrapped up. Larry slipped out to the men's room, and Phyllis stopped by with the check. "I hope you guys whip Richmond bad. I've got friends who live over there, and those folks are downright arrogant when it comes to football."

"We'll do our best," Bill replied. "I think we've got a plan that will make it happen." He grabbed the check and handed her a five-dollar tip. Five bucks was more than the check, but he owed her booth rent.

Larry caught up with Bill, and they headed to the register. "I think we've got a plan," he said. "What do you think?"

"We'll know soon enough."

# 15 | Doris Rages

## *Bart*

"Get back in here you ungrateful wretch!" Doris was screaming, and Bart knew what would happen next. He was always astounded by the ferocity of her temper. "Get in here, you little shit! I'll tell you when you can leave."

Bart hung near the door jamb, close enough to qualify as being in the room, but out of harm's way. Or so he thought. A coffee cup whizzed by his ear and shattered on the wall in the hall. "You bastard! I wish you had never been born! If I had known what a pain in the ass you were going to be, I would never have married your father!"

Bart studied her face. He was older now and less afraid she would really hurt him. It had not always been that way. When he was eight years old she terrified him and hurt him more than once. Now he outweighed her by fifty pounds. She was a wiry, skinny woman. Mean and skinny. She did have a good right arm. He'd give her that. Another cup zipped by. He ducked behind the door jam, and the cup smashed into the wall.

Her face was drawn, the skin tight and pale across her cheekbones like the leather drumhead he had seen at the Indian Museum in Raleigh. She looked dead.

Bart had seen a dead man once. It was at the funeral home. His friend's family ran the funeral home, and Beacham snuck him in even though it was against the rules. The dead guy had been pale and drawn, too. That was what Doris looked like, except that her ears were bright red.

He tried to work out what had pissed her off. Nobody was in the house when he came home. There was a hollow knot where his stomach belonged. He was famished after school and football practice.

He rummaged in the refrigerator and found leftover roast from the night before, then cut himself a good-sized hunk and ate it standing over the kitchen sink. It was delicious.

Gravy ran from the corner of his mouth down his chin. He swiped at it with the back of his free hand and chewed slowly, savoring the rich texture of the meat and the saltiness of the gravy. He could've eaten the whole roast standing there, but knew that would send her over the edge. He left the remainder in the pot and shoved it back in the fridge.

He had nearly finished cleaning up when he heard the porch door slam. Bart tried to get things perfect before she got to the kitchen, but he didn't quite make it. Doris clip-clipped into the room on her tiny little feet and saw him wiping the last of the gravy from his chin. And that set her off.

"Have you been eating that pot roast in the refrigerator?" She started shrill and escalated quickly. "I was saving that for supper. You should have known that! Can't you just once in your whole life think about someone other than yourself?"

"But Mom," he began. It was a concession to his dad. He didn't think of her as mom at all. He wished she was as dead as the guy at the funeral home.

"But Mom, I came home from school and I was starving. No one was here. I didn't know when you'd get here or what we would have for supper. So I fixed myself a snack. I didn't know we were going to have the roast for supper, I swear."

"That's just like you! That's just like a man. Just feed your face and don't worry about anyone else. You're just like all the rest."

It was clear to Bart that this wasn't about him. Or the pot roast.

"I'm sorry, Mom, I swear I am. I was just hungry, that's all. When are we going to have supper, anyway?"

"*We* are going to have supper in about thirty minutes. *You* just ate yours. I don't know what you are going to have. You can fix yourself a peanut butter sandwich, or find something in the pantry. Or you can starve to death for all I care.

"Here you are, eating us out of house and home when you know money is tight, and that damn church don't pay your daddy enough to buy a pot to piss in."

Stephanie clomped into the room, leg braces clattering. Bart got a quick reprieve when Doris turned her attention elsewhere. Her face softened as she bent to face her child. She spoke slowly, clearly, and more gently than normal.

"Honey, I know the trip to the doctor wears you out. You were a good girl and I'm proud of you. Why don't you go to your room and play for a few minutes? Or you can watch television. I'll call you when supper is ready."

Stephanie looked up at her mom through Coke-bottle thick glasses. The glasses were so heavy that her face had perpetual red marks where the nose pads rested. She smiled broadly, blue eyes sparkling, then gurgled what passed for speech. Doris seemed to understand. She smiled and patted the tiny, bent child on top of the head as Stephanie hobbled from the room.

Bart watched Stephanie leave and wondered what life must be like for her. It had to be tough. Watching Doris care for Stephanie made him lonely. Tears pooled at the bottom of his eyes, but he didn't have long to grieve.

Doris was back in attack mode. "I'm getting ready to fix supper for me and Stephanie. We're having the rest of the goddamn roast for supper. Since you've been a selfish pig and already eaten more than your share, I don't know what you'll be eating." Her voice rose, and he could tell she was getting spun up again.

"Mom," he decided to see if this would work. "Mom, I wish you wouldn't say 'goddamn.' If not for your sake, or Stephanie's, then how about for Daddy's sake? You know he doesn't like it."

"Goddamn him, too. I don't give a good goddamn whether he likes it or not. You tell me this, you little shit. If God loves us all so much, like your daddy the preacher says he does, then why do we have to scrimp and scratch to get by? Why do we have Stephanie, the biggest batch of medical problems ever rolled into one sack of skin? Why do we have to deal with all this crap? Why? Tell me that, if God loves us so much!"

"But…" Bart didn't know where to start. Truth told, he had wondered the same thing about Stephanie. Why would a loving God let a baby like her get born in the first place? She couldn't half hear or see or walk. Could hardly talk. Everybody would be better off, Stephanie included, if she had died the day she was born.

Bart would never admit it, but he sort of blamed Stephanie for getting him into this whole mess. He suspected that his stepmother would be easier to deal with if Stephanie had been a regular, normal baby.

"But Mom," he began anew, "you remember what Daddy preached a couple of weeks ago? About God saying, 'I will never leave you nor forsake you.' It's in the story…"

"Stop it! No more of that God shit! You sound just like your daddy. Are you people crazy? There is no God. You've all got your heads stuck up your asses. You can't see the world like it really is!"

Oh boy.

Bart looked at her with sad eyes. He'd heard her say many things, lots of them far more profane than this. He'd never heard her say that there was no God. He felt sick to his stomach.

He tried once more. "Mom, there *has* to be God. Even with Stephanie and no money and Daddy working all the time at the church, there has to be a God. Look at how beautiful the world is. Life is just too good…"

"You," she interrupted him, "are your daddy's child after all! Spouting all that God shit. And all this time I thought you were like that slut who gave you birth. But you're not. You're exactly like your Daddy."

"Okay, that's it!" Bart was infuriated now. He needed to get out of Doris' range. "I'm not gonna stand here and listen to you call my mama names."

He was headed for the door when the first cup flew. He stayed long enough for a second round, and then he had had enough. Bart headed to the stairs.

"Come back here this instant!" Doris screamed.

He ignored her and took the stairs two at a time, landing heavily on the step at the top of the flight. He glanced backwards and saw she had not followed him. Good. There was a God after all. He closed his door and slumped on the bed.

The late afternoon sunlight splashed across the bed, and the spread was warm and soft. Bart rested his head on the pillow and began to sob softly. The salt from the tears ran down his checks and merged with the last of the gravy on his upper lip. He cried and prayed and prayed and cried until he finally slipped off into a dreamless sleep.

It was eight twenty-three when he woke up.

Bart had to pee some kind of bad, so he tiptoed to the door and opened it quietly. The television was on in the den. He guessed that Stephanie was sound asleep, his Daddy was still at the church, and Doris had nodded off in front of the television.

He crept down the hall, took a leak and brushed his teeth, then changed into his pajamas. He was soon back in the bed alongside a pile of textbooks.

Bart picked up the history book. He was surprised how much he liked history. On the one hand, reading was hard for him, and that was a handicap. On the other hand, the stories about Paul Revere, Patrick Henry, Stonewall Jackson, and Robert E. Lee fascinated him. He bet some of those guys hadn't been any good at school either. Maybe he had half a chance.

What he really needed to study was math. He was already dying in that class. He set the other books aside and picked up the math book.

The corner of the page was dog-eared; it was easy to find his place.

Bart stared at the page. He would have been no more lost if the text-book had been in Hebrew. He studied the first problem and the sample solution. His eyes blurred, and he realized this wasn't a good night to study math. The row with Doris had sucked all the life out of him.

Why in the world had Daddy married that woman? She wasn't as pretty as his real mom, or as kind. And she sure wasn't as rich. Maybe she was good in bed? If you translate all that anger into energy for sex, you might have something…

His hand drifted off his stomach and beneath the waistband of his pajamas. He thought about slipping the *Playboy* out from between the mattress and box springs. Sometimes he used it for inspiration. Tonight he didn't need any inspiration.

The familiar fullness returned. It was so much better than when it popped up unexpectedly in the middle of class. Girls were lucky. They had periods and all that, but they never got called to the board to work a math problem in the middle of raging hard-on. Had to try to tuck it up behind your belt buckle. Ouch.

Girls had it better in another way, too. If they had a sex dream, it wasn't wet. They didn't wake up in a puddle, and then have to make up the bed so no one knew. His hand moved slowly now, and he settled into a rhythm.

He'd never had sex with a girl, never even gotten close. Had squeezed a bosom once or twice, but that was it. Never had his hand in anyone's pants. Bart was getting behind. Hell, he was fifteen, going on sixteen. He was almost a man. But the girls his age weren't interested in him because he had flunked two grades. And the girls in his class were afraid he was too fast for them. At this rate, he would die a virgin.

His hand moved faster now, and his breath was ragged. A slide show ran in his head. He'd seen pictures and even snuck into an X-rated movie once. He had a good idea how things unfolded. He focused on his favor-ite image: a slender, tan, brown-haired girl who once lived across the street. He saw her with her ankles locked around his back. They moved together, and their pace began to quicken.

Bart felt his legs tighten and was briefly aware that most of his weight was on his heels and his shoulders. His back was arched, and there was no weight on his hips at all. He wasn't in his head anymore. He was all sensation, and the sensation was heat that gathered deep inside him. His hand moved faster, and his eyes shut tight. And then the heat was everywhere and his breathing was fast and there was release and he felt gobs of wetness splash onto his stomach.

What was warm and viscous quickly became cold and runny. Bart reached for the bedside Kleenex and mopped up his stomach. His vision was foggy, and it was all he could do to stay awake. He tossed the wadded tissues at the trashcan beside the door, missed, and then switched off the lamp on the bedside table. He was asleep before the bulb got cold.

# 16 | Richmond Pirates

## *Franklin*

The bus bumped down the road as Franklin stared at the bright red stars stenciled on his helmet. They had played eight games and he had eight stars. No one had more. Not even Bart. He gazed out the window as the cotton fields whizzed by. Cotton had just been harvested and the leavings in the fields looked like snow. Laurel Hill came into view and the bus coasted to a stop at the lone light. Eighty-five years ago, Franklin's great-great-grandfather had lived here. Though he soon moved eight miles east to Laurinburg, the family still considered Laurel Hill its ancestral home. The bus rolled on. Five of their eight games had been on the road. He was getting used to the ride, sitting at the back of the bus thinking about football and combat.

Franklin felt a deep kinship to warriors down through history. His teammates did not seem to get it. So he sat alone at the back of the bus, deeply connected to the Goths, the Vandals, and the Roman Legions, but strangely distant from his teammates.

The bus swerved suddenly and Coach Wittenburg slammed on the brakes. Duffle bags flew through the air, and a couple of guys landed on their butts. "Damn! What was that?" The team stared out the left side of the bus.

"It's a stupid deer," Coach Wittenburg shouted from the driver's seat. "I saw him, but I figured he had enough sense to stay on the shoulder. Maybe there's a doe on the other side of the road. You know, a buck ain't got a lick of sense when there's loving involved. Are you men okay?"

No one was hurt, but the tone in the bus suddenly became more serious. Coach McInnis stood in the aisle, his hands on the luggage rack above each row of seats. "All right, men, listen up! We'll be at the field in ten minutes. I want to talk about the opportunity you have tonight. We're getting ready to play the Richmond Pirates. What do you know about them?"

"They always beat us!" a voice near the front of the bus yelled out.

"You're damn straight they always beat us," the coach responded. "How many of you have fathers who played for the Fighting Scots?" A smattering of hands went up, but Franklin's hand was not among them. His Daddy did many things well, but playing football was not one of them.

"What have your dads told you about the Pirates?"

"They are a football factory," one voice hollered.

"They play dirty," another voice roared.

"They could roll out eleven old ladies in wheelchairs and still whip our butts," said a third.

"Everything you say is true," the coach shouted back. "No Fighting Scot football team has beaten these guys in thirty years. They have our number. Are we gonna let that continue?"

"No!" the whole team answered in unison.

"I can't hear you! Are we gonna let the Pirates whip our butts?"

"NO!" the entire team screamed.

"All right, here's what we are gonna do. We're gonna have the best warm-ups we've had all year. Then we're gonna win the toss and, when we do, we're gonna defer so the defense can take the field first. We're gonna take the fight right to these suckers. We're gonna rip their heads off. We're gonna play hard and smart and clean and tough, and we are going to pound the shit out of these guys. And when we do, I'm gonna take you all to the Honey Cone for burgers and shakes after the game. What do you say to that?"

"Yeah!" came the response.

"I can't hear you! What do you say to burgers and shakes after we whip these guys' butts?"

"YEAH!" It was a thunderous reply.

Bill McInnis called it like a psychic. The warm-ups were focused and intense. When Bart and the other captain went out for the coin toss, they won, just like Coach predicted. They also deferred until the second half. That move alone put the Pirates off-balance, and they never seemed to recover.

The Fighting Scots' kick-off was a high, end-over-end affair that seemed to stay in the air forever. When the Pirate receiver caught the ball, he also caught a crushing tackle from Bart Wagram and fumbled immediately.

It was no wonder. Bart buried an arm across the guy's nose. That Pirate player probably wouldn't be able to breathe for a week. Franklin felt a moment's compassion for the guy. He also remembered what Bart said when he knocked out the guy at Mars Hill: "Tough shit for the guy. If he didn't want to get hit he should have joined the damn chess club."

When the Pirate kick-returner dropped the ball, one of Bart's team-mates smothered it on the twenty-two yard line. The Scots were in business. Two plays later, they scored. The point after touchdown was perfect. Less than two minutes had elapsed, and the Scots were ahead seven to nothing.

The Richmond offense came out after the ensuing kick-off, and it was clear they expected business as usual. You could see it in the way they walked. The offense sauntered to the line like the Scots were chopped liver.

Two plays later, the Pirates were lining up to watch the Scots kick another extra point. A blistering pass rush yielded an interception and the Scots' second touchdown.

Franklin was as shocked as the Pirates. They were up 14-0, and the offense had only been on the field for two plays. At this rate, Franklin wouldn't need to take a shower after the game. Heck, at this rate he wasn't even going to earn his burger and shake.

The entire game unfolded like the first two minutes. It was unreal, like living the best dream you ever had. The score was 21-0 by the end of the first quarter, and the Pirate fans were mute. At the end of the second quarter it was 35-0.

At halftime Coach McInnis warned them that a wounded animal is more dangerous than a healthy one. He talked about not letting up, about how people are more likely to remember how you finish than how you start. Franklin's teammates weren't listening. Heck, he wasn't really listening either. It was hard to listen when it was this easy, when guys were already talking about what they were gonna eat at the Honey Cone.

As planned, the Scots received the kick-off to open the second half. The first team offense took the field. Coach had promised he would play the second unit the entire fourth quarter, and Franklin knew his day was almost over.

Harvey called the play, and Franklin trotted to the line and bent over the ball. He looked up to see a new nose guard directly in front of him. No surprise there. Franklin had been blowing the other guy back three and four yards on every play.

Franklin checked out the new opponent. The guy wasn't an inch over 5'4". He was a squat, stumpy dude with bad acne. If this guy was a worse player than the last guy, the whole thing was going to be too easy.

Harvey slipped his hands under Franklin's rump and called the signals. Franklin snapped the ball, and the new opponent crashed into him, smashing a forearm full across his larynx. Franklin fell backwards, stunned. The play swept right end for four yards, but Franklin couldn't talk. He could barely breathe. He staggered to his feet and made his way back to the huddle, breath rasping in and out. A teammate noticed his difficulty. "You all right, man?"

"Yeah," Franklin croaked, his voice barely audible.

The next play was a short swing pass to the left flat. Franklin bent over the ball and glared at his opponent. Stumpy Man grinned back.

Franklin snapped the ball and, aiming directly for Stumpy Man's chin, brought a forearm up sharply. His arm met nothing but air, and the officials whistled the play dead instantly.

Franklin turned to see Harvey gingerly pick himself up off the ground, while Stumpy Man stood over him, gloating. What the hell happened?

The stupid nose guard had scrambled between Franklin's legs. Not slowed by even a hint of a block, Stumpy Man had gotten to the quarterback before Harvey could set himself to throw. The play was an eight-yard loss, and it was a miracle there was no fumble. It was third down and fourteen yards to go. Franklin was embarrassed. And more than a little pissed.

"Hey, man, I'm sorry about that," Franklin said to Harvey. "That squatty little bastard is making me look like an idiot. How about we run right at him?"

"I don't know, man. It's already third down, and we've got fourteen yards to go."

"Come on, man," Franklin begged. "We're beating these guys senseless. Let me give this guy what he deserves."

"All right. What the hell. Let's sneak it at them. Quarterback sneak on 'set.' You guys pay attention and don't jump offside. This one is for Franklin. Receivers split wide. We're gonna show pass and then shove it down their throats. Remember, on 'set'!"

Franklin broke the huddle and bent over the ball. Stumpy Man smirked at him. "Coming your way, asshole," Franklin growled.

"Fat chance," Stumpy Man replied.

"Down. Set!" The play exploded around Franklin. He hit Stumpy like a locomotive, then flattened him and kept going. He even managed to cleat Stumpy full on the arm as he fell limp before the onslaught.

Harvey followed as Franklin bulled his way into the secondary and took out the middle linebacker, then he broke left behind the flanker. A couple of jukes and one straight-arm later, the Scots had six more points.

When they lined up for the extra point, Stumpy Man was there, but he had lost his smirk. Blood trickled from the corner of his mouth.

"Cocksucker," he growled at Franklin.

Franklin grinned. "Your momma was a great teacher." The ball sailed through the uprights, and the score was 42-0.

Coach didn't put the first unit back on the field after this series, but the second team played as well as the first. The Scots scored once more, and the second unit defense kept the Pirates out of the end zone. It was a great game to watch, the best game the team had played all year.

It was clearly not Franklin's best game. He remembered Coach's half-time admonition. Coach warned them about a wounded animal, and he was right. That sawed-off pissant had damn near broken Franklin's voice box.

Coach spoke about not letting up and about people remembering how you finish more than how you start.

Franklin was embarrassed by the sack on Harvey, but hoped people would remember how he finished; running right up the gut of the defense, bowling over Short Stuff and stomping his arm, before laying the middle linebacker out like a dead man at a wake.

Coach McInnis called them together after the game and saluted their performance. "Don't forget how good this feels. Don't ever forget. You've done something no one in Laurinburg has done in thirty years. You didn't let them back in the game, you kept after them, and you beat them as a team effort. I couldn't be more proud of you. Now let's go eat some burgers!"

Franklin had a Tummyfull, the biggest burger on the menu, and a chocolate shake. He savored the moment: the guys, the smell of sweat and burgers and dirt all rolled together. Franklin was proud of how he had finished.

# 17 | Seeking Help

## *Doris Wagram*

Doris grabbed the heavy black phone. Her hand shook so badly it was hard to get her fingers into the holes on the phone's dial. She couldn't believe she was doing this; it wasn't like her.

The phone rang once, then again, and once more. She was about to hang up when a cheerful voice greeted her: "Good morning. This is Laurinburg Presbyterian Church. How may I help you?"

"Can I please speak to Reverend Inman?" Her voice was almost a whisper. "It's about a personal matter."

"Certainly. May I tell him who is calling?"

"I sorry, but I can't give my name just yet. Tell him it's an old family friend." Doris hated to be secretive, but she couldn't let anyone know what she was doing.

"I'll be happy to tell him. Let me put you on hold, and I'll be right back."

She sat with the phone to her ear. Out the window, leaves were beginning to change colors, and trees swayed in a light breeze. It was a beautiful day, but Doris felt like she was watching the world, not living in it. Like life was going on around her, but without her.

"Good morning. This is Robert Inman. How may I help you?"

Doris exhaled deeply. Maybe she *could* believe in God. This voice was certainly an answer to prayer. "Oh Reverend Inman, this is Doris Wagram, only I used to be Doris Calhoun." The words tumbled out of her mouth. "You may not remember me. I went to the Junior-Senior

Prom with your son Bobby right before our high school graduation. You might remember…"

"Of course I remember you, Doris. That was a beautiful dress you wore. The yellow was the perfect color for you."

Doris blushed. Truth be told, she had always had more of crush on Reverend Inman than on Bobby. She was astonished he remembered her dress all these years later.

"How are you, Doris? I haven't seen you in years. It's hard to believe in a town as small as this, but it's true."

"I'm fine, Reverend Inman. Well, actually, I'm not so fine at all. I need someone to talk to, and you were the only person I could think of. You were always kind to me, plus I thought you would be good at keeping confidences. That's really important. I can't go to the minister at my church. And, well, I need someone to talk to." Her voice trailed off.

"Well Doris, I'd be happy to meet with you. Let me grab my calendar. When were you thinking about?"

"Now." Doris was surprised at her urgency. "How about right now? I could be there in fifteen minutes."

"Well…let me see…" Doris could hear papers shuffling. "That will work. I have some time this morning before a noon meeting. I'll let the ladies in the office know you are coming. Do you know how to find the office entrance here at the church?"

That's how, less than twelve minutes later, Doris Calhoun Wagram wound up parked in the parking lot at Laurinburg Presbyterian Church. She reached up and moved the car's rearview mirror so she could freshen her lipstick and check her teeth. Her teeth were fine, so she blotted the fresh lipstick with a tissue and snapped her pocketbook shut.

Doris wondered what she was going to say when she met with Reverend Inman. The whole thing happened so quickly that she hadn't thought about that part. What would she say? *What was the matter with her?* Why was her stomach in a knot? Why did she always have a headache? She didn't know. She just knew she had to start somewhere. So she opened the car door and stepped into a sunny day, kissed with a hint of fall.

Sure enough, the office ladies were expecting her. She didn't know what Reverend Inman told them, but they were nice as could be. They offered her a cup of coffee and made her comfortable in the small sitting area adjacent to the office. Doris had a sense of impending doom, like she imagined kids felt when they went to the principal's office.

She settled into the chair and watched the office staff at work. They seemed to move through their work effortlessly, almost like ballet dancers. Doris' life was like running uphill through cold molasses. Everything required immense effort. She envied their effortlessness.

"Hi, Doris. It's so good to see you again." Reverend Inman spoke quietly as he extended his hand. The sound of his voice startled her. She had been so focused on the office ladies that she didn't notice as he walked up.

"Oh, Reverend Inman, it's so good to see you again." She rose from her chair to shake his hand, then wondered if that was correct protocol. There were no cotillion lessons in her childhood home. She thought about giving him a hug instead, but decided against it. "I think of Bobby often. How is he doing?"

"He's fine. He graduated from Presbyterian College and went to Columbia Seminary in Decatur, near Atlanta. He's serving a small church in the mountains of north Georgia. It's a beautiful place, but way too cold for me in the winter. What have you been up to since we last saw each other?"

Doris' eyes darted around the office, and Reverend Inman realized that she wanted to talk without being overheard. He nodded in acknowledgement.

"Come on to my office, you're welcome to bring your coffee, and let's sit and catch up." He looked over at the taller of the two office ladies, "Lois, if anyone calls for me will you please take a message? Doris and I will probably meet for an hour or so, and I'll return calls when we are done. I've got a meeting at noon, so I'll surely be done by then."

"Certainly," Lois replied. Then, "It was nice to meet you, Doris."

Doris hadn't been treated like a real person in she-did-not-know-when. She nearly burst into tears at Lois' kindness, but stuffed the impulse. "It was nice to meet you as well. Thank you so much for the coffee."

They walked down a short hall and turned right into Reverend Inman's office. When she stepped into the space, Doris noticed that only the right half of the room was a working office. The left half was a sitting area that reminded her of the parlor in her childhood home. That was the parlor where she and Bobby sat and talked during their few dates before the Prom. And the same parlor where he first kissed her.

"Why don't we sit over here?" Reverend Inman gestured to the sitting area. There was a small couch and a couple of wingback chairs. A coffee table held a heavy green glass ashtray and a set of brass coasters. There was an end table with a box of tissues and a large book of some sort. The book had a picture on the front, a building with a big golden dome. It looked like she imagined the Holy Land might look, all bright and sunny with a brilliant blue sky.

Doris realized that Reverend Inman was waiting for her to choose a seat. She stepped around the coffee table and settled into a corner of the small couch. It was soft and comfortable; she could feel it envelope her.

Reverend Inman sat in the wingback chair closest to her. He was so close she could have stretched out her left leg and touched his foot with hers. She glanced up to see him looking at her, and then looked away and stared deeply into the paper cup that held her coffee.

"How can I help you?" He said it so kindly and matter-of-factly that she wondered why this had seemed like such a big deal.

Doris took a deep breath to reply, but her throat wouldn't work. She glanced up from her coffee cup and tried again. Nothing. She forced a thin smile and tried once more.

No words came out, but this time she felt a hot streak of tears begin

122

to trace down her cheeks. She buried her head in her left hand and began to sob, great shuddering sobs that shook her whole body. She set her coffee on the table so it would not spill.

"It's too much. It's just way too much." Her voice had somehow gotten back on its feet. She was making real words.

"I can't stand it," she said. Then more forcefully, "I just can't stand it anymore. It's more than any one woman should have to bear." Her sobbing tapered and she looked up at Reverend Inman. He was gazing at her, resting the Kleenex in his lap. He extended it, and she tugged a tissue from the box.

"What's too much, Doris? What can't you stand?"

And now she knew why this had seemed like such a big deal. Now she had to tell the truth about her life to another human being. She felt heaviness in her gut, like she had eaten a bowl of ball bearings for breakfast instead of her usual raisin bran. Where would she start?

"Well, Reverend Inman…"

He held up his hand, like a cop stopping traffic, and spoke gently.

"Doris, let me ask you a favor. I know your parents taught you to respect your elders. We taught Bobby the same thing. Still, now that you are an adult yourself, please just call me Robert. It's my name, after all. And I was Robert long before I was Reverend Anything."

Doris giggled to herself at the thought of calling him Reverend Anything. "Well, Robert." The name was awkward in her mouth. She started over.

"Well, Robert, I'm having a hard time. I'm having a hard time as a wife to Ricky Wagram, as a stepmother to his son Bart, and as a mother to my handicapped daughter, Stephanie. I'm mad and I'm sad and I just can't seem to get myself together." She began to sniffle, pausing to wipe her eyes with the now damp tissue.

The sniffling spell didn't last long. She looked up, and Robert Inman was looking at her like nothing she could say would surprise or disappoint him.

"I don't know where to start. I've never done this before." Her voice trailed off and her eyes filled with tears. She dabbed the tears away, but one escaped and rolled slowly down her left cheek.

"Well, Doris, there's no wrong way to talk about your life. Why don't you tell me how you were feeling right before you called this morning?"

"I felt like I was going to die. Like I couldn't breathe and was suffocating. I was, I *am*, overwhelmed. It's just too much; it's *way* too much." She blew her nose softly into the shreds of the tissue.

"What is it that is too much?"

"It's all too much. Ricky's never home, and Stephanie is a fulltime job, and Bart, well you know how boys are when their hormones hit. I'm all by myself, and I know that half the town is talking about me, and I'm angry, and every time I go to church I know that people are looking at me and I just can't stand it anymore." She paused to take a breath and looked up at Robert. He extended the Kleenex box once more, and she wondered what she saw in his eyes.

"It sounds like too much. It also sounds lonely. What is the hardest part right now?"

Doris took a long breath and sighed. She twisted the Kleenex over and over until it began to drop tiny pieces of white lint onto her blue skirt. One more deep breath and she began.

"I guess the hardest part is the family stuff. I can't do anything about how people look at me or what they say. But the family stuff is so hard and I feel like I am getting it all wrong."

"I see," he said. "How are you getting it all wrong?"

Doris realized that she had never in her life been listened to in the way that Robert Inman was listening to her. He didn't seem to have any job in the world except to pay attention to her, and he was doing his job well. She felt heard, loved, and cared for. She wondered if this was how God listened to prayers, with one hundred percent concentration.

"I don't know. It seems like I am getting it *all* wrong. I married Ricky Wagram after his first wife left him. Mary Catherine Fitzhugh was his first wife, and she is Bart's birth mother. I think Bart blames me for her leaving."

Doris paused, then continued angrily, "Bart's always resented me, and it's not my fault! That bitch was gone long before I ever got there!" Stillness settled over the room. Doris was afraid to look up at Reverend Wagram. She finally chanced a glance.

"That'd be a tough place for anyone," he said. He didn't seem to have noticed that she called Mary Catherine a bitch.

"It is. It's a really tough place to be. Bart blames me for his mama leaving, and he's got her up on a pedestal, like she's some kind of saint. Hell, she was the one having sex before they got married. She's the reason Ricky couldn't finish school at that hotshot Ivy League college he went to right out of high school.

"Anyway, Bart's had a hard time in school forever. He can't read very well, and that puts him behind in every other subject. Plus he's becoming a man. Ricky's never home, so Bart never gets any Daddy time, and a woman cannot teach a boy to be a man."

Reverend Inman nodded. "I'd say you've got that right."

Doris seemed to be gaining momentum, and she jumped right back in to her story. "Bart's already two grades behind, he's in eighth grade and should be in tenth. He was held back in fourth grade, and he failed eighth grade last year. I don't know what we're gonna do with him."

"What does Bart like to do? What does he do well?"

"He loves sports and is playing football right now. They are doing great so far, and he's the best player on the team. They haven't lost a single game. But he just aggravates the dickens out of me. Sometimes I want to pinch his head off. I'll admit to being a little rough with him when he was a child. He can push all my buttons.

"I never really abused him, but I'm not saying I never hit him. Those days are over now. He outweighs me by fifty pounds, and he knows it. He's never raised his hand toward me, but there'll be no more spankings for him.

"Bart has a hot head. I've seen it when he talks about football prac-tice or the kids in his class. You can tell I've got one, too, and that makes us a bad match."

She stopped to catch her breath. "I'm embarrassed to tell you this, but last week I found a stash of those men's magazines in his room. You know what I mean, *Playboy* and the like. They were stuck between the mattress and the box springs. Can you believe it?

"I don't know what I'm going to do about that, either. My family was all girls except for my daddy, and he wasn't the manly man type. For one thing, he didn't know which end of a wrench to hold. He didn't hunt or fish or fix cars or any of that other manly stuff. He certainly wasn't a jock like Ricky and Bart."

She looked up at Reverend Inman. "Tell me, Robert, how did your wife handle being a preacher's wife and having sons and all of that?"

"Well, Doris, I guess you'd have to ask her yourself. I can't speak for her. What I can tell you is this: your circumstances and hers are different in many ways. Comparing yourself to her, or to anyone else, is probably not a good idea. You mentioned your daughter. Tell me a bit about her."

Doris' face fell.

"Oh, Stephanie." She shook her head slightly, paused and sighed. "I always wanted a daughter, but that's one decision I'd take back in an instant. I love that little girl. And I wish she had never been born.

"It was my first pregnancy, and it was difficult from day one. I threw up the entire nine months. I kept telling myself it would get better once the baby was born. Fat chance.

"Something went wrong in the delivery and she will never have a normal life. Neither will I. Sometimes I wish she was dead. I wish I was dead, too. Put us both out of our misery."

With that, Doris began to weep. She bent low at the waist, wrapped her arms around her knees and rocked slowly back and forth. She moaned low and deep.

Robert Inman had never heard this sound, and he didn't know how to respond. He took the tissues from his lap, set them on the coffee table, and slowly stood up. Doris didn't appear to notice. She just sat there rocking back and forth.

He stepped around the coffee table and sat beside her on the small sofa, perched just on the edge of the cushions. Then he leaned forward and gently placed his left hand on Doris's back. He didn't say a word. Just sat and prayed for Doris, with his hand resting lightly in the middle of her back.

He wasn't even sure how to pray. Heaven knows, she had a lot of challenges, and none of them seemed likely to disappear anytime soon. So he prayed for God's peace to surround her, for God's boundless shalom to enfold her like warm towels from the dryer.

Some of his classmates in seminary said this was a lazy prayer, that you should always ask God for exactly what you wanted.

Robert was certain they were wrong. Anyhow, what's the use throwing in with a God who doesn't already know what you need? That's not very omniscient, after all.

Doris' back was hot beneath his hand, hot and a bit damp. As Robert prayed, her tears and moaning resolved to gentle sobbing. He didn't know how long they sat there. He didn't even know what time it was when he moved beside her on the sofa. They had been meeting for almost an hour. Robert glanced at his watch, then puzzled over how to communicate compassion and still wrap up before his noon meeting.

He gave up and decided to surrender: to sink back into God, to pray, and to see how God would get him out of this mess. It worked more often than one would think.

Doris composed herself and sat up. As she did, Robert slipped his hand off her back and slid to the far side of the loveseat. Her eyes were bloodshot and puffy. He could see streaks of make-up running down her face where the tears had been.

"I've got to get going," she said. "I know you've got other appointments. Thanks for seeing me on such short notice."

Then with a half-laugh she said, "I'm a real mess, aren't I? I'm a mess and my life is a mess!"

He chuckled with her, and then added, "You don't have to make fun of your pain for me to care about you. Would you like to meet again?"

"Yes, I would," she said. "It's so helpful to have someone listen and tell me I'm not crazy."

"Well, let's pick a date," he said as he rose to get his calendar.

# 18 | Tragedy

## *Bart*

Bart headed up the back porch stairs. Something was up, but he couldn't tell what.

When he got home from practice, his daddy's car was in the driveway. Bart was surprised. Ricky never got home this early. Especially on Tuesday, when he visited sick people in the hospital and prepared his sermon for Wednesday night.

But there he was, sitting in the kitchen, talking to Doris. Life went better for Bart when his daddy was home. Maybe this was going to be a good night.

He could see them through the window as he rounded the corner to the back steps, Doris had her arm around Ricky, who was holding his head in his hands. Bart took the back steps two at a time, and was in the kitchen almost before they heard him coming. They were shocked when he threw the door open.

"Hey, Dad. I didn't expect to see you here." The old man often missed supper. "Are you going to eat with us tonight?"

Ricky jerked free from Doris. "Nope, I've got to get back to the church. I just dropped by for a minute on my way from visiting at the hospital."

Bart stared at his Daddy. Something wasn't right.

Ricky's face was strained. Like he was trying to fake being chipper when he actually felt awful. Bart knew that look. He used it himself when he was sick but wanted to go school because of some special event, like field day. He had certainly seen Doris use a plastic smile when she tried to convince people everything was fine in their home life.

Bart looked directly at Ricky. "Is something wrong?"

He and his Daddy had an understanding, they did not lie to each other. *The whole system breaks down if you don't tell the truth.* Ricky said that to Bart when Bart was six years old and lied about some trifle. And the two of them had kept the pact. It was a way they treated each other as equals, these two refugees from the good times of the past.

"No. Nothing's wrong." Bart could read the lie as it slipped from his Daddy's mouth.

"I just stopped by on the way home to spend a few minutes with Doris. We were just sitting here talking."

Bart's eyes shifted to Doris. Somehow she looked softer than usual. Like she cared. Like she had a heart.

Something was up, but nobody was talking. Bart felt like they were waiting for him to leave.

"Well, I'm gonna go upstairs and take a look at my math homework. Holler at me before you leave, so I can tell you goodbye."

And that's when he slogged up the stairs. His feet hit the treads heavily as he puzzled over his daddy's lie. He wanted to put it aside, since he couldn't fix it. He had other things to worry about, like football and classes and the fact that he was afraid he would fail math again.

True to his word, Bart sat down in his straight-backed chair and shoved aside the pile of junk that had accumulated atop his desk. He opened his math book to today's chapter and found the set of problems Miss McIntyre assigned. There were ten of them.

He attacked the first problem and nailed it. The next three problems came easy as well. Maybe it did help to pay attention in class, he had really listened when Miss Kate was explained how to do the homework. He couldn't do problems five or six, so he skipped them and finished the final four.

Eight of ten problems done, and he was pretty sure they were all correct. That was some kind of record. Maybe tomorrow he'd get called on to work a problem at the board. They'd all be surprised when he nailed it.

Bart glanced at the clock on the bedside table and realized he had been working math problems for an hour. He never got lost in his homework, but solving the problems had engrossed him.

He got up, stretched, and took a leak. Then he cupped his hands under the stream of water in the sink and took a good long drink. The windows in his bedroom were open, and a breeze ruffled his math papers and sent them drifting to the floor.

Bart had just gathered them when the phone rang. He let it ring, figuring someone downstairs would get it. It was never for him anyway, and the kitchen phone was hanging on the wall right above where his daddy and Doris had been sitting.

No one got it. The phone rang again. Bart wondered if his father was leaving, and Doris had gone out to see him off.

He headed to the hall table where the phone sat. It gave one more raucous ring before Bart got there and snatched the handset from the cradle to stop the racket. He figured for sure they were outside now, and was just about to say "hello" when he realized someone downstairs had also answered. He placed his hand softly over the mouthpiece of the phone and pressed the handset against his ear.

"Hey, Ricky." Bart knew the voice but couldn't place it. "Hey Ricky, it's Alexander."

Oh yeah, Uncle Alex. His Mama's younger brother. Bart always thought of Alex as his own brother, too. They were only six years apart, and they had had some big fun over the years. That was all before Alex went off to that prep school in Virginia. Now he didn't seem to have much time for the things that went on in Laurinburg.

"Look, I just got here, and I told Mom I'd call you with an update. They said you dropped by earlier. It doesn't look good. She's got swelling of the brain and is in a deep coma. They have patched up all her lacerations, and she doesn't have a single broken bone, but it doesn't look good. The…"

"What are her chances?" Ricky interrupted Uncle Alex, and his voice sounded funny. It was thick and full at the back of his throat.

"The doctors are saying it's "wait and see." They are also saying there is only a fifteen to twenty percent chance she'll make it. It's not the news you wanted, I know. It's not the news I wanted to give you. But I wanted to keep you in the loop."

"Thanks." Ricky croaked the word out.

"You told Bart anything yet?"

"No, not yet."

"Don't keep him in the dark too long. It's not fair."

"The whole thing's not fair." Bart thought he heard his daddy choke back a sob, then Ricky added "There's nothing fair about it."

"You got that right."

"Call me if anything changes."

"I will."

The line clicked dead, and Bart eased the black handset back into the cradle.

So that was it. Something had happened to his Mama.

He felt lightheaded and leaned against the wall. He thought he might throw up. It felt like taking a hard hit in football. It took a minute to regain your bearings. A coach once told him how to handle hard licks. "Open your eyes and take out your mouthpiece. If you can still see and you have all your teeth, there's nothing to worry about. The rest of it will heal."

Maybe in football, Bart thought. But not for this.

He steadied himself with a hand on the wall and made his way down the hall to his bedroom. He sat on the bed and looked around. His mind wouldn't work right. He tried to think about being alive and about what it would be like to be dead.

This was the same room where, two minutes ago, his biggest worry was whether his daddy was going to slip away without telling him good-bye. Now it looked like his mama was gonna slip away for good. Maybe even before he got to see her again.

Bart dissolved into silent sobs that shook his entire body. He slumped over on the pillow, throwing his bare feet on the quilt at the end of the bed. He rolled over, face down in the pillow, and wept noiselessly.

He had learned to cry without making noise not long after Ricky married Doris. Right after she exiled him upstairs. *The boy needs his own space*, she said.

He was only six years old, but Doris sent him to the big, dark upstairs anyway. He was alone, night after night. She had heard him crying once, came up to see what was going on, and reamed him. Told him he was a sissy and a crybaby and he needed to grow up and act like a man.

He didn't stop crying. He just stopped making noise when he cried. Now Bart cried into the pillow and thought about his mother, the mother he had already lost once.

Eventually the sobbing stopped.

You can only cry so much. Then you get all exhausted and cried out. Even if you are still sad and sick with worry, crying doesn't work anymore. It took less than fifteen minutes for Bart to reach this point. He was cried out. He was getting hungry. And his daddy still hadn't called up to him.

Bart got up from the bed, put on his shoes, and took a quick look in the mirror. His hair was flat on one side, but didn't look too bad. He headed downstairs. No one was in the kitchen, so he glanced out the window to see if his daddy's car was in the driveway. It was. He hadn't left without saying goodbye.

Bart opened the swinging door that separated the kitchen from the dining room and the living room. There was his daddy, across the dining room, sitting on the couch in the living room. He was slumped over on Doris' shoulder. Bart couldn't see his eyes. Doris stared straight ahead, looking directly through Bart. Bart could see her eyes, but couldn't read the look on her face. Sniffling came from Doris' shoulder, where Ricky's head was buried.

Bart swallowed hard and took a deep breath. "Dad?" he said. "Dad, what happened to Mama?"

Ricky moved his head slightly, like it was too heavy to move at all. He turned to face Bart. His eyes were vacant, and it was clear he had been crying.

"Dad?" Bart tried again.

"How'd you know something happened to your mama?" His daddy spoke in a tinny voice that Bart had never heard before.

"I, well, um, I picked up the phone at the same time you did and heard Uncle Alex talking to you. What happened? Is she gonna be all right? Can I go see her?"

"It was a freak accident. She got hit by a car while she was crossing the street downtown. She'd just come out of the drugstore and was talking to someone. I guess she got distracted. She stepped right in front of Willard Roberson's cab. He swerved to miss her, but that just made it worse. Hit her broadside. It happened about two-thirty this afternoon. That's why I was at the hospital, and why I came by here."

"You lied to me!" The veins in Bart's neck bulged as he shouted. "You lied when you said nothing was wrong! Mama is lying up in the hospital busted all to pieces and you lied to me so you wouldn't have to tell me the truth. You chicken shit..."

"Bart! That's quite enough." It was Doris. "If you are going to –"

"The boy's right." Ricky cut her off. "You're right, Bart. I did lie to you. And it was a chicken shit thing to do. I just didn't know how, or what, I was going to tell you. So I lied to buy some time. I'm sorry. You deserve better." Bart's father dropped his head and began to sob.

Bart noticed that Doris wasn't telling Ricky to be a man and knock it off with the crying. But there was no need to fight that fight now.

"Aw, it's all right." Bart began to sniffle, too. "How bad is it? Have you seen her at the hospital? Can I go see her? What's going to happen to her?"

"It's bad, Bart. It's real bad. I went up to the hospital as soon as I heard, but they wouldn't let me see her. She's in the intensive care unit. They won't let anybody in except her mama and daddy. Won't even let your uncles in."

"Is she gonna –" Bart started the sentence but the end of it got hung up in his throat. "Is she gonna be all right?"

"I don't know. I honestly don't know. The doctors aren't very encouraging. They say she's got a lot of swelling in her brain, and she's unconscious. She had a bunch of cuts and scrapes from the accident but no broken bones. They've patched all that stuff up. It's not a big deal. It's the coma that has got us all worried. She took a hard lick from the car, and then landed on the back of her head in the road."

"Well, what are we gonna do?"

"There is nothing we can do, Bart. Nothing but wait and hope and pray."

"Can I go see her?" Bart knew the answer before he asked the question. But he had to ask it anyway.

"You can't see her, son. Remember? They aren't letting anyone in but your Grandmama and Poppa Fitzhugh. Even they can't stay but fifteen minutes every four hours. And your mama doesn't know they are there when they do go into the room. They say she's hooked up to all these machines checking on her heart rate and breathing and brain waves. Maybe you and I can go see her when she comes out of the coma. We'll just have to wait and see."

"Why don't I fix us something to eat?" Doris said. Bart had forgotten she was in the room. "We've got to eat anyway, and I know you two must be hungry."

Those were the kindest words Bart had ever heard Doris say. He realized that he really was hungry, and glanced at his watch. It was late.

"Sounds good," Bart said. "I'm hungry."

They made their way to the kitchen and tag-teamed the fixing of supper. Nothing fancy, they just put stuff on the table, and everyone made their own meal. There was pimento cheese and peanut butter, a few slices of tomato from the tail-end of the garden, and two pieces of leftover fried chicken from Sunday dinner. Potato salad came out of the fridge, and half a cake and a few other things. Everybody seemed to eat hearty, though for the life of him Bart couldn't tell you what he ate five minutes after the meal was over.

They cleaned up. And then they waited.

Ricky decided not to go back to the church after all, said the whole church would understand if tomorrow night's sermon wasn't his finest. The phone didn't ring.

Bart tried to read his history chapters, but couldn't focus. He asked once more about going to the hospital, but it was no use. It was just as well. He wasn't sure he wanted to be hanging around the hospital if there was no chance of seeing his mama.

He tried to remember what his mother looked like. Right now Bart could not bring her face up to save his soul. If he had known he might never see her again, he would have looked more closely at her the last time they were together.

Everyone said she was pretty. He knew she had blond hair, blue eyes, and a nice figure. None of that told him what she looked like. There were twenty girls in his class who were pretty in that way: shapely, with short blonde hair and blue eyes. None of them looked like his mama.

Bart got up and paced, finally walking to the bookshelf. Doris had purged most of the photos of Mary Catherine once she took over management of the house, but a few remained. Bart noticed that every picture of his mama also had him in it. There was not a single photo of Ricky and Mary Catherine together.

He found one he liked; it looked like it was taken at a carnival. He was on a carousel horse, and Mama had her arm around his waist. He was grinning from ear to ear, and she was smiling broadly. Bart stared into the picture for a long time, trying to memorize her face.

Still the phone didn't ring. And there was no way to call the hospital, since there was no pay phone in the ICU waiting room. Ricky wouldn't call even if there were a phone. There was no need asking people for information they didn't have. Uncle Alex said he would call. If there were news, he'd call.

Doris and Ricky talked a little, mostly about nothing. Bart didn't join in. He couldn't understand how they could talk at all. And if they were going to talk, why not just go ahead and talk about the only thing that mattered, the most important thing that was happening? Why didn't they talk about whether his mama was going to die?

Finally, Bart gave up and went to bed. It was nine-thirty. He usually didn't hit the rack this early, but he was tired and sitting around wasn't getting him anywhere. He told them all good night, headed up the stairs, and was in bed in fifteen minutes.

The window was still open, and Bart could see the stars out past the tree limbs. He wondered if God really existed. And if there were a God, what God was doing right now. Was God getting ready to throw his mama a big old welcome home party? Or was He hard at work reducing the swelling in her brain so she could get well and Bart could see her again?

Either way, it seemed she was in good hands.

Bart couldn't say the same about himself.

Bart prayed, just in case. He prayed for his mama's healing. He prayed that, if God did heal her, He'd heal her completely and not leave her clomping around like Stephanie, drooling all over the place. And then he was asleep.

Bart roused and squinted at his bedside clock. Five-twelve. He was surprised he had been able to sleep so long. Surprised he had slept at all. And now he was surprised to be awake, the clock wasn't supposed to go off until six-fifteen. Had he heard something? He stopped breathing and listened closely.

There it was. The slight sound of footfalls on the steps. He heard the door swing open and peeked out through nearly-shut eyes. Dad.

"Bart?" Ricky said it softly. Bart played possum and waited. "Bart, it's me." His father sat down on the bed, and Bart glanced out through eyes at half-mast. "Hey, you awake?"

"Yeah. I heard you coming. So…what's the news?"

"Bad." A sob shook his Daddy's body.

"Alex called about forty-five minutes ago. Your mama died without ever waking up." Ricky bent over to hug him. Bart felt claustrophobic. He couldn't breathe with his Daddy so close.

"Damn," Bart said.

# 19 | Funeral

## *Bart*

Bart walked up the steps of The First Methodist Church. They glared bright white in the early fall sunshine, and he squinted against the light.

He often went to this church as a child, especially when his parents were together. This was Grandmama and Poppa Fitzhugh's church. He remembered sitting between his Grandmama and his Mama, happily sandwiched between these two people who loved him so. That was a long time ago.

When his Mama and Daddy divorced, it felt like his mother's family divorced him too. He never understood that, especially as a little kid. It was bad enough to lose your mother, but to lose your grandparents too? It wasn't right.

The tight collar of the dress shirt pinched Bart's neck, especially where the knot of the tie rode hard across his Adam's apple. He was hot in the navy blazer. People at his grandparents' church always dressed up like this.

He pulled open the heavy wooden door of the church and stepped into the cool dark. The church seemed smaller and sadder than he remembered. There were lots of flowers up front, enormous round bouquets on little green wire stands.

Bart headed to the front of the sanctuary and idly sniffed the flowers. A bee buzzed in the center of one of the sweet smelling blooms. One arrangement had a deep blue ribbon with *We'll Miss You Always* written in silver glitter.

Bart moved to a side aisle, then halfway to the back of the church where he sat on one of the padded pews. No one else was in the church. Bart was glad to be alone.

Everything had been crazy-tense at the house. He had to get out or lose his mind. Ricky told him to go on ahead; they would drive with Stephanie in a few minutes. It wasn't far to the church, and Bart didn't mind the walk. It would have been okay if he weren't wearing so many clothes. As it was, he was hot and sweaty when he reached the church. The cool inside was a relief.

Bart heard a mechanical sound and a big commotion at the back of the sanctuary, and figured it was his daddy trying to get Stephanie up the stairs. Her leg braces often made a racket. He turned to look, but it wasn't his daddy. It was some man dressed in a black suit. There was another man behind him, dressed identically. The men had some sort of cart they were struggling to get in the door.

The cart was gold colored and designed to expand and collapse accordion-style. When the men got the cart fully into the church, they unfolded it and rolled it to the front of the church, where they painstakingly centered it beneath the pulpit. Then they surrounded the whole thing with a green velvet skirt.

Once they attached the skirt, the men strode down the center aisle and out of the church. No one said a word to him.

A short time later commotion again broke out at the back of the church. This had to be his family. Bart turned to look.

All he could see was someone's backside sticking in the door. He heard grunting, and then someone said, "Easy, now. Easy, Earl. Careful. That's got it. A little more to the right. Okay, Earl, see if you can grab this door, and we ought to be home free."

The door opened wide, and two men eased through it, one on either side of a long, dark, polished wooden box. These were the men Bart had seen earlier. They shifted the box in their hands and turned to face the front of the church. The men had picked up two helpers, and all four of them had on suits exactly alike. One of the men had gray hair that stuck up funny in the back. He looked a bit like Alfalfa on *The Little Rascals*.

The four men walked carefully down the aisle and lowered the box onto the cart. Bart realized that, once again, his mama had gotten to church before his daddy.

As the men left the church, one peeled off and spoke softly to Bart. "I'm so sorry about your loss, son. It has to be a shock. She was a good woman."

The man paused, and Bart swallowed hard. "Your family is gathering in the church parlor. You might want to head back there. We are starting in just a few minutes."

"Thanks," Bart whispered. It was all he could manage.

# *Franklin*

Franklin watched the whole team jam onto the bus. The bus felt like an oven and smelled like stale sweat. It was littered with debris from the last game: sucked-out orange wedges, bloody band-aids, an odd mouthpiece here and there. There was one lone sock.

In some ways, this trip felt like a regular football game. You had to be there on time, you traveled together, and you had to be in uniform. Most of his teammates sat in the bus seats they took for travel to games. But this was different. They weren't going to a stadium. They were going to a church. They were going to Bart's mother's funeral. Franklin had on his stiff Sunday shirt. He was hot and could feel sweat rolling down his back. It was funny to look at the guys, dressed up and all. No run-over sneakers or t-shirts with funny sayings. Most people had on a tie. Franklin was the only one wearing a sport coat.

He knew it would be this way when his mother told him to wear it. He knew no one else would have on a jacket. But whose mother listens when it comes to putting on dress-up clothes? Franklin gave in. As his Daddy often said: *"Son, this ain't a hill you want to die on."*

141

They bumped through town, and Franklin realized it was hot because they were going so slowly. There was a stoplight every block. It was nothing like speeding down the back roads between Laurinburg and the nearby towns where they played their games.

Franklin glanced at his teammates. Their faces were tight. No one was talking. It was like before a game, anticipation laced with fear and adrenaline. The bus lurched away from a stoplight and continued to the church. Franklin knew Bart's daddy was a preacher. Who preaches when the preacher's ex-wife dies?

He could see the Methodist Church up ahead. The brakes squealed as the bus turned into the parking lot. The right rear wheels caught the curb, and the bus rocked violently before it came to a halt. The guys stood up and began to shamble off the bus. A teammate stumbled, lurched forward, and bunched the line. "Watch it!" someone cried out. That was it. No one else said a word.

Coach McInnis called the team to the shade of an ancient oak tree beside the dirt parking lot. "Huddle up, guys," he said. His next line was always *quiet down*. There was no need for that today. Coach's face looked strained. "All right guys, listen up. I know most of you go to church somewhere, but not many of you go here. Some of you don't go at all. And that's fine.

"I wanted to remind you that not all churches are alike. This may not be like any church you have ever been in before. Not all people do church in the same way. Some people who attend church do it very quietly. And some people are louder and more excitable. And that's all right, too.

"These people have lost someone they love and they will be sad. Bart has lost his mama, and that's the saddest thing of all. We are here because we are a team, and teammates support each other when bad things happen. And losing your mama is…is a…"

Coach stopped. There was an awkward pause, and Franklin saw his lower lip tremble. He was chewing it hard, and his eyes were wet. He started over.

"Losing your mama is one of the hardest things that can happen to someone. I know. My mother died when I was fifteen." Coach spit the words out, and now he was crying. So were some of the other guys. Franklin wasn't crying, but his chest ached in the vicinity of his heart.

Coach wrapped it up quickly after that. His voice was clipped as he spoke through tight, white lips, "We are here to show Bart we care about him and to be sad with him. If this church does not do church the same way you do church, please don't make fun of it. Act like the gentlemen I know you are. Now let's join hands and pray."

It was like a ballgame. They always did this right before kick-off, held hands and prayed The Lord's Prayer. When they had finished praying, the team climbed the steep bright stairs to the church and filed into the cool quiet of the sanctuary. The funeral home must have known they were coming, because there were four pews on the left side of the sanctuary reserved for them. The boys shuffled down the aisle and clomped into the pews. Something about adolescent boys isn't quiet or graceful.

Franklin looked around and was surprised. It was early, way early, and the place was more than half-full. There were chairs down the center aisle just like at Christmas and Easter. Franklin knew how much work it was to put them there, because he had often helped do it. He also knew that if they put a person in each seat, and filled up the balcony, there would be almost five hundred people there. This was a big crowd for Laurinburg. Franklin guessed it was because Bart's Mom was the mayor's daughter.

There was a polished wood casket at the front of the church. Thank God the lid was down. Franklin hoped it stayed down. He had heard that families sometimes left the casket open so people could walk by to see the dead person one last time and say goodbye. The whole idea gave him the heebie-jeebies.

He checked his watch. It was one forty. Coach had wanted to get to the church in plenty of time. Turned out it was a good thing they were there early. It gave everyone a chance to get settled and cool.

At fifteen minutes until two, Franklin saw Dr. Mueller slip onto the bench behind the organ console. He had liked her since he was a little kid. She had a twinkle in her eye and always looked like she was up to mischief. Franklin guessed she was at least as old as his own grandparents, but she looked at him with eyes that said, *"let's get in trouble!"* He wanted to be like that when he was old.

When the organ began playing, the pace picked up. A couple of the guys pointed to rows at the front of the sanctuary on the right. Bart's family had just entered the church. Bart's grandparents, Mayor and Mrs. Fitzhugh, sat on the front row with a bunch of people Franklin did not know. Their faces were pale and tight. Franklin's eyes filled at the thought of losing a *child*. Until now, it had never occurred to him that, in addition to being Bart's mama, Mary Catherine Fitzhugh Wagram was their child, their daughter, their little girl.

The second row held Bart and his Daddy, plus a little girl in leg braces. Bart looked more mad than sad as he sat next to his Daddy. Franklin wondered about the little girl, wondered if Bart had a little sister. He had never said anything about it.

Beside the girl sat a small, sad looking woman that Franklin had never seen. Maybe it was Bart's stepmother. Franklin knew Bart didn't like her, but that didn't say much. Bart didn't like anybody.

Franklin glanced up and saw Reverend Wells walk towards the pulpit. He announced the first hymn, A Mighty Fortress Is Our God, and the congregation stood, shuffled about for hymn books, and turned to the appointed page.

# Bart

Bart stood up, grabbed the hymn book, flipped to the right place, and shoved it over to his right so he and his Daddy could sing from the same book. His Daddy's jaw muscles were clenched tight, like he was chewing gum. Bart knew he wasn't. Ricky Wagram didn't believe in chewing gum in church.

Bart saw his dad's jaw muscles, but couldn't read anything else. What was he thinking? In that box lay his high school sweetheart, his Homecoming Queen, his head cheerleader, his ex-wife. In that shiny box was Bart's mama. Whatever went wrong between them, Bart knew that his daddy still loved his mama. How could he not?

And what in the world did his daddy see in Doris? Bart leaned forward and looked to his right, past his daddy, past Stephanie, to Doris. He remembered the scene in the church parlor, not five minutes ago. The family gathered to file into the church. Bart wanted to sit with Grandmama and Poppa Fitzhugh plus his daddy. This was the family Bart was been born into, the one he loved and longed for even now. The one he had lost forever.

Doris would have none of it. She threw a hissy-fit, so they rushed to devise a different seating arrangement.

He was glad she had shown her ass in front of the whole family. Maybe now they would know what he was up against, and someone would believe him. When Bart thought about Doris, he wanted to break something.

The hymn ended, and everyone sat. Bart had never been to a funeral at this church, but he knew the drill from the times he had come to worship with Grandmama and Poppa Fitzhugh. It would be boring compared to the church where his daddy was the preacher, or the little trailer church that his mama went to.

Sing-pray-talk. Sing-pray-talk. Amen. That's how he and his mama joked about Grandmama and Poppa Fitzhugh's church. If the Holy Spirit ever moved in this church, they kept it mighty quiet. In fact, if the Spirit ever moved *mightily*, they'd ask Him to leave.

Bart chuckled, even as tears pooled in his eyes. His mama had been a fun and funny person. He wondered why she and his daddy couldn't make it work.

The preacher called them to prayer, and Bart zoned out. He knew how to do this because preacher's kids get a lot of practice. Just keep an ear open to hear the "Amen," then look up when you hear it.

Bart worried that he never got to tell his mama good-bye. He should have acted like he was going to bed, then crawled out the window, jumped off the back porch roof, and gone to see her by himself. It was night. No one would have seen him. He bet there weren't even a lot of people working in the hospital at night. He could have snuck around until he found the ICU and walked right in.

He would have liked to have said goodbye while she was still alive, even if she wasn't awake. He guessed he could pray to God or Jesus so they would tell his mama what was on his mind, but Bart didn't know where he stood with all that Jesus stuff. He had hung around church his whole life, so he could ace the Jesus test. He just wasn't sure the stuff on the test was the truth.

When the preacher said "Amen," Bart opened his eyes on cue. He checked the order of worship and saw they were right on schedule. It was time to talk. Reverend Wells read a couple of familiar passages from the Bible, looked out on the congregation, and began to speak. Bart listened closely. There was a fair amount that was news to him.

The preacher talked about all the ways Bart's mom had served the community of Laurinburg, and the joy she brought to the world through her service. There was a bunch of stuff she did, working with the Junior Service League, helping start the library guild, volunteering at the Red Cross, that was news to Bart.

What wasn't news was the next thing he heard: "*Everywhere Mary Catherine went, she seemed to carry the light of Christ with her. She brought light to a dark and hurting world. And the world is a brighter place for our having known her, and a darker place for her having left us.*"

Bart's eyes again filled with tears. There was nothing he could do about it. He couldn't even swallow. Perhaps it was the dumb tie over his Adams's apple, or maybe it was the lump in this throat. He tried to sniffle without making noise. He wanted to slump over on his Daddy and weep.

Reverend Wells was still talking about his mama. Bart had a hard time thinking of her as Mary Catherine. To him, she was just Mama. He tried to focus on the words. This seemed important in a way that regular church was not. Bart needed to hear these words about this woman he loved so much, the only person who really loved him just for who he was.

*"More than anything else though, more than her good works, more than her many contributions to the town, we will remember Mary Catherine for her love of people. Anyone whose life was touched by Mary Catherine can attest to that."* Bart felt the puddle of tears beneath each eye overflow and trace down his cheeks.

*"When I met with her family yesterday, they all talked about what it was like to be with her. About how she always had time for the person she was with, about how she was lovingly present, no matter how busy she was. Mary Catherine truly valued people over projects.*

*"The longer I live, the more convinced I am that, at His essence, God is pure, sweet, redeeming love. That God truly loves us more than we dare hope or imagine. And that God loves us always and in all ways. Mary Catherine Fitzhugh was one of the ways we all got a foretaste of God's love, a little bit of heaven here on earth. For that I am profoundly thankful. And I'm sure you join me in that thanks."*

Tears streamed down Bart's face and dripped onto his blazer. He could feel his daddy crying. The pew was shaking beneath them. Bart did not want to cry in front of his teammates, but he could not stop.

He glanced quickly over his left shoulder to see if his teammates were watching. They weren't. They all were crying, too. They weren't even trying to hide it. Bart could see them wipe tears out of their eyes. He could hear their sniffles.

"Hallelujah! God is good!" A shout rocked the sanctuary. It was disorienting, even for Bart. After that, things got so quiet in the church that you could hear the air conditioner hum. Then there was a second shout, "Hallelujah! Our sister has gone to God! Praise the Lord!"

Bart instantly figured out what was happening. It was a lady from the trailer church his Mama and Daddy had attended while they were dating. His mama went back to that church when his parents split.

Bart was tickled. He was sad, but he was also tickled. He found himself laughing through his tears, and realized his daddy was laughing, too. The whole pew was shaking, and now it was shaking harder than ever.

Bart would bet every *Playboy* magazine stowed under his mattress that no one had ever shouted *Hallelujah* in the First Methodist Church. He glanced around. Most folks looked like they had seen a ghost, and it wasn't the Holy Ghost. His teammates' eyes were bugging out of their heads.

He wanted to laugh out loud, but knew he'd catch hell. His daddy would understand, but Doris would get her underwear all in a knot with *what will people think, you laughing out loud at your own mother's funeral?*

Bart jerked back to reality, to his mama lying in the polished wooden box, to the rip in his heart and the gaping hole in his life. Since no one else felt the movement of the Spirit, the rest of the service was predictably uneventful. Bart's eyes stayed wet, and the lump in his throat never went away.

Bart's mama had nailed the Methodist Church routine: sing-pray-talk, sing-pray-talk, Amen. He wondered if she could see the service from heaven. The thought of his Mom watching from heaven was consoling.

They stood for the last hymn, and Bart was relieved it was almost over. He was exhausted. All he had done for the last four days was shake hands with people, eat funeral food, and try to be nice.

He had also cried, but only when no one could see it. He cried until his nose was red and the pillow was wet with tears and snot. He cried until he was out of tears, then lay on his bed heaving dry sobs and clutching the stuffed monkey he had retrieved from the toy chest in his closet.

Grandmama and Poppa Fitzhugh had given him the little brown monkey when he was just a kid. Bart once asked his mama if that monkey had lived at her house when she was little, if they were sisters.

She laughed so hard that tears ran down her face.

The hymn ended, and Bart tried to remember what would happen next. He was thirsty as the dickens and needed a drink. The family was going to gather in the church parlor; maybe he could grab a drink then.

While Bart's family was in the parlor, the rest of the folks would file out of the church and walk around to the graveyard in the back. Mary Catherine was going to be buried in the Fitzhugh family plot since she wasn't a Wagram any more. Bart wondered if there was any way he could be buried with the Fitzhughs. Especially with Mama.

The tall funeral hall man, the one with gray hair that stuck up funny in the back, stood at the end of the pew directly in front of Bart. Grandmama and Poppa Fitzhugh rose and headed to the parlor, with Bart and his daddy following. Stephanie clomped along behind them, with Doris at her side.

## *Franklin*

Franklin watched Bart walk slowly to the front of the church and out the door to the right of the pulpit. The toughest thing about the funeral was looking at Bart and his daddy when the minister spoke about Bart's mama. They were the picture of broken-hearted, all gray-looking, with their color washed out.

Franklin's grief was once-removed. He didn't know Bart's mama. He was sad about the loss, but it was not *his* loss. He didn't feel the gut-clenching grief that swelled in him every time he thought about losing a member of his own family.

Franklin remembered what Reverend Wells said about Bart's mama. It was a heartfelt tribute, and Franklin could feel his eyes fill with tears. All he could think was this: *Bart's mom must have been a different breed of cat from her son.*

Still, Franklin was strangely sad for Bart. He was surprised. They were on the same team, but Bart had tormented Franklin all year long. Bart was an asshole, of that there was no doubt. But Bart was also human, and Franklin could see that in the waves of emotion that broke across his face during the service. Franklin had seen the tears streaming down Bart's face. And once, when that lady gave out with the shout, it looked like Bart and his old man were going to break out laughing.

The shout. Now that was something.

Franklin almost jumped out of his skin when that lady gave out with the first shout. His heart was thumping like a horse's heart in the last seconds of the Kentucky Derby. And the second shout nearly did him in.

He chewed on the lady's words: "Hallelujah! God is good! Hallelujah! Our sister has gone to God! Praise God!" There was not much to disagree with there. Franklin believed that God was good. He believed that people went to be with God after they died. And he certainly believed that God was worthy of praise.

The holy-roller lady got it right. Franklin decided that her shout would be his prayer for Bart's Mom. He closed his eyes and breathed in deeply. Then he prayed, "Oh God, I praise You because You are good. Please welcome Bart's mama into heaven. And thank you, O God."

"Ouch!" Franklin cried out before he even knew it. His head snapped around and up.

"You gonna sit there all day, or what?" Danny had kicked him in the shin. The kick wasn't too hard, but Franklin wasn't expecting a kick while he was sitting there praying. His shin throbbed a bit, and he struggled to orient himself.

"All right all ready. Give me a second will you? I was just thinking about Bart and his mama."

"Well think while you're walking. Everybody else is out of the church, and I'm blocked in by some guy who's sitting here in a trance." Danny gestured toward the aisle and Franklin saw that the church was largely empty. He limped to the aisle, and then gimped his way toward the back of the church.

# 20 | Graveyard

## *Franklin*

Franklin's teammates talked quietly as they walked into the heat and glare of mid-afternoon. The conversations were evenly split between "The Shout" and Bart's crying during the funeral. No one knew he had it in him.

The boys made their way out of the church and looped around the building toward the graveyard on the knoll in back of the church. Because they were sitting near the front of the sanctuary, they were the last ones out of the church.

They hurried to catch up, past the swing set and sand pile for the pre-school, by the picnic shelter, and up behind the shed where the custodian kept his lawnmower. By the time they cleared the shed, they had moved to the middle of the pack of mourners and could see some of what was going on ahead of them.

The front of the procession had entered the cemetery gates and started up the hill. Franklin looked around and was reminded how old the graveyard was. Some of the headstones dated back a hundred years. The Methodists had been in Laurinburg a long time.

Franklin's shin ached from Danny's kick, and the throbbing got worse as they walked up the hill. Twenty or so yards in front of him, he could see eight stout men with Miss Fitzhugh's casket on their shoulders. He recognized them as the guys who were sitting behind Bart's family at the service. The pall bearers were tall, and the casket blocked his view. Franklin wondered if Bart and his daddy were at the head of this sad parade, and he politely pushed through the crowd trying to make some progress

The line slowed, and Franklin ran smack into the people in front of him. They had stopped at a small level spot on the side of the hill. Through the crowd he saw two big green funeral tents. Under one tent was a shiny metal structure that surrounded an open hole. Through the side rails, Franklin could see the gaping darkness of the grave.

Under the other tent stood thirty folding chairs, sitting on lengths of green matting. The chairs faced the grave. The matting was supposed to look like grass, but it didn't. It was curled on the edges from where it had been rolled in storage and looked even less real than the fake grass his parents put in his Easter basket when he was a kid.

Franklin noticed a big granite monument with *Fitzhugh* carved on it. It never occurred to him that Bart's mama wouldn't be buried with the Wagrams. Franklin only knew her as *Bart Wagram's Mama*. But she'd be spending eternity with her own people.

From where he stood, Franklin could see everything. He saw the pall bearers slide the casket onto the rollers of the shiny metal frame, and heard the polished wooden box clatter into place.

Franklin noticed that the floral arrangements from the church lined the area behind the grave. He found his favorite, the one with the deep blue ribbon and *We'll Miss You Always* written in glitter.

He thought about Bart's mama and was sad all over again. Maybe Bart was an asshole because he was mad that his mama had left him and his daddy all alone. Franklin didn't know much about psychology, but the theory seemed to make a certain kind of sense. The crowd parted a bit, and Franklin saw Mr. and Mrs. Fitzhugh making their way to seats under the tent. They looked bent and fragile, like the funeral had sucked the life out of them.

Ricky Wagram followed, with Bart at his side. Then came the rest, filing slowly into the folding chairs. They sat down all at once, as if they had practiced.

Except for Bart's stepmother and his little sister, Franklin didn't recognize the rest of the group. Maybe it was other family. He had noticed that funerals brought out relatives you had never seen before, just like weddings.

For some reason Franklin wanted to be in the shelter of people he knew. It was too late. He had gotten separated from his teammates as they walked up the hill, and none of them was anywhere around.

Reverend Wells had been chatting with the Fitzhughs but, as the last of the crowd arrived, he pulled away from the family and moved to the middle of the funeral tent. The backs of his knees grazed the silver metal railing supporting the casket. He gazed gently at the group.

Conversation waned, and the crowd quieted in concentric waves like ripples in a pond, beginning with the folks closest to the preacher. The quiet traveled out until the whole place shushed. The only sounds were those of late fall in the south: birds and tree frogs and cicadas. The mourners looked expectantly at Reverend Wells.

He began with a brief prayer, then read a passage from the Bible. It was the passage from Ecclesiastes about "ashes to ashes and dust to dust."

Franklin wondered how long it took a body to turn to dust, especially if it was embalmed and in an airtight casket with a big metal vault. He guessed it eventually happened. It was hard to believe that everyone he loved would eventually return to dust.

Next Reverend Wells sprinkled some dirt on the casket and spoke a few more words, commending Bart's mama to God's love and care. He said a brief benediction and that was that. The service was over. Franklin figured they were headed to the bus and back to school.

And then there was a tremendous wailing. A high-pitched, prehistoric, keening sound unlike anything Franklin had ever heard. He couldn't wrap his mind around it. It was like a wounded animal, or a baby who needs to be fed. Or like a lonesome wolf; he had once heard that sound on a nature program on television.

Before Franklin could sort it out, there was an uproar among the

Fitzhugh family under the tent. The knot of mourners parted briefly, and Bart launched himself from the group like he was throwing a body block. He flew through the air, sailed past Reverend Wells, and landed limp and wailing on his Mama's casket. The hardass look was gone.

"Mama!" He wailed. "Mama! Mama!" He was sobbing like a child. His daddy, his grandparents, and Reverend Wells all bent to console him. Bart was still there when his teammates left and headed back to the bus.

No one said a word on the ride back to school.

# Bart

Bart hung his head and straggled to the black funeral home Cadillac. He could hear Stephanie clanking along behind him, her braces clicking at every step. The walk down the hill was tough on her. Someone opened the car door and Bart climbed in. The inside of the car was like a tomb, dark and close.

The tears on Bart's cheeks had begun to dry, and his skin felt tight and too small for his face.

# 21 | Preparation

## *Bill McInnis*

Bill McInnis, and everyone else in town, wondered how the last game of the season would turn out. In the first place, the Fighting Scots had an open date, their second of the season. It would be two full weeks between games when they finally teed it up against Mars Hill. That wasn't the half of it. Bill and Larry had planned to give the guys a break during the off week, and then ramp up the intensity of practice in the days before the last game. The team needed to be fresh and peak just as they met Mars Hill. But all that was before Mary Catherine Fitzhugh stepped into the path of Mr. Roberson's cab.

Coach McInnis spent the next four days trying to help a bunch of thirteen-year-olds reckon with tragedy. And he had to do it while reliving the death of his own mother. The first move was to visit Bart and Ricky Wagram. It was one of the hardest things he had ever done.

Bill went to the house before news of Mary Catherine's death was out in the community. A lone car was in the driveway, and he wondered if anyone was home. He made his way to the back door, no one used the front door in Laurinburg, and knocked quietly. An enormous black lab, tail wagging wildly, sidled up to him and nuzzled his hand.

Ricky Wagram appeared through the window to the kitchen and crept toward the door. He was drawn and gray. Bart followed his Dad and he looked worse.

Ricky greeted Bill, thanked him for coming, and welcomed him into the kitchen. The dog followed eagerly. Unsure what to do next, they stood awkwardly around the table, trying not to look at each other. Only the dog was comfortable, with his tail thumping against a table leg.

Bill took the coffee Ricky offered and chose a chair. The three men sat down, and the dog settled under the table. Silence weighed on the room.

Bart looked from Coach McInnis to his dad and back. Ricky stared unseeing past Bill into the backyard. Bill took a breath and eased into the conversation.

His thoughts were a jumble. He wasn't at all sure that what he was going to say would make any sense, or any difference. But he had to do something. How do you ignore it when one of your players loses a parent? He had experienced it, had been ignored himself. He could not do that to Bart.

So Bill mumbled his condolences and said how sorry he was. Then they sat in silence while he prayed that Bart and Ricky would make it through the days ahead. It would have to be grace. No one could do it alone.

After that visit, Bill picked up with his to-do list. He cancelled practice and planned the team bus trip to the funeral. He paid a sympathy call on Mayor and Mrs. Fitzhugh. Mostly he cried.

He thought he had finished crying about his mama, and was surprised when the grief hit him. But he cried until his eyes were red and his nose ran and his breathing was raw and ragged. He would never forget the pain, and he vowed that he would help Bart in a way that no one had helped him.

All of Tuesday was dedicated to the funeral. When it was over, Bill was exhausted. He slumped in his favorite chair, staring at the television, an unopened newspaper in his lap.

The last straw was when Bart threw himself past Reverend Wells and onto his mother's coffin. Bill felt a sharp pain in his chest and wondered about broken hearts. Wondered if it was a real medical diagnosis, if a broken heart could kill you. It had damn near killed him.

Bill was fifteen when his mother died. It was cancer, although no one spoke the word back then. He watched her go from a vital, fit, athletic woman to a skin-and-bones corpse in less than ninety days. Even now, he couldn't believe how quickly it had happened.

This woman, who could outrun him until he was fourteen, shriveled as he watched. At the end, the only part of her that looked right was her eyes. They shone out at him exactly like they always had, bright with life and light, full of love and joy.

He bit his lip as his eyes brimmed. His situation had been hard enough. Bart's was far worse.

Bart had a daddy he idolized, but Ricky was never at home. And he had a stepmother he loathed with a passion that bordered on hatred. Bill had no idea what was going on there.

What Bill *did* know was that lots of people in Laurinburg didn't like Doris, thought she had come gunning for Ricky when he was wounded and lonely. Bill had no reason to question that assumption.

That wasn't the worst of it for Bart. He began life with a beautiful, loving mother. She appeared to have divorced him when she divorced his father. And now he had a half-sister who sucked up all the love and care in his new family circle.

Bill reflected on the anger that fueled Bart's life. The kid had plenty to be angry about. And now there was this.

Larry and Bill worked the boys like rented mules in the days after the funeral. Wednesday and Thursday were like a mini-preseason camp, the coaches broke the team into position groups and focused on fundamentals. The guys went after it wide open, blocking and tackling, practicing double-teams and trap blocks, stripping the ball from the ball carrier. Both coaches noticed the amped-up level of violence.

The hits were more vicious than at the beginning of the season. Tacklers planted their face squarely in the chest of the ball carrier, then drove him backwards, legs churning and dirt flying from their cleats. Blockers opened gaping holes, annihilating defenders who should have made the tackle. Defenders wiped blood from their scarred knuckles onto their pants, then lined up for the next play. There was a lot of grunting and snorting, but no complaining. It was a ferocious two days of practice.

Something was missing, though. The coaches couldn't tell what it was.

Whatever was missing, it wasn't Bart Wagram. Bart came back to practice the Wednesday after the funeral. Coach McInnis told Bart to take as much time as he needed, but what Bart needed was to hit somebody.

That first day back, a couple of guys tried to console Bart. He wasn't having any of it. He shrugged off their comments and walked away. Bill McInnis knew that feeling.

Bart joined in practice like nothing had happened. Maybe it hadn't. Bill didn't know how much Bart had gotten to see Mary Catherine anyhow. Maybe things were pretty much like they had always been. But something was different.

What was different was this: Bart was playing like a lunatic. He had always been ferocious. His motor always ran wide open. But now he was brutal, even to teammates.

Larry Wittenburg noticed it when he was running a drill with the linebackers. Bart hit Danny so hard that Danny's helmet flew off. Then he threw Danny to the ground and stood over him, glaring.

Coach whistled sharply to end the drill and hollered at Bart. "All right already, don't kill the guy! Save it for Mars Hill." Bart didn't speak, just trotted to the back of the line to wait his turn.

Again and again, Bart hit his teammates with a ferocity that bordered on criminal assault. It was contagious. By Thursday, fights were breaking out on almost every drill, whether or not Bart was involved. The coaches whistled a break and conferred. The madness had gone far enough. They decided to run the guys, and then send them home.

Bill McInnis called the team together and announced a scrimmage for the next day. Then he whistled them to the line for running drills and wind sprints.

# *Franklin*

Linemen hate running drills, and Franklin was no exception. He hated them especially today. He had felt out-of-sorts during the entire practice, like he wanted to break something. Running would not help.

First were the sprints. Then it was running backwards. Then running sideways. Then it was crabbing forward and backward on all fours. The torture was endless. His breath came in sharp rasps, and his chest ached. He felt burning in his thighs and his calves. Finally, Coach whistled them into a circle and sent them home. He reminded them of tomorrow's scrimmage and told them to be there in game uniforms at 3:45.

Franklin's route home took him by the ice house. Sometimes there were chunks of ice left below the hopper of the crusher. If he were lucky, he would find a chunk to suck on as he walked the last mile. He hoped today he was lucky.

Everyone arrived early for the scrimmage. It felt like a game day. The coaches chose sides like kids do on a playground. They flipped a coin; Coach Wittenburg called tails while it was in the air. It landed tails, so he went first and chose Bart.

Franklin wound up on Coach McInnis's team, along with Harvey and most of the offense. It looked like they had half a chance to win. Franklin was flattered to be the third player Coach selected, and the sixth overall. Maybe Coach saw him and Harvey as a package deal. A quarterback isn't much good unless someone can snap him the ball.

With Bart on the opposing side, Franklin knew it would be a long afternoon. He had seen how Bart was playing in practice, and Bart would face him every play. Fine. Playing against Bart would help him get ready for whatever Mars Hill threw at him. *That which does not kill us makes us stronger.* And Bart hadn't killed him. Yet.

The scrimmage was savage. Bart and Franklin fought to a draw, which Franklin considered a moral victory. Bart tried the old fist-to-the-crotch trick, but Franklin was ready. He had bought himself a cup after the first episode.

Not long after Bart hammered him in the groin, Franklin managed to get a good solid stomp of his cleats into Bart's instep. Bart scrambled up, limping and screaming and swearing, ready to fight. The coaches broke it up, and Franklin was grateful.

He was also surprised. *Why* did he provoke Bart? The guy was hard enough to handle anyway. But dammit, Franklin was sick of the abuse. He wished he were strong enough and brave enough to kick Bart Wagram's ass all over the field.

The brutality continued; someone got dinged up every play. The coaches exchanged glances and shook their heads. After thirty minutes of ferocious scrimmage, Coach whistled the boys together, wished them well, and sent them home. They didn't even have to run sprints.

The week after the funeral was a strange one for Franklin. He found himself looking at Bart and wondering what it would be like to have your mama die.

When he had this thought, his chest ached and a lump formed in his throat. He had this experience every day. It started the day Bart threw himself onto his mama's casket, and was still happening a week later.

Franklin would sit at the supper table and try to imagine the scene without one of his parents, like he had erased them from the picture. However hard he tried, he could not make the scene work. He could not see himself without both parents and his bratty little sister. And this left him thinking about Bart.

Bart's deal was a different; Franklin knew that. For one thing, his mama was already out of the house. But she wasn't out of the *picture*, not like she was now, dead and buried up behind the Methodist Church. What would it be like to never see your mama again?

At Franklin's church they had a time in the Sunday service when people could offer prayer concerns aloud. Reverend Wells would pray this long-ass prayer and then offer an opportunity for the congregation to *add your prayer concerns at this time.* People rarely spoke into the silence.

On the Sunday after Bart's mama died, Franklin was astonished when the words "Bart Wagram and his family" leapt from his mouth into the silence. Franklin's mama was so startled she jumped. He felt the pew wobble beneath them. Bart was on Franklin's mind. Big time.

That wasn't the only thing on Franklin's mind. The Scots had a chance to go undefeated. He couldn't believe it. Last year he had been a goof-up, playing on a team that barely broke even. His teammates had kicked his butt every day.

This year he was a starter on a team that might go undefeated. He was holding his own in practice against a *man.*

This year football seemed so important. Like the most important thing he had ever done. Certainly more important than Scouts, or school, or anything that happened in the youth group at church. The anticipation of going undefeated was almost more than Franklin could stand.

# Bart

It didn't take Bart long to realize that, if he thought about his mama being dead, he would go crazy. He simply could not think about it. So he didn't.

He completely shut out the events of the last few days: eating supper with his daddy and Doris, waiting for the call from the hospital, the moment on Sunday morning when his daddy told him his mama was dead.

He didn't think about eating the funeral food brought in by people he didn't know. He didn't think about being all dressed up or the bee he saw buzzing around the flowers at the church. He didn't think about the flower arrangement with the ribbon, the one that said, *We'll Miss You Always.*

And he damn sure didn't think about throwing himself onto the coffin before they lowered it into the ground. He didn't think about Mama, closed up in that dark casket inside that shiny vault six feet under all that dirt. And he didn't think about the hole in his heart. He especially didn't think that.

Instead, Bart thought about how much he hated Doris. And about how much he liked football. And about how he liked flattening anyone who got in his way.

He thought about how he would never get a date and how he hated school and how some of those girls in *Playboy* didn't seem a whole lot older than he was.

Bart thought about all that. And he thought about how much he wanted to pure and simple knock the crap out of somebody.

He was mad, and he didn't even know why. People die. That's how it works. His mother died a little early, but so what? She was already gone, anyhow. She left him when she left his father. So get over it.

But he was still mad, and the best thing he could do with his anger was take it to football practice. On the Wednesday after the funeral he had tried to kill Danny. He had knocked Danny's helmet off, then thrown the son-of-a-bitch to the ground.

"Hell," Bart thought. "Danny's one of the good ones. What's going on here?"

He did not know. He only knew that the moment he knocked the shit out of Danny was the best he had felt since he found out his mama was in the hospital.

# 22 | Showdown

## *Bart*

Bart didn't know what else was going to happen in the Mars Hill game, but he knew this much, someone was going to pay. He had never been to Mars Hill. Didn't even know where the place was until it popped up on the schedule. He found it on a map, some little one-horse burg way out in the sticks. He didn't care, didn't care about anybody or anything. He just cared that someone was going to pay. He'd see to that.

## *Franklin*

Franklin was nervous and couldn't figure out why. He'd gone through the same pre-game ritual as always. This time it didn't yield the expected results. He couldn't ease into his usual studied readiness and deep will-to-kill.

This bus ride was like every bus ride; people sat in the same seats, mostly by themselves. Franklin sat in the back, on the left-hand side. He lowered the window, and cool air flooded the bus.

## *Bill McInnis*

Coach McInnis sat in the front of the bus, right behind Larry Wittenburg, who was driving. Even in the chill of fall, the bus seats were hot. He felt his pants sticking to the cracked brown vinyl upholstery.

Bill looked over the top of Larry's head and out the windshield. The white lines of the highway flashed by, and he knew they would soon be in Mars Hill. *Mars Hill. That's somewhere in the Bible isn't it?* He couldn't remember where, and gave up trying. His mind should be on the football game, not Bible trivia.

Bill didn't know much about this team. The game had been a last-minute addition to round out the schedule at ten games. It was the perfect number of games for guys this age. They would have to play ten games in high school, even on the jayvee squad.

Mars Hill didn't play in the same athletic conference with Laurinburg. They played teams farther west, which made it hard to pick up the phone and get a scouting report. Bill had sniffed around a bit, and he knew this game would be a cat fight.

He was glad it was the last game of the year. This was a great team, and they had certainly jelled, but the last two weeks had been tough. Bill's heart ached for Bart, and he was as sick of practice as the boys were. He looked forward to thinking about something besides football, and he was ready to be home with his family after work.

The bus groaned to a stop, and Bill realized they were on the outskirts of Mars Hill. He stood to address the boys as they drove the last few miles to the football stadium on the south side of town.

## *Franklin*

Coach was talking, but Bart wasn't listening. From his spot at the back of the bus Franklin could see everything. Bart was staring out the window, eyes blank. The muscle on the side of his left jaw, directly in front of the earlobe, was bulging, just like it had been at the funeral. Bart had his teeth clenched.

What Franklin didn't know was what the clenched jaw meant for this game. Sometimes Bart got so angry and out-of-control that he hurt the team's chances. Franklin had seen it last week in practice, when Bart destroyed Danny in the nutcracker drill, then stood over Danny like a gladiator over a victim. It didn't seem right to gloat over a teammate.

Coach kept talking while Franklin watched Bart. There was really no need to listen, Coach said the same thing before every game. Franklin not only knew the speech, he could recite it.

In the game a few weeks ago, the one against Huntersville, Bart had been so revved up he was wild. It was like Franklin against Rock Wilkins, except it didn't work out as well.

Bart was so juiced that he missed tackles, got caught out of position, and misread plays. It didn't matter against Huntersville. They were so bad they couldn't have beaten The Little Sisters of the Poor. But Franklin didn't know about Mars Hill. This might be a different deal.

The bus jerked to a stop just as Coach wrapped up his pre-game talk. Franklin grabbed his helmet and checked for his mouthpiece, tucked inside the helmet webbing. His mama thought that was gross, but it was the cleanest place on the field. The team clattered off the bus and filed through the gate in the cinder block wall surrounding the field.

## Coach McInnis

The Scots' warm-ups were loud and energetic, lots of shouting and exhortation. Coach McInnis noted that Mars Hill looked sharp and disciplined. They executed their warm-ups like a military drill team. Their uniforms were old and faded; they had once been dark green, but were now green-going-to-gray. The words, "Green Wave" were stenciled in white across the jerseys, right above the numbers.

Bill counted the green helmets at the far end of the field. Each team had about the same number of players, and the players appeared to be of similar size. He was glad to see the Scots weren't overmatched, but the Mars Hill team was still a mystery to him.

An official whistled warm-ups to an end and called for the captains. Franklin watched as Harvey and Bart headed to the center of the field. The Scots won the toss and elected to defer to the second half. It was the same strategy they had used against Richmond. Mars Hill chose to receive the kick-off. The game was on.

# Franklin

Danny's kickoff was a high, end-over-end affair that came down at the fifteen yard line. Franklin saw the kick-returner's eyes lock onto the ball, his arms open and waiting. From the corner of his eye, Franklin also saw a blur. It was Bart, streaking down the sideline, screaming.

Bart got to the receiver half a beat before the ball did, driving his helmet under the receiver's chin and violently snapping the opponent's head up and back. The player's helmet flew off and bounced crazily toward the sideline while Bart drove him into the ground like a tent stake. The ball caromed around the field and settled on the twelve-yard line. It was covered by a swarm of Scots.

The Fighting Scots' sideline erupted in a cheer. Bart was up in a flash, standing over his fallen opponent in full-on gladiator mode. He let out a primal scream, but his delight was short-lived.

Whistles sounded all over the field, and red penalty flags hit the ground from every official. When the officials sorted it all out, there were two infractions: violating the neutral zone around the receiver, and unsportsmanlike conduct because Bart used his head as a weapon. The official called it "spearing." No one mentioned the gloating.

The Green Wave team got the ball on the thirty yard line, and Bart got a warning from the referee. *One more stunt like that, son, and you're out of the game.* Coach McInnis called timeout. Seventeen seconds had ticked off the clock.

That first play set the tone for the whole quarter: vicious hits, mental errors, and lots of penalties. The referees were earning every dime they were getting paid. The Green Wave, helped by Bart's penalty, drove the ball all the way to the Scot's eighteen yard line, then fumbled. The Scots' offense took over.

On the first series, Franklin realized the linebacker opposite him was a mean motor scooter. In the space of three plays, the guy slugged Franklin in the groin, tried to gouge his left eyeball, and spit in his face. It was like playing against Bart.

The next play was a pass play, and Franklin was ready. The opponent bulled into Franklin, and Franklin stomped hard on the guy's right foot, grinding his cleats deep and hard into the bastard's toes and instep. He heard the guy scream and saw the receiver burst through a seam in the secondary for a fourteen yard gain. On the way back to the huddle, Franklin stopped one of the officials and spoke quietly, "Excuse me, sir. Please keep an eye on the guy in front of me; he's playing dirty."

"Thanks. I'll do that," the official said.

The Scots broke the huddle, and Franklin bent over the ball to snap it. "Hey, shithead, your ass is grass." It was the linebacker, limping slightly.

Franklin snapped the ball. A flash of yellow-red light tore through his field of vision. He lost sight of the linebacker and everything else. Whistles blew. Franklin sat up to see what had happened, but everything was blurry. He could make out a knot of striped shirts standing about ten yards from him. He overheard one official: "These guys are crazy. If we aren't careful, we could lose control of this game."

When the officials finished their conference, the penalty was unanimous. It was unsportsmanlike conduct against the Green Wave middle linebacker. The official warned the Mars Hill coach, the coach removed the offending player, and the referee stepped off a fifteen-yard penalty.

Franklin's head throbbed in time to the beating of his heart. Boom-boom, boom-boom. He had never been hit that hard. Even by Bart. First down, Fighting Scots. The official blew his whistle. Franklin shook his head to clear the cobwebs and staggered back to the huddle.

The Scots' drive stalled soon after the first down, and Franklin trotted a crooked path to the sideline as the defense took the field. Coach Wittenburg grabbed him by the facemask as he came off the field. "Nice job, Franklin. You okay?"

"Yeah. Got a bad headache. Did you see what he did?" Franklin was still unclear about the play that gave him the headache.

"Hit you straight across the side of the head with his entire arm. The ref said one more stunt like that and he's out of the game. Same goes for Bart. You sure you are okay?"

"Yeah, I'll be fine." Franklin spoke with more confidence than he felt. "That sucker really rang my chimes."

"Take a blow, man, and get some water. You'll be good to go in a minute."

Franklin smiled despite the headache. It was a standing joke among the players. *Take a blow and get some water.* Coach Wittenburg would prescribe that for everything: concussion, broken leg, heart attack. Nothing in the world that three minutes rest and half a cup of lukewarm water wouldn't cure.

The entire first half was a cat fight. Franklin's vision got back to normal the middle of the second quarter, but the headache never went away. Even as the official blew the whistle to signal the end of the half, Franklin's head was keeping rhythm with his pulse. *Boom-boom. Boom-boom.* He would check the trainer's kit for some aspirin. Maybe that would take the edge off.

The halftime score was 0–0. It was astounding that no one had been sent to the hospital. Coach led the team on a slow trot to the far end zone where the managers had water coolers and a tube of paper cups. They also laid out a bunch of sliced oranges on a tray. By the time he scrounged up the aspirin, Franklin was the last player to arrive.

He grabbed a cup of water and a couple of orange slices, then slumped down in the dew-wet grass. Harvey and Coach Wittenburg were talking by the corner of the end zone, probably selecting the first series of plays for the second half. Franklin's head pounded. He stuck an orange slice in his mouth, and reached up to massage his temples. The aspirin was taking its own sweet time kicking in.

# *Bart*

Bart grabbed three orange sections and a cup of water, then took a seat directly beneath the goal post and leaned against the upright. He was not happy. First the idiot official called a penalty on him during the opening kick-off, and then he had to contend with double-team blocks for the rest of the half. He was getting his share of tackles, but he had to work for them. Bart stuck one of the orange slices into his mouth and stared at the fingers of his right hand. The skin was peeled back on all of his knuckles except the thumb. Dried blood was a rusty brown where it had caked on top of his hand. His right hip was nasty where he had wiped blood during the first half. He liked how it looked.

Though Bart was getting slammed, he fought through the blocks every time. This game was the toughest of the season. Most of the time practice was tougher for Bart than the games. A half-smile creased his face. In a million years he would have never guessed, when the season began, that Franklin Gibson would be the toughest opponent he would face.

He stole a glance at Franklin, who was across the way holding his head in his hands. Bart had seen the linebacker club Franklin. He had also seen Franklin stomp the bastard's foot. That trick had earned the Scots fifteen yards and a first down. Not bad, he thought. Maybe I've taught Franklin a thing or two.

Bart wondered if Franklin had tried the trick where he flexed his arm and lifted a finger to draw the defense offside. Maybe he was saving it for later.

# Coach McInnis

Bill McInnis couldn't figure out what to say, so he hadn't said any-thing. He sat atop a cooler with a cup of water in his hand, sucking on an orange and looking at the carnage. Franklin was holding his head in his hands. He was lucky he wasn't carrying his head under his arm. That forearm across the head was vicious and illegal; the other guy should have been ejected.

Bill's eyes searched out Bart. His pants were a bloody mess. He was getting clobbered, but holding up. The Green Wave was neutralizing him, putting two people on him every play. Someone was going to have to pick up the slack if the Scots were to have a chance.

Bill sucked down the last of his water. It was stale and tasted like the old galvanized water cooler. He crumpled the cup and tossed it on the pile. The scoreboard clock showed less than ten minutes remaining in the half time. If he was going to say something, he had better get to it. Maybe it would come to him as he talked.

"All right men, circle up. Shake a leg; we haven't got all night." The boys gathered around him, some standing, many of them kneeling with their hands on top of their helmets. Franklin looked dazed from having his chimes rung. Bart looked tired. Tired and mad, but ready for whatever was thrown at him.

Speechifying was the only part of coaching that overwhelmed Bill. The players always looked at him like he knew exactly what to say, like they were absolutely committed to doing whatever he suggested. He took a deep breath.

"Well guys, when the season started this is where we hoped to wind up. This is what you've worked for all year. The last half of this game is the only thing that stands between you and an undefeated season." He glanced around, his gaze taking in each player individually. He wanted each player to know he was talking to him.

"These guys are tough. And they are playing hard. Ask Bart. He's got two men on him every play. They're tough, they're playing hard and they're mean and they're dirty. Ask Franklin. The guy in front of him brutalized him on the play when the officials called the penalty. He should have been kicked out then and there. But we don't have control over that, and we're not gonna waste energy worrying about it.

"What you *do* have control over is the next twenty-four minutes. What you *do* have control over is whether or not you step up to the challenge of whipping the Green Wave in this half. What you *do* have control over is this: how well you execute, how much you keep your emotions in check, how willing you are to put it all on the line to show each other what you are made of.

"We're receiving the kick-off. Harvey has already got the first series of plays. What I want you to do is go out there and focus. Focus and execute. You boys have an opportunity to do something really special here. You can be the first undefeated Fighting Scots team in a genera-tion. Let's go get 'em!"

The team circled up and placed their hands one atop the other until there was an enormous stack of hands in the middle of a sweaty huddle. Steam poured out of the knot of teammates. A cheer rang out, and the boys sprinted to their spots in the warm-up formation. There were seven minutes left in halftime. Bill's speech had taken less than three minutes, but he said all he knew to say.

Bart and Harvey ran the team through a quick and spirited series of warm-ups, and they returned to the sidelines energized and manic. Whatever was missing in the run-up to the game was back, and Bill was glad to see it. They needed all the help they could get. The receiving team lined up to take the kick-off.

# Bart

Bart was glad he was on the receiving team. He was so jazzed he would explode if he didn't hit someone soon. He lined up in the short backfield. It was a great position. You rarely got to catch the ball, but you could always destroy someone with a blind side block. Opponents were so focused on the ball carrier they didn't remember to watch for you. It almost wasn't fair. Bart liked it that way. He didn't care about fair. He wanted savage.

An official placed the ball on the tee. It was the same guy who had given Bart static for that early hit on the kick-returner during the game's opening kick-off. Bart considered knocking the crap out of the official. He wondered if he could make it look like an accident. Probably not. The official was old, fat, and slow. Like Coach said, Bart would just have to let it go. He didn't have any control over the zebras. He'd just have to take it out on someone else.

A whistle sounded, the official signaled for the kick-off, and the kicker moved toward the ball.

# Franklin

As the whistle sounded, Franklin lined up and tried to focus on the ball. His headache was pushing everything else to the background. The kicker trotted toward the ball, picking up speed as he ran. That's when Franklin noticed the guy had a funny gait, like he wasn't really going to boom the ball when he hit it.

"Watch out! Onside kick!" Franklin screamed as the kicker's foot met the ball. Bingo. He was on the money.

The kicker punched the ball and it squibbed crazily across the field, spinning like a top. As it spun through the first line of Fighting Scots, a mad scramble broke out. Franklin knew he couldn't pick up the ball and run with it, knew it was past him anyway. He saw two Green Wave players converging as they moved toward the ball, and he took them both out with a vicious block. It was crisp, surgical, ferocious. Behind him the melee continued.

"Get him! Get him!" Franklin heard yelling, then the same primal scream he had heard in the first half. Bart. Bart must have the ball. Franklin turned and saw Bart lower his helmet and bowl over two opponents, plus the official who had called the penalty in the first half. Fighting Scots' ball, first and ten, on the forty-one yard line. Bart danced toward the sideline as his teammates cheered wildly. The chunky official struggled to his feet holding his side. Franklin called for the huddle. The Scots were in business.

The first play was a disaster. A blitzing defender overwhelmed the Scots' line and stopped the runner for no gain. The second play worked pretty well; Danny swept right end for seven yards. Now it was third and three. Franklin ran to catch up with Harvey before the team huddled. "Give me a long count," he wheezed. "It's a guaranteed five yards."

"You sure?" Harvey asked. "This is a big one. We gotta get this first down."

"Positive. I've got this guy's number. If it works like I think it will, the guy in front of me gets ejected."

The team huddled around Harvey as he called the play. He told them not to move until the third count. "Listen up and focus; this is a big one. You've got to get this snap count right. We've got to execute like Coach said." They broke the huddle and lined up over the ball. Third and three, ball on the Scots' forty-eight yard line.

Franklin bent over the ball. He could see the defensive linemen crouched in their stances, could hear the breathing of the linebacker standing less than a foot from his hands. He saw the tendons in the guy's lower leg as he strained forward. The guy was set to blitz. This was going to work out just fine.

"Ready! Down! Set!" Harvey was screaming the signals now, louder than usual, perhaps to confuse the defenders.

"Hut one!" No one moved, though Franklin could see the defender inch closer to the line of scrimmage. Franklin readied himself.

"Hut two!" Harvey screamed it, and Franklin flexed his forearms and lifted his right index finger ever so slightly. Pandemonium erupted.

Two Green Wave defensive tackles launched themselves into their Fighting Scot opponents. Whistles shrilled. The linebacker opposite Franklin flattened him, kneeing him in the helmet, and torpedoing Harvey. More whistles sounded as Franklin rolled across the field, holding the sides of his helmet with both hands. His headache was worse than ever.

"Number fifty-two, Green Team, you're out of here!" The fat official jerked his thumb toward the bench like an umpire calling a batter out.

To Franklin it sounded like the referee was making the call from far, far away. He could hear the official well enough, but it was as if he were watching the whole thing unfold on a television with bad reception.

"Hey man, I didn't do nothing." The Green Wave linebacker wasn't going down without a fight. "He drew me offside. I swear he did. Ask the others..."

"Son, that's enough out of you. You're ejected from this ballgame." The official turned toward the Mars Hill bench. "Coach, number fifty-two is out of the game. He kneed the center in the head."

Franklin struggled to a kneeling position and watched. His opponent's shoulders drooped for a moment as he trudged to the sidelines. When he got within earshot of his teammates, he squared his shoulders and resumed his protest. "I didn't do nothing, man. That sumbitch moved his hands. I swear he did! Ask the other guys. Coach, this ain't right!"

The Mars Hill coach waved the player over and sent in the second team linebacker. Franklin had faced this guy earlier in the game. He was a cupcake. This would be easy. Or it would be easy if he didn't throw up, which is what he felt like doing. He put his right hand on the ground and braced himself as he struggled to his feet.

The officials conferred briefly, but there was no question what the call would be: unsportsmanlike conduct on the Green Wave, fifteen yards, first down Fighting Scots at the Mars Hill thirty-seven line. The official walked off the penalty, and the Scots were on their opponent's side of the field for the first time.

Coach McInnis called timeout and Harvey trotted to the sideline. By now, Franklin had made his way to the knot of players at mid-field. The managers ran onto the field with water buckets and dippers. Franklin's teammates sucked the water down. Even with the throbbing in his temples, the scene amused him. They were like puppies around a water bowl.

The line judge whistled for the clock to start, and Franklin huddled the players around Harvey. "Okay guys, this is it. We're going for the end zone right now." Harvey called a pass: two receivers out, everyone else staying home to block. "Hold 'em out guys. This could be the difference in the game. On one. We'll catch 'em back on their heels after the last play."

The Scots broke the huddle and lined up. Franklin fought a wave of nausea as he bent over the ball. Harvey approached the line and began to call the signals: "Ready! Down! Set! Hut one!"

Franklin snapped the ball and met the advance of the new linebacker. Harvey faked to Danny up the middle, then faded back with the ball concealed behind his right thigh. The two receivers streaked for the end zone, one on a post pattern and one on a hitch-and-go.

There was nothing tricky about this play except the fake up the middle and the ball behind Harvey's thigh. This was all about focus and execution: block the rushers, beat the defenders, catch the ball, and score six points.

That's exactly what happened.

The Scots' flanker lost his defender when he threw the hitch-and-go at him, the cornerback slipped and fell. The other defenders had gone for the fake to Danny and were too far out of position to recover. The flanker streaked down the field, and Harvey laid the ball out for him just as pretty as you please. The trailing official raised his hands, and the Scots were up 6-0. The extra point was automatic, sailing through with plenty of room to spare. The score was 7-0. Two minutes and thirty-eight seconds had ticked off the clock.

And that was the end of that. The lone touchdown took all the energy out of both teams, out of the crowd, out of the whole place. Mars Hill Legion Field lost the electricity it had had for the past hour and a half.

The rest of the game was hard fought, but it was nothing like the first half or the first series in the second half. The hitting was spirited, but the execution only so-so. There were fumbles and busted plays and missed assignments by both teams. Even the savagery went down a notch or two.

The Green Wave mounted a long, time-consuming drive in the fourth quarter. It ended with a fumble on the Scots' seventeen yard line. There were five minutes left in the game when the Scots recovered the ball, but the Green Wave had all of their timeouts left.

The Fighting Scots ran out the clock with nine consecutive running plays. They swept left end and dove over right tackle. They waited through timeouts and then trapped over the left side of the line. They snuck the ball up the middle and pitched it wide right. By the time the clock had ticked to 0:00, the Scots were waiting in the huddle, bent at the waist with their hands on their knees, gasping for breath. Franklin looked around; they all looked like they were going to puke.

The official blew his whistle and lifted the ball high over his head to signal "game over." The Fighting Scot sideline erupted in a cheer, and Franklin saw some of the guys trying to hoist Coach McInnis on their shoulders. He looked around for someone to congratulate and found Harvey standing behind him. Franklin slapped him on the butt. "Nice game, man. We did it."

"Yeah, we did," Harvey said.

Franklin thought he was going to cry, but couldn't understand why. He coughed to choke it down. "Way to go man; that was a beautiful pass."

"Thanks. You know I never would have had a chance to throw it if you hadn't gotten us those fifteen yards on the penalty. How's your head?"

"It hurts like the dickens."

## Bill McInnis

Bill McInnis felt the guys trying to lift him off the ground and wished they wouldn't do it. He didn't want to ride around like a Roman emperor. He wasn't much of a showboat, never had been. No need to show up the other coach on his home field in front of the home crowd. Not only was it bad form, it could be dangerous. He had seen some wicked brawls *after* games.

He felt his feet pulled away from the ground and looked over to see Bart Wagram hoisting him up on the right side. There was no use protesting. These guys had earned a celebration. Anyway, Bart was as big as Bill was. Bill felt himself go higher in the air. Now Danny was under Bill's left hip, and Bill felt himself relax a bit. If you had to ride on two shoulders, these were the two biggest studs on the team.

Bill looked across the field and saw Harvey and Franklin greet the Green Wave players for post-game handshakes. Franklin was so much bigger than Harvey that sometimes in the huddle you couldn't see Harvey at all. They were an odd pair, a good pair. And between them they had won this game.

This was the first time Bill had seen Franklin do that thing with his hands. Larry told him about it weeks ago, but he had never seen it with his own eyes, that slight flex of the forearms, the lifting of that single index finger.

Bill almost felt sorry for the Green Wave player who got ejected; he really had been duped. But then he thought about Franklin: chunky, slow and smart, from a family that didn't do sports at all. His only real athletic trait was his brain, and he was playing the hand he was dealt. You had to admire that.

By now the rest of the team had finished the post-game handshakes and joined in the victory procession. They were chanting the same victory song the high school team used:

> *We are the Scots, the mighty, mighty Scots!*
> *Everywhere we go, people want to know,*
> *Who we are? So we tell them:*
> *We are the Scots, the mighty, mighty Scots!"*

Over and over they chanted it, until the tune was long gone and all that remained was a sing-song rhythm. Bill noted that most of his players would never have to cut football practice to attend chorus rehearsal.

The procession snaked toward the team bus, which was parked behind the end zone nearest the gate. Bill noticed that the field was clearing fast, and there were uniformed sheriff's deputies milling about. He sighed in relief. The Green Wave had given the Scots all they could handle. He was glad there would be no after-game fracas as a postscript to an already rough night.

As they reached the bus, the boys lowered Bill to the ground and gathered around him in an expectant circle. He hated speech-making, but it was easier when you won. Especially when you were undefeated. The whole team was looking to him to acknowledge it, to name this thing they had all done.

The bus door gaped open where the managers and trainers had begun stowing the water coolers and other gear. Bill McInnis climbed onto the first step and turned to face his team. They quieted immediately.

"All right men, listen up. This was the toughest game of the season, by far. These guys were good and they were mean. They played hard. Occasionally they even played dirty. And in spite of all that, you won. I couldn't be more proud of you.

"You have done something no Fighting Scots football team has done in a generation, you have gone undefeated!" A cheer erupted from the team, and then a chant: "10 and 0! 10 and 0!" Bill waited a moment for the cheering to abate.

"We'll have lots more time to talk about what we've done, and we'll do that. But this is not a time for talking. This is a time for remembering, for feeling, for savoring. I'm gonna shut up and let you feel what it's like to be a winner. Let you remember all the hard work that brought you to this place. Let you savor what it is like to set a goal, push yourself to reach it, and accomplish something no one else in your community has accomplished in a long, long time.

"This, men, is what it feels like to be a winner. You are all winners, each and every one of you. I am very proud of you. And I love you. Let's close with a quick prayer."

They all bowed their heads and prayed the Lord's Prayer. The "debtor" folks and the "trespasses" folks still tried to shout each other down.

## Bart

Bart blinked back tears, surprised they were there in the first place. His right thigh was a bloody mess where he had wiped his busted hand throughout the game. The second half hadn't done him any favors. His hand looked like he had stuck it in the meat grinder at the A&P supermarket. But that wasn't the reason for the tears. He'd been busted up plenty of times before.

Bart never cried. He'd been fine when time ran out and they had won the game. He had loved parading Coach around the field. So what was up with this? Coach said "I love you" and now he was sniffling like a baby.

# Franklin

As the team clambered onto the bus and pulled out of the stadium, Franklin's head throbbed. When they reached the open road, he realized that he still couldn't see right. The lights of the oncoming cars looked like starbursts, fuzzy on the edges. Even with the bus moving and cool fresh air blasting him through the window, he felt woozy, like he might throw-up.

Franklin's stomach clenched and he strained to get his mouth over the lower edge of the window. He was able to holler out to Coach McInnis before he began to retch violently.

# 23 | Concussed

## *Franklin*

Once he threw up, Franklin felt better. His head still hurt and his vision was out of whack, but the queasy feeling was gone.

Coach McInnis raced to the back of the bus the minute Franklin began barfing. He quickly decided the bus would stop by the hospital on the way into Laurinburg. Bill would stay with Franklin at the hospital while Larry returned to the school with the rest of the team. Bill told Franklin not to worry. He just wanted to stop by the hospital *to be on the safe side.*

Franklin rode on through the night with Coach sitting across the aisle. He was so sleepy he could barely keep his eyes open. Coach chattered non-stop, like Julie when she went out with friends and ate too much sugar.

It was all Franklin could do to hold up his end of the conversation. He felt himself drifting off to sleep and slumped over on the side of the bus. The cold metal of the bus cooled his face, still flushed from the game. His breathing was rhythmic and his eyelids were at half-mast and headed down.

Franklin remembered what he learned studying for his first aid merit badge. Caregivers weren't supposed to let the victim of a concussion fall asleep. It was dangerous. And then it occurred to him: *That's why Coach is talking so much. He's afraid I'll fall asleep.* Another sign of concussion was a pounding headache. Franklin had that symptom for sure. He wondered if his pupils were unequally dilated.

Fear swept over Franklin. Even in the postgame rush of testosterone and adrenaline, anxiety squeezed him tight.

"Franklin! Franklin, can you hear me?" It was Coach McInnis, shouting. The noise magnified the pounding in Franklin's head.

"Sure, Coach. I can hear you. Why?"

"I've been asking you questions and it's like you're not even here."

"Sorry, Coach. I must have drifted off for a minute."

"What month is it, Franklin?"

"Come on, Coach. That's too easy. It's November. It's Wednesday. I think the date is the 17th."

"Okay, showboat. You just seem a little dazed, is all. Here's another one. Who's the President of the United States?"

"Lyndon Johnson. I can even tell you what kind of dogs he has, beagles. Two of 'em, a boy named 'Him' and a girl named 'Her'."

"How many fingers am I holding up?"

"Two. It looks like Churchill's victory sign."

"All right. You made a hundred."

Coach McInnis finished his questioning, but Franklin could tell he was concerned. "You made a hundred, but I suspect it's only because you're smart. How's the headache?"

"It hurts, Coach. If I hold still, it's bearable. If I move at all, it pounds like the little hammer you see in the television ads for headache pills."

"What about your stomach?"

"The nausea has gone away, but I still can't see right. By the end of the game all the Mars Hill players looked like big gray-green blobs. I couldn't even read the numbers on their jerseys. I just blocked the closest blob."

"Well it worked. That was as good a fourth quarter drive as I've seen all year. You guys manhandled them. We ran nine consecutive plays, right up the gut of their defense. I've never seen a team eat clock like you guys did."

"Yeah, it was some drive." Franklin felt the energy of the final drive run through him again. "At the end of the game, it was like the clock was a separate team. In my mind I kept chanting, 'Go clock, go! Go clock, go!' It seemed to take forever."

The bus rumbled over the railroad crossing on the west side of Laurinburg. A few minutes later they pulled up in front of the hospital emergency department. The brakes squealed and the bus rolled to a stop.

Coach McInnis and Franklin made their way down the aisle to the front of the bus. Several players shouted encouragement to Franklin. He slapped palms with Danny and Ricky. At the front of the bus, Coach draped an arm over Franklin's shoulder and turned to say a few words.

"Men, that was a great game tonight. I'm proud of each of you. Coach Wittenburg is going to take you back to the school while I stay here to get Franklin's head checked out. We just want to make sure that he didn't dislodge the sawdust in his noggin."

A few guys chuckled at the coach's lame joke.

"That play with the long count, the one where we drew them offside, may have been the difference in the game. And that's the one where Franklin got his chimes rung. Let's give Franklin a hand before he heads in to see the doctor."

The cheer was loud and long. Franklin could see the faces of his teammates in the half light of the bus, cheering with passion, "Frank-lin! Frank-lin! Frank-lin!" He raised his helmet, and gave them a half wave.

Franklin and Coach then clattered down the steps of the bus and made their way to the sidewalk. They turned to watch as the bus chugged into the dark.

The waiting room lights glared bright, and the pounding in Franklin's head intensified. He was glad no one else was waiting for treatment. Maybe this wouldn't take long. The lady at the window got the information she needed, and then he sat down while Coach went to find a pay phone.

It was awkward to sit in a chair wearing a football uniform. Franklin had a big butt anyhow; with hip pads he could barely wedge himself into the chair. He hadn't been sitting there ninety seconds when a nurse with a clipboard came out and motioned him back to the examination area. As he stood up, the chair stuck to his butt and stood up with him. Franklin was mortified.

The nurse helped Franklin out of his jersey and shoulder pads. He climbed onto the exam table, and she raised the portion of the table under his back and neck to make him more comfortable. Franklin was cold, and the wet t-shirt and cold metal exam table only made it worse. He asked for some cover. The nurse disappeared and returned with a warm blanket, which she spread over Franklin's shoulders and torso. She said the doctor would be in to examine him shortly. Franklin pulled the blanket up under his chin, stared up at the lights above the table, and immediately fell asleep.

## Bill McInnis

Coach McInnis found the pay phone in the lobby and unfolded the scrap of paper with the Gibson's phone number on it. He dropped a coin and dialed the number. Franklin's Dad answered on the third ring.

"Harold, this is Bill McInnis." Coach was glad he had gotten Harold and not Betsy. Harold would take this news better than Betsy would.

"There's no cause for worry, but you need to meet me at the emergency room as soon as you can. Franklin took a hard lick in the Mars Hill game, and we brought him to the hospital to get checked out."

"How is he? Is he badly hurt?" Bill could hear the edge in Harold's voice. Perhaps he would have been better off talking to Betsy.

"Nah. He's dirty but doesn't have a scratch on him. He did say he had a headache and was seeing double. And he threw up on the bus ride back. I thought we ought to let a doctor take a look at him."

"What happened? How did he get hurt?"

"He got kneed in the head. It was a big-time cheap shot. They threw the guy out for the play.

"By the way, I'm not sure we would have won the game if it hadn't been for Franklin. He's a real sparkplug on the offensive line. He's not the most athletic player we've got, but he's smart and he's sneaky."

"He got all his athletic ability from me. The 'sneaky and smart' came from Betsy, but don't you dare tell her I said it. What room is he in?"

"He doesn't have a room. They're just checking him out in the emergency area. I doubt they will keep him overnight. Like I said, it's just a precaution."

"Got it. I'll be there as quickly as I can. Thanks for going ahead and getting him to the hospital. I don't like to take chances with stuff that happens to the head. See you in a few minutes."

Coach McInnis hung up the phone and stopped by the restroom. He glanced at his watch: 10:15. It was getting late. He made a quick call to his wife, and then went to find Franklin.

The waiting area was empty when Coach McInnis walked through it. Wednesday night was evidently a slow night in the emergency business. He ducked through the swinging doors to the treatment area and asked a nurse where to find Franklin.

Bill hurried into the examination room and stopped short. Franklin was lying on the table covered with a white blanket. In profile he looked like a corpse. Bill strode quickly to the table and stared hard at Franklin's chest. He saw what he was looking for as the blanket rose and fell in rhythm with Franklin's breathing. Only then did Bill himself begin to breathe. He breathed deeply through his nose, inhaling the hospital scent of alcohol and pine-scented disinfectant.

There was a rustling at the door, and the room filled with people. Harold Gibson came in, trailed by a nurse and the on-call doctor. Bill recognized the doctor immediately; it was George Creed. Doctor Creed had delivered half the people in town, and he *loved* Fighting Scot athletics. Bill noticed how Doc stepped between Harold Gibson and Franklin, partially blocking Harold's view of Franklin lying on the table.

"Well, it looks like we've got ourselves a crowd here," Dr. Creed spoke first. "Does everyone know each other?" They all nodded in assent.

"Who can tell me what happened?" Doc Creed was down to business.

Bill McInnis laid out the events of the game: how Franklin got clubbed upside the head in the first half, and then got kneed in the second half. He made sure everyone knew that the Fighting Scots would have lost the game if not for Franklin.

Bill talked about Franklin's headache, his sensitivity to light, the wooziness, and the nausea. He soft-pedaled this part, even though he knew Doc Creed needed the whole story. Bill didn't want to worry Franklin's Dad unnecessarily.

Doc took it all in and turned to Harold Gibson, "Has Franklin ever had any other head injuries of consequence? Ever lost consciousness?"

Harold shook his head "no."

"Ever fall hard off his bike, a ladder, or anything of that sort?"

"Not that I can think of."

"All right, then. Let's have a look. Why don't the two of you take a seat in the waiting area? This shouldn't take long. I'll call you back in when I've finished my examination."

The nurse led Harold out the door. Bill McInnis lagged behind for a last word with the doctor. "Doc, I didn't want to scare Harold, but Franklin has been complaining of a bad headache for the last two and a half hours. He even took a couple of aspirin at halftime. He was very sleepy on the drive back from Mars Hill. I talked to him the whole trip to keep him from drifting off."

George's eyebrows lifted slightly. "Anything else?"

"Nope. That's it." Bill was ashamed he hadn't given Doc Creed all the information from the get go. But he knew it would have frightened Franklin's daddy.

"Thanks. You better head out to the waiting area before they come back to find you."

"Got it." Bill knew he needed to hurry, but he had one more question. "Do you think he's gonna be all right?"

"I don't know. We'll just have to see what happens."

Bill sighed, then headed for the door just as the nurse came looking for him. "We wondered where you were," she said. "Will you shut that door on your way out?" Bill pulled the door shut behind him and headed down the hall. He parted the swinging doors and saw Harold sitting across the empty waiting room.

# Harold Gibson

*Waiting is the hardest part of loving.* Harold Gibson had heard that somewhere, a sermon maybe, or a poem. He checked his watch again. It had been three minutes since he sat down, probably only ninety seconds since the nurse had left him. It seemed like an eternity. Where the heck was Bill?

"I'm sorry to have to get you out like this, but I thought you needed to be here."

Harold startled and looked up. It was Bill. Harold had been so lost in thought that he had not seen Bill come through the doors from the treatment area.

"How's Franklin? Did they tell you anything?" He realized how dumb the questions were as they left his mouth. How could Doc have found out anything important in the time that elapsed before Bill left the examination room?

"Nah, he hadn't even started the examination yet. I just told him a little about the game. We would have lost that game if it hadn't been for Franklin. Doc said he thought Franklin would be fine. He just wanted to look him over for a bit."

Bill was dismayed to hear the lie leap from his mouth. It was like he and Harold heard it at the same time, like he could *see* the lie hanging in the air. But he didn't take it back, didn't correct himself. It seemed like the most humane thing to say. Instead he offered up another prayer. *"O God, please make this thing turn out all right."*

Bill told Harold all the details of the game: how evenly matched the two teams were, how vicious the hitting had been, how much Franklin had improved over the year. He wasn't sure Harold was taking it all in. Maybe he was worried about Franklin, or maybe he just wasn't into sports.

Then they sat in silence, both watching the big clock above the nurses' station.

"Did Franklin have his wits about him on the bus ride home?" It was Harold.

"Oh yeah, he was quite lucid. He even made sense right after the two licks that gave him the headache." Bill told Harold all about Franklin drawing the middle linebacker offside on the touchdown drive. How he had just lifted a finger ever so slightly and created complete havoc.

Harold seemed to brighten at the story. Maybe he liked the sneaky part. Bill left out the part about Franklin stomping the guy's foot in the first half. That didn't remind him of something Harold Gibson would celebrate. Or Betsy either. Especially Betsy.

While they were talking, Bill snuck in the part about Franklin being sleepy on the bus ride, and about his taking two aspirin at halftime. It assuaged Bill's conscience a bit, telling the whole story. Plus Harold deserved to know.

Once again they fell silent. Bill checked his watch. They had only been waiting twenty-four minutes but it seemed like an eternity. Now it was pushing eleven o'clock. He was about to suggest that one of them go ask for an update when the nurse stepped through the swinging doors.

"Come on back, fellows. There's someone back here who wants to see you."

Bill and Harold jumped from their seats. Bill was surprised how fast Harold could move. He was quick for his size. They were in the examination room in a flash, and both were delighted by what they saw. Franklin was up, face full of color, chatting with Doc Creed.

Franklin's face brightened when Bill and Harold hit the door. "Hey, Coach. Hi, Dad. Did Coach tell you we beat 'em? Undefeated for the whole season! First time it has happened in years!" Franklin appeared pretty much back to normal. Bill McInnis breathed deeply for the first time in a couple of hours. Harold moved to Franklin and tousled his hair, then turned to George Creed.

"Well Doc, what's the verdict?"

"His head is hard as a rock. You couldn't bust it with a sledgehammer." Doc grinned, and continued. "He did take a pretty good lick, but I think he's gonna be fine. His vital signs are all normal, his pupils are dilating appropriately and in tandem. Everything looks good to me.

"I'd say take him home, scrub him off, and give him a good night's sleep. Oh, and give him the rest of the week off from school or any vigorous activity. Sorry, Franklin, I guess you're gonna have to watch television and read comic books for a couple of days. You can probably do whatever you want by Saturday. Too bad you have to miss a couple of days of school." Doc Creed shot him a wink.

Franklin smiled and felt his daddy wrap an arm around his shoulders. His daddy wasn't much on hugging. Franklin wasn't used to this. He liked it.

They made their way out of the treatment room to the lobby. While Harold wrapped up the paperwork with the admitting nurse, Coach McInnis and Franklin chatted. "That was a hell of a game you played, son. I'm sure your Daddy is proud of you, and so am I. We would not have won the game if you hadn't drawn that penalty on number fifty-two."

"I'm not sure I'd have done it if I knew he was going to kick me in the head."

"I wouldn't have wanted you to do it if I'd known he was going to kick you in the head." Coach grinned at Franklin and slapped him on the butt.

"Come on, Bill. I'll give you a ride back to the school so you can pick up your car," Harold said. "That is, unless you want to walk."

"Thanks. I'll skip the walk if it's all the same to you. I'm probably not as tired as Franklin, but I'm whupped. I'd love a ride."

The three of them headed to the parking lot, Franklin sandwiched between his daddy and his Coach. His head hurt, but the rest of him had never been happier.

# 24 | Celebration

## Bart

Bart stared out the window as the bus pulled into the night. The hospital got smaller and smaller, and then disappeared completely when they turned right onto Church Street. The bus headed for town as Bart thought about Franklin.

He had seen Franklin toss back the aspirin at halftime, watched him wobble on the field after the mega-hits, and heard him throwing up on the way home. None of that was good. Franklin really got his bell rung.

Bart had thrown everything he had at Franklin all year long: slaps to the head, fists to the groin, gouging, stomping, kicking. The kid just keep walking up to the line of scrimmage and going at it. The hell of it was that Franklin got better, and he got better *fast*. Bart had experienced it all season, and he had seen it tonight. Franklin was the toughest opponent Bart had faced all year. Bart knew where Franklin learned his tricks.

Bart's whole body ached, and he had a bit of a headache himself. He was glad *he* wasn't puking out the bus window. He didn't want to go to the hospital. He wanted to go home and tell his daddy all about the game.

The guys on the bus cheered and chanted while Bart mentally replayed the game. He remembered the double teams: one guy hitting him low while another one hit him high, trying to fold him in half. More than once he thought they were going to take out his knee.

Thank God that didn't happen. Those suckers were a handful, and dirty too. He knew the Scots were lucky to have escaped with a win. And they owed the win to Franklin as much as anyone.

Those two key plays were something special. No wonder Franklin's head ached. He had suckered that damn linebacker twice, and paid for it both times with his head. Bart knew what it was like to be tricked by Franklin. He wasn't the strongest kid in the world, but Franklin could outthink you in a second.

Bart remembered the play that set up the touchdown. Here's what the Mars Hill player had been up against: on defense, you attack at the first hint of movement. If a cricket hops onto the ball, you jump. You didn't have time to think, because thinking gets you run over. They move; you move. It's that simple. Pure instinct and reflex.

Which is why Franklin's trick worked so well. The officials never saw him flex, never saw him raise that finger. All they saw was the entire Mars Hill team jump before the ball was snapped.

Fifteen yard penalty, ferocious linebacker ejected, first and ten in Mars Hill territory. It was just enough momentum to squeeze out the lone touchdown. All thanks to Franklin. Bart shook his head. Damn rich kid.

"Sing, man!" It was Danny, whacking Bart on the shoulder pads. Bart looked up. Everyone else had picked up the team chant. Most of them were hanging out the windows and beating on the side of the bus as they sang. Bart sang, but his heart wasn't in it. He was thinking about Franklin.

Coach Wittenburg took them to the middle of town and drove the length of Main Street to celebrate. Bart joined in as the boys waved and hooted and hollered. A few nightowl townspeople waved back. Not many had made it to the game, but they knew what was up. *Undefeated* is a big deal in any town, for any team, in any sport. Particularly in Laurinburg. Especially for football

After dragging Main Street, Coach ferried the boys to the school where they tumbled out of the bus. Most of them were sore now that the adrenaline had begun to fade. You could see it in how they walked, how they carried their shoulders, how gingerly they moved whatever body part had borne the brunt of the Green Wave assault.

Cars were idling in the parking lot, with parents waiting to pick up Bart's teammates. A few guys began to unlock their bikes from the fence around the practice field. The kids who lived closest had walked. They could start home any time.

But nobody left. Nobody wanted to leave. Bart didn't want to leave either. He wanted to feel this way forever. Being undefeated almost made up for having to repeat eighth grade.

Players milled around and parents joined them. Bart heard snatches of a dozen conversations. It pleased him to hear his name mentioned.

*Bart just annihilated the kick-returner and we got the fumble. But the official robbed us with a penalty.* That kid got it half-right, Bart thought. He did annihilate the guy with the ball. But the penalty wasn't robbery. Bart knew he got there early. He had leveled that pissant just to send a message to the other team. It worked.

*Then Franklin drew them offside, and their linebacker got kicked out of the game. You should have seen it. The guy kneed Franklin right in the head. We got fifteen yards on the penalty, and it was the first time we had been over the fifty yard line the entire game.*

Bart was still impressed by that play. He wondered how bad Franklin's head hurt now that he was in the hospital.

*Harvey laid that pass out there just as pretty as you please, and our guy snatched it and raced in for the only score of the game.* That was the ballgame, Bart thought. Undefeated. 10 and 0. Hadn't been done in thirty years.

Folks began to get into cars. Bart noticed that the teammates who left first were the ones being picked up by their mothers. He wondered if mothers understood what it was like to kick ass, to go 10 and 0, to be undefeated. It took a mama a long time to realize her boy was becoming a man.

Most moms wouldn't get it. They didn't understand football. But his mom, his real mom, knew more about the game than half his teammates. She had been a cheerleader, and she knew the game. She'd get it, and he couldn't wait to tell her. He'd call her first thing when he got home.

Then it hit him.

There wouldn't be any calling Mama to celebrate. Not tonight. Or ever. Bart turned away from the team and stepped into the darkness.

# 25 | Undefeated

## *Bart*

Bart wanted to stay and celebrate with the team, to enjoy the moment. But he started missing his mom and he had to get out. A breeze rustled the dry leaves still hanging on the limbs. Bart looked up through the trees at the moon. It was full, bright and white against a cloudless sky. The pit of his stomach felt hollow, like he was hungry. He had often felt that since his mama died. The breeze chilled him, and he shivered. His cheeks were wet where tears had traced down his face. He soldiered on.

The porch light was on as Bart walked up the drive, and he could see the wreath on the front door. Doris made the wreath. It was surprisingly pretty, with orange flowers and a couple of ears of Indian corn in the center.

That wreath was one of the things about his stepmom that didn't fit. How could such a hateful woman create something so beautiful? He couldn't figure her. She had been nicer to him since his mama died. He wondered if it would last.

Though the porch light was on, there were no lights in the living room. Bart made his way down the driveway to the back porch. He smiled when he saw his daddy's car parked in the driveway.

Bart's cleats made a clattering sound as he walked across the concrete landing at the base of the back steps. He took the steps carefully, stopping at the top to take off his shoes before stepping through the kitchen door.

"Hey!" he called out. "We won! Beat 'em by a touchdown! It was, "

"Shush!" Doris glared. "What are you thinking? Be quiet or you'll wake up Stephanie. We had a tough day. She had several seizures and I just now got her off to sleep."

"Oh." Enthusiasm drained from his voice. "Sorry. Where's Dad?

"He's in the study working. He said not to bother him."

Bart knew the second part was a lie. Doris hid behind Ricky when she wasn't willing to say what she wanted. He headed down the hall to the small room his daddy used as a study.

"I said don't disturb him!" Doris hissed from the kitchen.

Bart ignored her and opened the door.

"Hey man! We won!" Bart said it as loudly as he dared, with enthu-siasm back in his voice.

Ricky Wagram turned. His eyes were red and bloodshot. There was a lot of that going around.

"Come on in, sport!" His daddy was whispering, but clearly excited to hear about the game. "Tell me all about it."

"Man, it was great. It was the toughest game of the year. They were really good. No one could score, and the hitting was ferocious. We beat each other senseless, and there were lots of penalties. I even got one myself." As words tumbled out of Bart's mouth, he could see his daddy breathing it all in. The more they talked, the better each of them felt.

Bart told his daddy everything, including the penalty when he inten-tionally hit the kick returner early, before the ball arrived. His dad said Bart was lucky not to get thrown out of the game.

He told about lucking up and knocking the referee on his ass, though he used "butt" when he told the story. Ricky smiled. Bart could tell that his Dad thought it was pretty cool, even though he tried not to let on.

Bart told Ricky about Franklin's foot-stomping trick in the first half, and drawing the guy offside in the second. He told about how the Mars Hill guy got thrown out even though he was innocent. Bart saw a flash of recognition in his dad's face. He knew his dad would get this. Some things can only be discussed with people who have lived them. Bart had read that soldiers feel the same way about their battlefield experiences.

Bart recounted the lone touchdown, and by then they were both having a hard time keeping their voices quiet. His dad was jazzed. Ricky asked a bunch of questions about the routes the receivers ran and the coverage patterns of the defense. He even asked stuff that Bart couldn't answer, though he had seen the whole game.

Bart knew his dad was visualizing the action, living himself into each play: the quick snap count, the dropping back. Two receivers streaking for the end zone, the linemen smashing into each other, grunting and straining. And then the pass, a perfect strike whipped downfield and laid out so the receiver could gather it in and dash to the end zone. Ricky lit up, and Bart knew he had relived the whole play.

Bart wished he could have seen his daddy play football. Ricky had lived this stuff, lived it even more than Bart. He got *it*.

Bart knew his dad got it, but Bart also realized that football was a different thing to his father than it was to him. He couldn't explain it any more than that. When his daddy talked about football, it was like he was reading poetry. He talked about the flow of the game, and it sounded fluid, like ballet.

For Bart there was no "pretty". There was only struggle: violent collisions, hurt and be hurt. There was inflicting pain, and there was experiencing pain. Bart had done his share of both.

They talked until Bart told his dad every single detail about the contest. Doris had long since stuck her head in to say she was going to bed. Ricky glanced up briefly, "I'll be there in a little while." Then he dove back into their conversation. It was the most time the two of them had spent with each other in months.

Bart explained all about Franklin getting clubbed in the head in the first half and kneed in the head in the second. He told his dad that the Scots probably would not have scored if Franklin hadn't given them a little momentum with that second-half penalty, the one that got them over midfield for the first time.

And then Bart surprised himself.

He told his dad he was worried about Franklin. Bart saw Ricky soften; saw what it was that made him a good minister. Now his questions were gentle and earnest. What were Franklin's symptoms? How had they been treated?

By the time he gave all the details on Franklin, Bart was sad again. He remembered winning the game and being undefeated, but sadness over his mom and worry about Franklin trumped the undefeated season. His slumped forward and held his head in his hands.

Ricky reached out and put a hand on Bart's shoulder. "Would you like me to pray for Franklin?"

Bart nodded *yes.*

"Gracious and loving God," Ricky began and Bart noticed he wasn't using a church voice. Ricky was praying like it was just him and Bart and God in the room. "Gracious and loving God, we thank you that you have given us bodies to use and the joy of running and playing and winning. I thank you that Bart got through this game with no serious injuries.

"We pray tonight for Bart's teammate and friend, Franklin." Bart looked up at the word *friend,* but his daddy's eyes were shut tight.

"We pray that you will work miraculous healing in Franklin. Healing in Franklin's body, in his mind, and in his soul. Guide the doctors who care for him. Support his parents as they gather around their son in concern. Comfort Franklin as he lies in the hospital, afraid and in pain." This was the first time it occurred to Bart that Franklin might be afraid.

"Oh God, in your wisdom restore Franklin to health and bring him back to his family soon. We pray all this in your name, O God, You who knew us when we were knit together in our mother's womb. AMEN."

There were tears in Bart's eyes and his nose was running. He swiped at his nose with the back of his hand and looked up at his dad. "Thanks. That means a lot."

"You're welcome, son. Praying for people is the best part of this job. Now you better take a shower and get to bed. You're starting to stink up my study." Ricky grinned at him.

Bart stood to leave and was surprised when his daddy rose to hug him. "I'm proud of you son. You're a fine young man. I'll check to see if Franklin is in the hospital when I do visitation tomorrow. If he's still there, I'll go see him, okay?"

"Sure," Bart said. "That would be great."

# 26 | Foreboding

## *Franklin*

Franklin didn't want to rest. His teammates were heroes the Thursday after the game. They got special recognition on Friday afternoon at a school-wide assembly. The entire team went on stage while the band played the fight song. Everyone cheered and hooted and hollered. It was a big deal.

Would Franklin's mama let him go? No she would not.

He pleaded to go, even if he only went for the assembly. Not possible. That would have been too easy. He had to lie around the house while his mother hovered over him like a hen over a day-old chick.

Resting on Thursday morning wasn't so hard because his head still hurt and he was a bit woozy. By afternoon he was fine and lobbying hard to go to the Friday assembly. His Mama didn't buy it. It was a *no sale* from the get-go.

"Franklin, head injuries are a serious thing. I can't believe you want to shrug this off like it is one more skinned knuckle." She was warming to her topic.

"First you got *clubbed* in the head, and then you were *kicked* in the head." She came down hard on the verbs. "You cannot go to the assembly. You cannot go to school. You cannot even go outside. Go lie down before I have to call your father.

"I can't believe I let you play football anyway." She was on a roll. "It's one thing when you are a pudgy little eight-year-old, running into people and falling down. But some of those people you are playing with are men. I mean, have you taken a hard look at Bart Wagram? You could really get hurt. I read in the newspaper about a boy your age who got killed playing football somewhere up north."

Betsy Gibson's antennae were always alert for anyone Franklin's age who got killed doing anything. Franklin wished someone would fall out of a chair and die while doing math homework. He'd be sure to show her that clipping.

He considered her question. *Had he taken a hard look at Bart Wagram?* Franklin had seen enough of Bart Wagram to last a lifetime.

Franklin headed back to school on Monday. His teachers asked about the head injury and wished him well. They excused him from the homework assigned over the days he missed, and he was grateful for that.

For most students the general buzz of the game and the undefeated season had faded. The weekend intervened, and people moved on. Franklin would never get to savor the victory in the same way his teammates had savored it. He hated to have missed all the celebrating.

Classes went well in the morning. He easily picked up what the teachers were talking about. It was a beautiful day and most teachers had the windows open. Franklin could see the fall colors on the trees, could feel the breeze slipping through the open windows, could hear the birds singing. Even though he was sitting in school, this was almost perfect. His head didn't hurt any more. His team was undefeated. Life was good.

Suddenly, Franklin realized he was hungry. Food had tasted peculiar immediately after the concussion, it was sort of a metallic taste, like chewing on aluminum foil. Nothing really tasted right again until Saturday afternoon, when his family ate lunch at the Honey Cone. He wondered what the cafeteria would be serving today. Whatever it was, he was going to eat his share.

As the last minutes of class passed, Franklin began to feel lightheaded and realized he needed to eat right away. The bell rang and he jumped up, trying to get a head start on the way to the cafeteria.

Franklin collided with Bart, who was heading down the aisle from the back of the room. "Hey man, watch where you're going!" Bart shoved Franklin.

Franklin pushed back. It was reflexive, like a football drill. Bart lost his balance and fell over a desk, landing on his butt. There was an awful racket.

"Boys!" The teacher was on them quickly, and the incident was over before it began. A couple of kids righted the overturned desk. Franklin and Bart eyed each other warily. Franklin wanted to kill Bart. But he wanted to run away at the same time.

He didn't do either. Instead he apologized.

"Hey man, I'm sorry. I didn't know what was going on and just responded when you shoved me. It was a reflex."

Bart didn't say anything the teacher could hear. He just leaned in close and whispered, "Your ass is grass."

# 27 | Rage

## *Kenneth*

Kenneth could not believe what he had just seen.

He tried to get it clear in his head, because he knew he would be asked a lot of questions. He wanted the answers locked down tight before the principal got to him. He knew all about his obligation *to tell the truth, the whole truth, and nothing but the truth, so help him God.* It was a serious obligation, and he took it seriously.

But he was in a pickle. Friends look after friends. That's part of the code.

Kenneth didn't know where the code stopped and the law began. Right now his primary interest was the facts. What *exactly* happened? He conjured the scene. He would tell it to himself so he could imagine telling it to others.

They were straggling in from recess, tired and dusty. Mrs. McClellan stopped by the office on a quick errand. She told the class to head upstairs and prepare; she would join them in two minutes.

Kenneth was at the back of the line and might have missed something at the beginning. He heard someone raise a voice, and the voice became a shout. It sounded liked an argument. Bart ripped into Franklin just as Kenneth walked through the classroom door.

"You peckerhead!" Bart was screaming. Kenneth was startled by how loud it was.

The word bounced off the cinderblock walls and the bare blinds over the windows. Students exchanged shocked glances. Some of them had never heard the word. A couple of guys looked like they were going to convulse with laughter.

"You stupid rich kid! You with your banker daddy and your perfect family! You think you're such a hotshot, big deal football player. Hell, if you weren't your daddy's kid, you wouldn't even get to play."

Kenneth had known Franklin since they were three years old. Franklin hated this stuff. He said you could change lots of things about yourself, but not your parents. *You can't pick 'em and you can't ditch 'em.* It wasn't Franklin's doing that his last name was plastered on half the businesses in town.

"You fat sack of shit!" Bart pressed his attack. Kenneth wondered if Bart had ever seen Franklin go off. Surely it had happened at least once during football season. Maybe not. Franklin and Kenneth were pretty tight. He would have heard about it.

Kenneth had a hint how this might turn out. Franklin was more scared than he let on. But scared people don't always run.

Franklin told him once, "When you grow up fat, you learn to turn around and take your beating *now*. Someone like me has no chance to outrun trouble. And I ain't good at fighting when I'm tired."

Kenneth had seen Franklin fight. It was a mistake to underestimate him. He would beat you with his brain, that and his passion. He couldn't outrun trouble, but Kenneth had seen him outthink it many times. And Franklin could out-hate anyone Kenneth ever met.

When they were in fourth grade, Kenneth saw Franklin take a stick to the school bully, a seventh grader. Franklin beat him without mercy. The last anyone saw of that guy, he was running away screaming threats over his shoulder.

After the fight, Franklin had collapsed, sobbing, into a heap. But the bully never bothered them again.

Kenneth listened closely to Bart's rant. Most of the stuff Bart was saying wasn't true. Kenneth had been to every home game, and was surprised how good Franklin had become. He was a *real* player, not some fat guy taking up space. Kenneth saw Franklin's eyes fill with tears. Bart was relentless.

"You crybaby! I ought to kick your fat…"

Bart never finished the sentence.

"Bastard!" Franklin screamed it so loudly that it echoed through the room. He lunged at Bart. Kids scrambled out of the way. Shrieks joined Bart's and Franklin's curses. Desks toppled. Books flew. Franklin grabbed Bart by the neck, and the two of them landed in a mad, writhing tangle.

It was hard to tell what was happening. For a second Bart was on top, and Kenneth saw him punch Franklin squarely on the nose. The two of them rolled across the floor and slammed into a cabinet. The globe on top of the cabinet toppled onto the thrashing melee, then rolled off the pile and across the floor. When it stopped rolling, there was a bright smear of blood across the South Pacific.

"Someone stop them!" Kenneth couldn't tell who screamed, but no one moved. This fight pitted the oldest and strongest guy in the school against the biggest and heaviest. No one wanted a piece of this action.

Now Franklin was on top, if only briefly. He flailed at Bart with little effect. Bart punched Franklin hard on the chin, and they again rolled across the floor. The classroom was in shambles. All the desks were overturned, and students lined the walls, staring bug-eyed. The blood from Franklin's nose was smeared on the floor and covered the front of his yellow shirt.

They writhed and wrestled and rolled once more. Now Franklin was on top. This time he had Bart by the neck and seemed to have an advantage.

Kenneth was as surprised as anyone. Looking at them, you would have put all your money on Bart. He was two years older, a lot more muscled, and a hell of a lot faster.

None of that mattered here. Not in these close confines. Terrain determines tactics. Bart couldn't get away.

Franklin leaned forward with his hands around Bart's neck. His nose was a foot away from Bart. He squeezed Bart's neck so hard that the tendons in his forearms stood out.

Kenneth could see the veins around Bart's temples bulge, as his eyes went wide. Bart was partially pinned by overturned desks, and he had Franklin's one-hundred-eighty pounds on top of him.

"Asshole!" Franklin yelled, and he began to slam Bart's head on the bloody tile. Wham.

"Bastard!" Wham.

"Son of a bitch!" Wham. Wham.

Bart's eyes widened, then rolled back in his head. Terror was all Kenneth saw in those eyes.

Franklin was out of his mind. His eyes looked like something from a horror movie. If the pupils had gone bright red, Kenneth would not have been shocked. Franklin tightened his hold on Bart's neck. He smashed Bart's head once more to the floor. "Son of a bitch!" He screamed, and it was louder yet. Bart's face was going purple.

Wham. "Bastard!"

Wham. "Asshole! Take it back. You know I earned my place on the team. Take it back. Say it. Say it, you son of a bitch!"

Wham! went Bart's head again. Something had to happen. Franklin was going to kill the guy. Not many people would have been sad. But still.

Franklin smashed Bart's head to the ground. "Say it, you asshole. Say I earned my place on the team! Say it or I will kill you, so help me God!"

Bart's face was getting bluer and bluer. Franklin's face was contorted. He was slamming Bart's head so hard that Kenneth could feel each blow through his feet.

Kenneth could only see the whites of Bart's eyes, the whites with a tiny bit of pupil at the top under the eyelids. Bart opened his mouth, but no words came out. Kenneth wondered what a person looks like just before he dies. He might be seeing it.

The door opened with a bang. "What in the world is going on in here?" Mrs. McClellan shouted. "Stop it, boys! Stop right this minute!" Wham! There was one last bang of Bart's head on the floor.

"Bastard," Franklin gasped. He slumped onto Bart, and they lay there in a blood-soaked pile.

"Whatever in the world is happening here?" Mrs. McClellan grabbed Franklin by the shoulders and moved to pull him off of Bart. Kenneth saw Franklin's face twist with emotion. Bart struggled weakly to get out from under Franklin and the overturned desks. A few students moved toward the pile and began to pull the desks away.

Franklin looked as beaten now as he had looked otherworldly thirty seconds before.

"Whatever is going on, class?" Mrs. McClellan demanded again. No one spoke. Bart got slowly to his feet. He looked like a death row inmate whose execution has just been commuted. When he spoke it was clear he had lost his voice but not his swagger.

"He just went crazy," Bart rasped. Franklin's choking had changed the timbre of Bart's voice. "I don't know what's wrong with him. I didn't do nothing, just teased him a little bit. All of a sudden he lost his mind."

By now Franklin was up, standing slumped next to Mrs. McClellan, his yellow shirt streaked with blood. He was sniffling. She put her arm around him, and Kenneth wondered what would happen next.

Mrs. McClellan was as self-assured as an airline captain taking a plane through heavy weather. "Class," she said, "I want you to straighten this place up and put everything back in order. Susan," (she was the smartest person in the school, probably in the whole town) "I want you to monitor what's going on.

"Bart, head down to the principal's office and sit in one of those chairs under the bulletin board outside the office. I'll be there shortly. On the way, stop by the restroom and see if you can get cleaned up. For heaven's sake, don't talk to anyone on the way. If anyone asks you what you are doing, tell them I'll be there to explain it all in five minutes."

The class looked at Bart. Bruises were beginning to appear on his neck, and there was puffiness under one eye. Bart was such a bully, they all wondered if anyone had ever beaten *him* up.

Kenneth thought Bart would protest Mrs. McClellan's directions, given his reported innocence. But Bart knew he'd just missed out on getting killed. He had only Mrs. McClellan to thank. He shuffled off to the principal's office with as much bravado as he could muster.

Mrs. McClellan turned to Franklin, and that's when everyone noticed he was crying.

She leaned over and whispered something to Franklin, and he nodded through his sobs. The two of them made their way to the door. As they were headed out, Mrs. McClellan turned and leveled her gaze at the class. "No more monkey business. This is quite enough for one day."

The door clicked shut and the class began to turn the desks upright.

# 28 | Recuperation

## *Bart*

Bart didn't know what happened. He couldn't remember much. All he knew was what people had told him, and the bits he had pulled from the haze of his memory. He chewed on the fragments, trying to shape the pieces into a story that made sense.

They were on their way in from recess when he started ragging Franklin about being a rich kid, about getting everything he had just because of his family's name. Bart knew it wasn't true, but Franklin was an easy target. He took it to heart. So Bart teased him all the way in from the playground, then down the hall and up the steps to the classroom.

He could see Franklin getting angry. A crimson flush ran up Franklin's neck and wrapped around his ears. The angrier he got, the more Bart teased him.

Franklin was a strange kid. He'd get mad and then he'd cry. Bart could tell Franklin was about to explode. He could see tears pooling in Franklin's eyes and, just as they got into the classroom, Franklin went berserk.

Bart remembered Franklin lunging at him as desks flew everywhere. He remembered Franklin landing on top of him, and he especially remembered that Franklin was heavier and more solid than he looked.

They rolled across the floor, and suddenly Franklin was astride Bart. He grabbed Bart by the neck and slammed his head against the floor. Over and over Franklin crashed Bart's head to the floor. Franklin was swearing like Doris swore when she used to beat Bart as a child.

211

That was all Bart had.

The head-slamming scrambled the rest of his memories into mush. People who saw the fight said Bart looked fine when he left the room. But he didn't remember it.

He didn't remember the walk to the principal's office or sitting on the bench outside the office. He didn't remember trying to think up a way to pin the whole episode on Franklin. And he sure didn't remember throwing up, or passing out, or anything about the ride in the ambulance.

The ambulance attendant was a member of Ricky Wagram's church. He told Ricky later that Bart had talked a blue streak on the way to the hospital, but that none of it made any sense. Something about his real mama, Franklin, and family. About being lonely. And especially about not being stupid.

Bart couldn't remember anything else until the next day. He opened his eyes and the room was all swimmy. He saw a bunch of faces hanging over his bed, but couldn't make out any of them. There was mumbling, but he couldn't understand that either.

Bart thought he heard his real mom say something. He concentrated hard so he could see her, but his eyes were fuzzy and slow to focus. When his eyes finally focused, he couldn't find her anywhere. He remembered she was dead.

Bart could see his daddy, some doctor he didn't know, and a couple of other faces. He struggled to form a sentence, to make his mouth work. Finally he spit out three simple words: "Where am I?" He was confused. Last thing he remembered was the fight at school.

Bart furrowed his brow to make the room stop swimming. His head hurt so bad he was afraid it might bust wide open. He had never had a headache like this. The lights were too bright and he was cold.

He soon realized why he was cold. Bart's backside was hanging out of the hospital gown. It didn't cover much.

He again tried to speak. It made perfect sense to him, but no one else could make it out.

He tried once more. "What happened? How'd I get here?" And then, "Man, my head really hurts!"

"Whoa," Bart's daddy spoke. Ricky was chalk-white, like people get before they faint. Bart had never seen him look like that. He needed to shave and he looked sad. "That's a lot of questions in a row. Let me take 'em in barbershop order.

"What happened is you got in a scuffle at school and wound up with a concussion. The ambulance brought you to the hospital yesterday, and the doctors admitted you so they could watch you until you regained consciousness. Your head hurts because of the concussion. The docs wanted to see how you recovered before they gave you any pain killers."

Bart had been sitting up slightly on his elbows, but all of a sudden he was exhausted. He slumped back on the pillow and closed his eyes. His head felt like a sledgehammer was driving a railroad spike into his skull.

He was too tired to talk. His eyes fluttered shut, and then opened. There was his daddy, two feet from his face. His breath stunk something awful. He must have given up brushing his teeth when he gave up shaving.

"I'm so glad you woke up," he said. "I was worried about you." Funny. He had tears in his eyes now, but he didn't look half as bad as he had looked a minute ago. Bart drifted off.

When next Bart opened his eyes, there was a whole new batch of people in the room. Mrs. McClellan was there from the school, and his dad was still there. Plus some man Bart didn't know. He was dressed in a suit. Mrs. McClellan spoke first.

"Hello Bart. I was just getting ready to go, and I'm glad you woke up before I left. The class sent you these." She handed him several brightly colored envelopes. There were two yellows, an orange, a green, and a blue.

*Damn nice of 'em* he thought, but he caught himself. "Thank you, ma'am. Please tell everyone I said *hello* and that I hope to be back soon." Bart was astounded how exhausting it was to make a sentence.

"I'm going to leave now and let you get some rest," Mrs. McClellan said. Bart was surprised when he wanted to hug her. She was always nice to him; a lot of the teachers weren't.

"Thank you for coming." It was all he could get out.

"I've had a good time chatting with your father and Mr. Gibson, so I'll leave you in their capable hands," she said. "You do know Franklin's father, Mr. Gibson?"

Bart nodded yes, but he had never met the man.

"Heal up quickly, Bart. We miss you and want you back as soon as possible." Bart waved weakly and she was gone. Nice lady. He hated to see her go.

Franklin's father stepped around to the side of the bed and loomed over Bart. He seemed nice enough. He was fleshy though, and soft. You could see where Franklin got it. Bart wondered if the old man had balls enough to slam someone's head against the floor like Franklin did. Probably not, from the looks of him.

"Bart," Mr. Gibson started, and it sounded just like Bart's daddy in his preaching voice. It's the voice adults use when they are trying to impress one another. Maybe they've all got one. Bart didn't know.

He halfway expected Mr. Gibson to break out in prayer but, being a banker, he dealt in gold, not God. "Bart, I am awfully sorry for what Franklin did yesterday. You can be sure he feels awful about it, too. What he did was wrong, and when you get to feeling better, he'll say that to you in person. For now I just wanted to come by, see how you were doing, and wish you well. I also brought you this." Franklin's dad handed Bart a small, cold container.

"Franklin told me it was your favorite flavor. I thought it might taste good to you."

Bart turned the container over in his hands. Where had he seen this before? It looked familiar, but his brain wasn't up to speed. Oh yeah, the Honey Cone! The team sometimes went there to celebrate after they won a game.

Bart ripped off the top; it was rocky road ice cream. It must have been hand-packed by Tarzan, because there appeared to be four scoops in the small container. Mr. Gibson handed him a spoon, and Bart dug in. He didn't realize how hungry he was until he started eating. He hadn't had anything to eat in twenty-four hours.

"Thanks, Mr. Gibson." Bart managed to get it out between spoon-fuls. The ice cream hit the spot, and he lit into it like a buzzard on a dead squirrel. Every bite cheered him a bit.

"Franklin tells me what a great ballplayer you are, and I've seen it for myself. Y'all have got quite a team. It wouldn't be the same without you plugging up the middle on defense."

"Thank you, sir."

"I'm really proud of you guys. It's the first time Franklin has played football at this level. I don't think he's done too badly."

"No sir," Bart said. "He's picked it up pretty quick. And he will lay you out with a block." Talking was hard work. Bart would much rather be eating ice cream.

"I'll tell him you said so. It will mean a lot coming from you. Franklin says you are the best player on the team."

"Thanks."

"I'm gonna let you get some rest and visit with your dad. I hope you enjoy the ice cream. And Franklin *will* be coming by to make amends as soon as you feel up to it."

*I bet he will,* Bart thought. "I'll look forward to that," he said. Then Mr. Banker Big-Shot Gibson was out the door with his soft pudgy self.

Now it was just Bart and his daddy. Bart felt *little,* like a kid who has just had his tonsils out. He wanted his daddy to take him in his arms and hug him. To rock him and make all the pain go away. To bring back his real mama and to get rid of Doris. He wanted so much and he wanted it so badly.

"How you doing, Kiddo?" his Daddy asked. He wasn't using his preaching voice, either. Bart could tell his Daddy was worried. Ricky was happy to be staring into Bart's eyes and not at his eyelids.

"Not bad, Buddyro." This was the name they used when they were joking around. "Not bad at all. Just awful tired." Bart felt his eyelids go heavy again, and the room went swimmy. "I need some sleep," he said.

"I'll be here when you wake up."

That was the last thing Bart remembered.

# 29 | Reconciliation

## *Betsy Gibson*

The straight plastic chair Franklin's mom sat in was hard and hot. Her bottom stuck to the seat. She shifted delicately, trying to unstick herself.

She was *beyond* distressed. No one in her family had ever had to go to the principal's office. Now, of all things, Franklin had been in a fight in front of his whole class. And Bart was in the hospital. As if that boy didn't have enough to bear.

Betsy had never gone to the principal's office except to receive an occasional award. Even that made her nervous. When she was named most outstanding student in her elementary school, she threw up in a potted plant right outside the principal's office. Even the memory of it made her queasy.

Franklin was a different child ever since he took up with that eighth-grade football team. She was against it from the start, but would Harold listen? No. Not a chance. Said Franklin was soft, and football might make a man out of him.

Shame washed over Betsy, like she had caused the fight herself. She shifted in the chair once more and checked the clock. She had been so worried about being late that she had gotten to the school far too early. They were meeting at 3 o'clock; even now it was only 2:48. Where was Harold? She didn't want him to be late.

This incident could go on Franklin's permanent record. He wasn't even in high school, and he might have already done the one thing that would keep him from being a Rhodes Scholar. That scholarship was her dream for Franklin.

The school secretary caught Betsy's eye. "Those chairs are terribly uncomfortable, aren't they? I wish I had something better to offer you. We don't often have adults waiting to see Mr. Bryant. May I get you some coffee? There's a pot in the workroom."

"No thanks, but that's awfully sweet of you."

A cup of coffee was the last thing Betsy Gibson needed. She had a nervous stomach in the best of times, which this wasn't. She tried to think of something else to say. *Do you think Franklin will get expelled? Does Bart have permanent brain damage? How in the world did this happen?* All these questions came to mind, but she kept them to herself. "Do you know my son, Franklin?" she asked.

"Oh yes," the secretary's eyes danced. "He is one of my favorite students. He's *so* polite. The teachers tell me he's smart as a whip. But what I like best is how kind he is to everyone: teachers, younger students, even the custodial staff. I know you are just sick about what happened, but there must be a good reason. That's not the Franklin I know."

Betsy relaxed a bit and inhaled deeply for the first time since she sat. Perhaps there was hope. "Thank you. He has always been an easy child up until now. This whole thing just breaks my heart. I don't know what to say."

"I remember when my boy was fourteen. Isn't that how old Franklin is?" Betsy nodded, though Franklin would not be fourteen until April. "Boys get that adolescent hormone surge and lose their minds. My son was crazy for a couple of years. Don't worry, honey, it'll all work out."

"Thanks. I sure hope so." She wondered where Harold was. It was 2:55, and it wasn't like him to cut it this close.

Just at that moment Harold burst into the room with The Rev. Wagram by his side. "We just came from the hospital. Sorry I wasn't here earlier. Ricky and I were talking about what it's like to be in eighth grade. We both had our share of tussles, didn't we?" Betsy was stunned by their good humor.

Her gaze shifted to Rev. Wagram. She couldn't believe Harold was calling him by his first name, like they were fraternity brothers. She seemed to remember that they had been in elementary school together, but then Harold had gone away to prep school in ninth grade.

Betsy looked at the two men smiling. They were goofy looking. Obviously, neither of them understood the *gravity* of this situation. Harold motioned to Rev. Wagram and did an introduction of sorts. "Betsy, this is Bart's father, Ricky Wagram. Ricky, this is my wife, Betsy." Ricky Wagram stepped forward and extended his hand.

"It's a pleasure to meet you," she said, "though I could die of embarrassment over the circumstances." She looked Ricky in the eye and thought she saw a twinkle. He was a handsome man, easy on the eyes.

The two men stood awkwardly for a minute, then Harold broke the silence. "I was just by the hospital to visit Bart, which is where I ran into Ricky. Bart seems to be feeling better. What do you think, Ricky?"

"Yeah, he's coming along. I suspect they'll let him out in a day or two. He says his head still hurts pretty bad. Franklin laid a whupping on him from what I understand."

"Oh, Rev. Wagram," Betsy stood up so she could look Bart's dad more nearly eye-to-eye, "I'm so sorry about that. I –"

"Don't worry about it," he waved her off. "And please call me Ricky.

"This is what boys do. I did it, and I'm sure Harold did it, too. Boys are like puppies, trying to work out who's in charge. The big surprise for me is that Franklin whipped Bart. The last time I was here it was because Bart whipped someone. He doesn't often lose."

Betsy took this in. Men were an alien species. She couldn't imagine Harold in a fight. A debate, certainly. An argument, perhaps. But not a fist fight. Never a fist fight.

"Let me get you to come to the principal's office," the school secretary spoke into the group. "He has slipped out his side door, but he'll be back shortly. I expect Mrs. McClellan any minute."

Harold and Ricky stepped aside and let the secretary lead. Betsy was close behind her. The office was bright and colorful. Betsy was surprised that it contained a large round table, and half-a-dozen decent chairs. The chairs had fabric-covered seats. What a relief.

The three of them stood around uncomfortably, trying to decide where to sit. Eventually Harold sat next to Betsy, with Ricky more or less across the table from the two of them. Principal Bryant came in before they were fully settled into their spots, and Mrs. McClellan was right behind him.

Mrs. McClellan chose the seat next to Ricky, and Principal Bryant sat between Mrs. McClellan and Harold. Except for the one chair between Betsy and Ricky, the table was now full.

The show was finally underway. Betsy tried to read the principal's face, but no luck. He was as calm and matter-of-fact as if they were discussing a bake sale to buy new playground equipment. Mrs. McClellan was positively cheery. Betsy was *clearly* the only one who fully grasped the seriousness of Franklin's nearly murderous attack on a minister's son.

Principal Bryant spoke up: "Have you three met each other?" They nodded.

He continued. "Good. I'm glad you all know each other. This is Mrs. McClellan. She was conducting class when Franklin and Bart had their little encounter. And I'm Daniel Bryant, the principal here. I know Rev. Wagram, but I have never met you, Mr. and Mrs. Gibson. It is always nice to get to know the parents of our students, although I am sure you would rather meet in different circumstances."

"Oh, Mr. Bryant, I could just die of embarrassment!" Betsy blurted it out even before it went through her brain

"Don't worry about it, Mrs. Gibson…"

"Please call me Betsy."

"Don't worry about it, Betsy. This is not the first fight between eighth-grade boys at this school. It's not even the first one this month. We don't condone fighting, and we can't have it for that matter, but I have every faith we can work this out." He smiled in a way that gave Betsy hope. Maybe Franklin still had a shot at the scholarship.

The principal continued, "Since Mrs. McClellan has more information than anyone else, let's hear from her first."

Mrs. McClellan looked at each of them in turn. "Thank you all for coming in today. I know you all are busy, and I want to tell you how much I appreciate your being here. It is much easier to help young people whose parents take an active role in their lives." Betsy noticed how warm Mrs. McClellan was. She was the kind of person you would want for a neighbor.

Mrs. McClellan detailed the events she saw and heard. They sounded remarkably like Franklin's account. Perhaps he had told it exactly as it happened. Betsy had always assumed Franklin was selectively reporting things to put himself in the best light. She felt ashamed for not believing him.

Mrs. McClellan mentioned that she had heard "a fair amount" of teasing from Bart targeted at Franklin, and that it had been going on the entire fall. Still, she said, she was surprised at Franklin's attack.

Surprised? Betsy was mortified, horrified, aghast. She didn't even have a word for it. Whoever would have thought it? Now five adults were sitting in the principal's office to decide the fate of her little boy.

Betsy remembered how sweet and round and pink Franklin was as a baby. Since she was a cradle member of the Methodist Church, Betsy had never said one word about this to anyone, but she always thought Franklin looked just like a little Buddha. He was so beatific, bouncing in his jump seat. And now, for all intents and purposes, he was on trial in the principal's office for felonious assault. Her heart thumped wildly.

"Does anyone have any facts to add to what Mrs. McClellan has said?" Principal Bryant's comment shattered Betsy's mental stroll down Catastrophe Lane. She shook her head no.

"Bart said he deserved it," Ricky Wagram spoke up. "Said he had been riding Franklin like a rented mule. He was surprised Franklin snapped. He didn't think Franklin had it in him."

"Well neither did I," Betsy added. "And I wish he had kept it in him where it belonged."

"Oh, honey, this is just what boys do." It was Harold. Betsy was going to kill him in the parking lot.

Harold continued, "I'm terribly sorry this happened, and I didn't expect it either. Franklin has never been much of a brawler. But testosterone is a powerful drug. And nobody has more testosterone than an adolescent boy.

"Franklin has told me he's sorry, and I take him at his word. I am going to drive him to the hospital this afternoon to apologize to Bart. He knows this type of behavior is unacceptable. I think he's learned his lesson."

Betsy fumed. One young man is half-dead in the hospital, my son is almost convicted of assault, and Harold thinks Franklin *has learned his lesson.* She would teach them both a lesson when she got them home.

Daniel Bryant addressed Ricky, "How does that sound to you, Rev. Wagram? Is an apology enough?"

"Certainly. It's more than enough. Like I said earlier, Bart told me he had been razzing Franklin unmercifully. I think Bart has probably learned a lesson from this, as well. It is possible to push people, even people who aren't naturally violent, too far. That's what Bart did, and he got a headache for his efforts.

"Anyway, you have been mighty forgiving of Bart the other times I have had to meet with you. It seems only fair that Bart and I extend the same forgiveness to Franklin."

"That's so gracious of you," Betsy said. "You don't know how much we appreciate this."

"What about you?" the principal turned to Mrs. McClellan. "What would it take to make this right in your classroom? How has this affected your class?"

Mrs. McClellan paused before she replied. "Well," she spoke deliberately, "I have been surprised how the class has responded. Franklin is clearly one of the leaders in the class, and his peers admire him a lot. They are glad he stuck up for himself. They had heard more of Bart's abuse than I had.

"With that said, the class has also been very concerned about Bart. The class, of its own initiative, even took time during recess to make get-well cards for Bart. I took them by the hospital, and Bart seemed to appreciate them."

"Rev. Wagram," Mrs. McClellan turned to address Bart's Dad, "I know Bart has had some challenges in school in years past, but I am enjoying having him in my class. It's pretty clear he likes me, and I like him as well. He is doing good work and, though he is obviously older and more physically mature than many of his classmates, he fits in well and tries to do his part."

"Thank you," Ricky's voice sounded thick as he continued. "Bart is quite fond of you, although I am sure he has never said it directly."

"Is there anything else we need to do here to help you, Mrs. McClellan?" Principal Bryant was trying to move the meeting to conclusion. Betsy wondered how often he had to do this.

"I don't think the group needs to do anything else," Mrs. McClellan responded. "That is, not if Rev. Wagram and the Gibsons are happy. I appreciate your joining us to talk about this. A teacher can do a lot, but a teacher cannot be a parent. It's obvious you are deeply involved in raising these boys you love so much."

The parents nodded their happiness, and it was clear to Harold and Betsy that they were free to go. Harold stood, and Betsy followed. They shook hands all around.

Betsy and Harold headed down the hall to the front door. She waited for Harold to speak, but he never did. She couldn't stand it any longer. "You think this is all very funny, don't you?"

"What do you mean?"

"You know exactly what I mean! Your son has beaten a classmate half senseless. The poor boy has been in the hospital three days, and he'll likely be there several more. We just left a meeting with the principal of your son's school, and your only contribution is, 'Oh, honey, this is just what boys *do*.' I would have killed you on the spot if I didn't think all those people would lay Franklin's aggression on me. You just don't get it, do you?"

Harold pushed on the heavy wooden door and held it open for Betsy. She stepped into the fall sunshine. "Don't get what, honey?"

She could feel heat rising in her neck and wondered if her skin was getting splotchy, as it often did when she was upset. She stopped dead on the walkway and looked straight at Harold.

"You don't get that your son has gone from a plump, pleasant seventh grader, one who never got in trouble and was a perfect gentleman, to some stranger I don't even know. You don't get that, if Ricky Wagram wasn't so understanding, we would be down at the jail, trying to explain why Franklin shouldn't be charged with assault as a juvenile offender.

"You don't get that this isn't some tussle on the elementary school playground. Bart is in the hospital with a concussion. A concussion is brain damage, for heaven's sake, and you act like they were arguing about who could use the sifter in the kindergarten sand pile. This is serious stuff, and you simply don't get it!"

Betsy felt her tension level drop. The outburst was cathartic. She noticed Harold's face go crimson, and wondered what got a rise from him.

"Betsy," he began. He was quiet and measured and rational, but she could see the anger flaring in his eyes. "Betsy, here's what I don't get. I don't get why you don't get that Franklin is turning into a man. He's not plump and pleasant anymore, and I'm damn glad for it. Life eats up the plump and pleasant. You can't run a business being plump and pleasant. At some point a boy has got to grow some balls. This fight is the first evidence I've seen of Franklin growing balls, and I'm damn happy for him.

And for us, too. Unless you have always dreamed of having a eunuch for a son.

"And there's another thing. *A woman cannot teach a boy to be a man.* It's not your world. You've admitted that you are mystified. Let this thing alone. Don't shame Franklin about this. We are going to do the same thing physicians do when they see a shadow they don't like on an x-ray; we are going to watch and wait.

"If beating the shit out of people becomes a pattern for Franklin, then I'll worry. For now, I want to celebrate. It looks like our little boy is learning how to make it in the world of men. Now, will you please just let this thing rest?"

*Beating the shit out of people.* Betsy could never remember hearing Harold swear. Nor could she ever remember him making such a lengthy statement about anything.

*A woman cannot teach a boy to be a man.* She guessed that was true. It certainly had the ring of truth. *Watch and wait…if this becomes a pattern…learning how to be a man…want to celebrate.*

This was all new territory to her. She had no brothers, and there were no men in her wider family of cousins. Harold certainly wasn't prototypically male. That's what she most liked about him when they met.

It was all so hard, and she had such big dreams for Franklin. There was no owner's manual for kids. It hadn't mattered up until now, but this adolescence thing was putting her through the wringer.

"Sure, honey," she finally said. "I think watchful waiting is a good idea." They walked together down the walkway, by the flagpole, and towards the parking lot. She laced the fingers of her left hand between the fingers of his right hand and leaned on his shoulder. She could smell his aftershave, and it comforted her.

They reached her car first, since Harold had gotten there after she did. Harold gave her a quick peck on the cheek. "It'll be all right, honey, I swear it will. This is what boys do when the hormones hit." He winked at her and she headed home.

# 30 | Redemption

## *Franklin*

Hospitals gave Franklin the willies.

You most always left with something cut open or something cut off, and frequently both. That didn't include when you left dead, wrapped in a white sheet in the back of the McDougald Funeral Home meat wagon. Franklin was afraid of hospitals.

Now he was walking to the front door of the hospital on an errand he didn't want to do in the first place. His daddy said it was the only decent thing to do. Said he might as well learn this lesson now. Said it took a big man to admit it when you had done something wrong.

Trouble was, Franklin didn't think he had done anything wrong. Bart had it coming. Franklin recited Bart's offenses: picking on him since the day football started, ragging him about his size, *hundreds* of dirty hits on the practice field. Then there was the last straw, the one that set off the whole episode, claiming Franklin only got to play on the football team because his daddy was a prominent banker.

It was a lie, and Bart knew it. That bastard had it coming.

*I am not sorry I attacked him. I wish I had done it two months ago, and more violently. It wouldn't bother me a bit to kill him.*

Franklin was doing it again. He often obsessed about something until he had pushed out all hope of doing the right thing. As his Scout leader said, "We agonize until we make our worst fears come true. That's when we squeeze out all hope of God doing anything redemptive." How in the world, he thought, could God redeem this episode with Bart?

Franklin reached the steps of the hospital. The late fall sun was warm on his back and a slight breeze played in the leaves. He turned and squinted into the sun. His father was idling at the pedestrian drop-off point. Franklin gave him a half-hearted wave. His dad waved back.

He climbed the steps and leaned into the heavy doors. Nothing happened. Then he saw the sticker: *Pull*. He pulled, and the door swung open. He was one step closer to Bart.

The information counter loomed in front of him, with a large sign saying *No unescorted children under the age of 14 beyond this point*. The two ladies standing guard looked like the ladies at the library check-out desk. They had on pink smocks.

He recalled his daddy's counsel: "Walk quickly like you know where you are going. Don't look at them. You'll get right by them with no trouble. This is as good a time as any to learn this lesson." Harold Gibson made everything into a lesson.

Franklin checked the directions on the crumpled sheet of paper. Take the elevators on the left of the information counter, just past the gift shop. Go to the third floor and take a right out of the elevator. Bart's room was down the hall on the left, room 321.

Franklin switched the container of ice cream from his left to his right hand. He stood up straight, sucked in his stomach, and acted like a man who knew exactly where he was going. Then he ran the gauntlet of smock ladies, walking briskly by the information counter without glancing up. He waited for one of the ladies to call out. "Excuse me! Young man! Excuse me! You need to check in here at the information desk."

It didn't happen. How did his daddy know this stuff?

Franklin made it to the elevators just as one opened. He stepped in, pressed the button for the third floor, and let out a sigh.

The doors closed slowly, and the elevator jerked upward. The hardest part was ahead. Franklin wondered what he'd say when he got to Bart's room. Too soon the elevator doors opened, and he stepped out on the third floor. He switched the ice cream from his right hand back to his left. Both palms were sweating now, even the one holding the ice cream.

Franklin got oriented and headed down the hall. Six doors down the hall on the left was room 321. Bart's name was printed on a slip of paper below the room number: Wagram, Bart; WM 15. Franklin leaned into the enormous wooden door, and it swung open silently.

Bart was in the bed with his eyes closed. He appeared to be asleep. Franklin tiptoed closer. That's when he saw the thick purple half-circles under Bart's eyes. They were dark and puffy. Franklin wondered if Bart's eyes were swollen shut.

Maybe Bart wasn't asleep at all. What if he couldn't open his eyes even when he tried? Franklin listened closely. Bart's breathing was deep and rhythmic. He was asleep. Perhaps the best thing to do was jot a quick note and leave the ice cream. A note would be so much easier. Franklin could tell his dad that Bart was asleep and he hated to wake him. They'd deal with the rest of it later.

He retrieved the scrap of paper with the directions and fished around for a pen. Darn it. Why don't you ever have a pen when you need one? Franklin scanned the room frantically. Now that he was committed to the note idea, he wanted to write the note, leave the ice cream, and get out.

He spotted a pen on the tray table beside the bed. He looked hard at Bart, still sleeping soundly, and tiptoed toward the pen.

Bart shifted in the bed, and Franklin froze.

Once Bart settled down, Franklin stepped toward the tray table, grabbed the pen, and quietly lifted it off the table. He set the ice cream down on the tray table and bent to his note, not daring to breathe. He used the palm of his left hand as a writing surface. The pen tickled as it moved across his hand.

*Dear Bart –*
*I came to see you, but you were asleep. Here's some ice cream.*
*It's Rocky Road, your favorite flavor. I hope you feel better soon.*

*Everyone in our class said to tell you "hello."*
    *See you soon,*
    *Franklin*

Franklin read the note. There was nothing in the note that was a lie or would be incriminating if it got back to his daddy. He could say he gave it an honest effort. His daddy would be satisfied. And he would have more time to think about what to say to Bart. Everyone would win.

Franklin shoved the ice cream closer to the sleeping Bart and propped the note up beside the container. A drop of condensation immediately blotted the note and stuck it fast to the ice cream. He took a final look at Bart, chanced a shallow breath, and then turned to leave. This worked out better than he had dared to hope.

He took one step, then another. Three more steps and he would be out the door.

"Hey, peckerhead, whatcha doing?" Bart said it so softly that Franklin wasn't sure he actually *heard* anything. He turned towards Bart, still lying in the bed, eyes apparently shut tight. Bart slowly lifted his right hand and raised the middle finger in salute.

"Whatcha doing in here, sneaking around like that? I've been watching you the whole time. Thought maybe you were gonna beat my head on the floor again." Bart chuckled at the last remark, and Franklin wondered why.

"Your daddy was in here the other day. Damn nice of him. He said you'd be coming by. Was this your idea or his?"

"Well, I just wanted to…um…bring you this ice cream…and…"

"So it *was* your old man's idea, huh? You brought ice cream, too. Is it Rocky Road? That's my favorite flavor. You bring a spoon? I'm hungry.

"The food here sucks. We have mystery meat and booger-bean soup for every meal. I bet I've lost weight, and I ain't got any to lose. When you've got the perfect body, a couple of ounces either way can make a big difference." Bart grinned like he was the funniest man on earth.

"No, I didn't bring spoons. Haven't you got any around here? What about that table over there?" Franklin gestured toward the bedside table, which held two flower arrangements, a water pitcher, and a telephone.

"Take a look, will you?" Bart nodded to the table. "It's hard for me to move with all these bruises."

Franklin strode quickly to the bedside table and yanked open the drawer. There was a kidney shaped blue plastic dish, the kind you throw up in, and one of those Bibles like you see in motels. Behind that was a box of Kleenex. He kept digging and finally spied four or five of those spork things, with a bowl like a spoon and tines like a fork. "Here you go! See if this will work." Franklin tossed a spork onto the tray table.

Bart ripped the top off the ice cream container, then used the spork to dig in. The spork broke immediately. "Piece of crap! Gimme another of these things, will you?"

Franklin retrieved the rest of the sporks, and threw them all on the tray table. "Maybe this'll keep you covered," he said, nodding toward the pile of sporks.

Bart was hungry. He ate half of the ice cream before taking a breather. "Man, if I eat this stuff too fast it gives me a monster headache. My head's about to bust. It's as bad as when you whipped my butt the other day." Bart winked at Franklin. Franklin didn't know how to respond.

"Here, I'm full. You want the rest?"

Franklin hesitated.

"Go ahead and eat it; I ain't got cooties. I'm in here for a concussion, not pneumonia. And concussions aren't contagious. Here, have some." Bart extended the container to Franklin, as Franklin tried to read his expression. "It's Rocky Road. Ain't that one of your favorites?"

It was, but Franklin was surprised Bart knew it. Rocky Road was what he always got when they were treated to ice cream after a big win. "Yeah, it is. Thanks. You sure you don't want it?"

"Nah, I'm full. Haven't had much of an appetite since you beat me up. Pull up a chair. No use standing while you eat." Bart gestured to a chair behind the tray table.

Franklin pulled the chair closer to the bed. He took the ice cream from Bart and sat on the edge of the chair. It looked like he was going to eat with the same spork Bart had used. It seemed rude to ask for a new one.

Franklin picked at the ice cream tentatively and took a bite. The rich taste of chocolate, toasted almonds, and miniature marshmallows washed across his mouth. He almost forgot his anxiety about making amends to Bart.

He took another bite, a larger one this time, and glanced up at Bart. Bart was looking back at Franklin with a wry grin. Franklin swallowed quickly and was about to say something when Bart spoke.

"Man, you really beat the shit out of me the other day. I didn't know you had it in you. My head has hurt like hell ever since then. What got into you to do that?"

So this was it. This was the hard part.

Franklin didn't know where to begin. He opened his mouth and words tumbled out. "You've ragged me all year, and I just got sick of that shit. You know I earned my spot on the team. My family doesn't have anything to do with it. I left everything I had on that field, every practice, every day. I'm not a great athlete like you, but I gave it all I had. You started ragging me, and I just went crazy."

"Crazy? You went apeshit! I thought you were going to kill me. Lucky for me Old Lady McClellan walked in and saved my ass. I tried to act like nothing happened and shrug it off. I remember leaving the room to go to the principal's office and wondering how in the hell I was gonna hang the whole thing on you. That's the last thing I remember for a day and a half. You really kicked my butt."

This seemed like the place to apologize.

"I'm really sorry, Bart. I know what I did was wrong. My daddy told me…"

"Screw your old man," Bart cut Franklin off. "Your daddy don't have anything to do with this. But you do know I'm going to have to whup you when I get out of this bed."

Franklin studied Bart's face. He couldn't tell if Bart was serious. He certainly looked serious, his gaze leveled through swollen eyes.

"I don't really want to do it," Bart continued, "but you don't leave me much choice, thrashing me in front of God and the whole class. Bad for my image, you know?"

"Well...um...I...um...I really don't much like to fight..."

"Cut the shit, man! I'm just kidding you." Bart grinned widely.

Franklin sank back in the chair. He stirred the remaining ice cream till it was the consistency of frozen custard, then looked up at Bart, who seemed to have gone all serious on him.

"Really, man, I should apologize to you. I've been thinking about it here in the hospital. I haven't done you right. You've worked your ass off out there on the field, and you've picked up the game real fast. I admire the hell out of how you wipe guys out when you downfield block. Really, I do. You're a headhunter. And you're a good guy, too."

"Well, thanks." Franklin was stunned.

"Your old man ever play football?"

"Nah, I don't think so. He was more the Latin Club type."

"I thought so. Well screw him. He's a nice guy and a big deal in town, but a guy that don't play the game is never gonna understand what happened the other day. We're like Marines, man. We might kill each other in training, but we'll fight anybody who messes with one of our own. We're like brothers."

Franklin had always wanted an older brother. No one at his house understood what a release it was to clobber someone on the football field. Even when you were scared. Even when it hurt. Even when you got knocked on your ass in return.

"We *are* like brothers," Franklin spoke. "Only not like Marines, because they are equals. You're more like the older brother I never had. You know how to do stuff, and you're good at sports, and people laugh at your jokes, and you're older and..."

"And I'm dumb as a rock." Bart added. "I've already flunked two grades. Ain't a girl my age who will go out with me because I'm so far behind. Ain't a girl your age who will go out with me because I'm too old. Yeah, I'm a prize, alright."

"Well, you're the best ballplayer we've got by a mile. If you weren't on the team, we never would have gone undefeated."

"Don't matter, does it? Stepmother didn't care enough to come to a single game." Bart said it softly, and Franklin saw Bart avert his eyes and blink rapidly.

"Ah, man, don't."

When Bart glanced back at Franklin, it was plain to see that part of the conversation was over.

"Thanks for the ice cream, peckerhead. Hey, hand me that note you stuck up there when you were sneaking around like some kind of spy."

Bart scanned the note quickly, then tossed it on the tray table.

"Tell all the folks in the class I said 'hi,' especially Old Lady McClellan. She's a good woman. Came by to see me the other day. Tell 'em I'll be back soon. Now get on out of here. Your old man is probably stroking out in the parking lot, wondering what we're doing. It was nice of him to send the ice cream."

"I'll tell him you said 'hello.' But the ice cream was my idea." Franklin made his way to the door.

"Thanks for letting me have some. It was great. See you later." He waved and crossed the threshold.

"One more thing," Bart hollered. Franklin stuck his head back into the room.

"Don't let your meat loaf." Bart gave Franklin a broad wink, and Franklin headed out the door toward the elevators.

He exhaled long and slow. That was harder than he thought it would be. Harder and better. He wondered what he'd tell his daddy. No need to tell him everything. He would leave out the part about trying to get in and out without talking to Bart.

The elevator opened, and Franklin stepped in. He was amazed how light he felt. Like he could leap up and touch the ceiling. He remembered the deep black circles under Bart's eyes, and ice cream and sporks and how Bart always called him peckerhead. He thought about what it must be like to feel stupid and about how Bart's stepmother didn't come to a single game.

All this ran through Franklin's head in the time it takes an elevator to drop two floors. When the doors opened he was light and tired and relieved and sad all at the same time. He floated past the reception ladies in their pink smocks and gave them a cheery wave. He pushed on the heavy front door and was surprised how easily it opened. Down the steps, across the walkway and into the parking lot he went. There was the car with his dad in it, and soon he was in it too.

"So, how'd it go?"

"Not bad. Bart said 'thanks' for the ice cream. He seems to be getting better. I expect he'll be out soon."

At this point Franklin shifted in the seat to face his daddy full-on.

"I really appreciate you and Mama. I appreciate your coming to the games when you can. I appreciate all you do. I never say it, but it means a lot."

His daddy smiled slightly.

"It's what parents do."

# Acknowledgements

When a writer in his seventh decade publishes a debut novel, many people deserve acknowledgement and thanks.

I begin with special thanks to those who taught me to love words, stories, and reading: my parents, my grandparents, and the public school teachers of Laurinburg and Scotland County. I am also in great debt to those who helped me learn my craft, especially Wallace Kaufman, the late Roberta Spear, Darnell Arnoult, Lynn York, and Pam Duncan.

Those who edited the manuscript (Brian Simpson, Martha Brown, Annie Jenkins, and Terri Erickson) improved it immeasurably. The story got shorter, tighter, and better every time one of you touched it.

Mike Simpson first saw promise in this manuscript, which was a tremendous gift.

Judy Dearlove is a writing partner *par excellence*. Thrown together at the Duke Writers' Workshop, we wrote our respective novels on parallel tracks over an entire decade. Thank you.

To my friends who have listened to me complain, bemoan, and celebrate, I offer heartfelt thanks. You are too numerous to name, but too important to omit; you know who you are.

Judy Jordan designed the cover and interior of the book, and helped shepherd the manuscript through the printing process. I could never had done either job myself.

To Laura, my wife and best friend: *How have you loved me? Let me count the ways.* I have turned our guest room into a writing studio and kept it upside down for an entire decade. I have piled countless versions of the manuscript everywhere. I have asked you to read multiple rewrites of every chapter, and you have done it with patience and good humor. You have tolerated all this and so much more. I am blessed and I know it. Thanks for everything. You are a gift beyond measure.

# Reading Group Guide

1.  Franklin and Bart are very aware of their differences. What differences struck you most? For most of the book, the boys never acknowledge the ways they are similar. What do Bart and Franklin have in common?

2.  The book is set in 1965. How might this story be different if it took place in the present day?

3.  It's clear that most people in Laurinburg either know each other or know someone who knows the person in question. How does this inform the book? In what size town did you live when you were in eighth grade? How was your experience similar to, or different from, the experiences Franklin and Bart had?

4.  Both Bart and Franklin would tell you their story was about football and conflict, but a great deal of the story also has religious overtones. How did the boys' different religious backgrounds inform the story? What do you make of the conversion Bart's grandfather experienced at the tent meeting? How did the presentation of religious themes compare to your own experience?

5.  If football is about conflict, religion, at its best, is about reconciliation and healing. What were the driving forces you noticed behind the reconciliation that took place in the narrative?

6.  Football is more than a contact sport; it is a *collision* sport. If you played football, did the scenes involving the game ring true?

    If you never played football, what feelings did the violence of the game elicit?

What was your response to some of the more-underhanded tactics (hitting opponents in the groin, stomping feet with cleats, setting an opponent up to get penalized, drawing an opponent offside) the players used?

7.    There is a story about a veteran football player who, in an interview, remarked: *Some people play football like it is a game. I never was one of those. I played the game like it was a referendum on my right to exist. It was societally sanctioned rage, and it saved my life.* Do you think this statement applies to Bart? How about Franklin? Why?

8.    As we move through the narrative, it is clear that Bart and Franklin are both thinking about what it means to be a man. In Chapter Two, the narrator tells us: *Bart stiffened his back, pulled himself up to his full height, and stood ramrod straight like a Marine.* In Chapter Thirty, the narrator describes Franklin walking by the reception desk at the hospital: *He stood up straight, sucked in his stomach, and acted like a man who knew exactly where he was going.*

It is easy to laugh at these caricatures, but they raise an important question. What behaviors are authentically male? How, if at all, are authentic male behaviors different from authentic female behaviors?

9.    When Doris Wagram goes for counseling with Robert Inman (Chapter Seventeen) she remarks: *A woman cannot teach a boy to be a man.* Franklin's father says the same thing after he and Franklin's mom meet with the school principal (Chapter Twenty-nine). What point do you think these characters are trying to convey with this statement? Do you agree?

10.    Reflect on the book's ending. Why do you think, after twenty-plus chapters of laying waste to each other, Franklin and Bart

were able to reach a rapprochement so quickly? What things do the boys have in common at the end of the book that they did not share at the beginning?

# A Conversation with Frank McNair

**Q:** How did you come to your life as a writer? Have you always written?

**A:** I have always *liked* to write. You would have to ask someone else if I have always been a legitimate writer. My love of writing began in Nancy Liles' third grade class when we were asked to write a poem. I somehow cobbled together four rhymed couplets, which I still remember and can still recite. I was hooked from that moment.

Most of my professional life required writing: proposals, market research summaries, strategy documents, and marketing plans. I wrote a couple of nonfiction books (*How You Make the Sale*, *The Golden Rules for Managers*) for the business market, and they were well received.

I keep up an active personal correspondence. I am extraverted and writing is, to me, just conversation on the page. I love to write.

**Q:** How did you begin the book?

**A:** *Life on the Line* had its beginnings in a class taught by Lynn York at the Duke Writers' Workshop in 2007. The first scene was the incident in Chapter One where Franklin surprises his football coach and knocks him down. I had no idea what would happen next.

**Q:** When you began the book, did you know how it would end?

**A:** Heavens no! I didn't even know it was a book. I just knew the first page and a half were pretty engaging, and I wanted to know what happened next. I wanted to see how the characters developed.

**Q:** What surprised you most about the book as it unfolded?

**A:** I was, and still am, surprised how layered and rich and complex the book became.

Who knew there would be a funeral, or a religious conversion in the middle of a summer tent meeting? Who knew there would be an undefeated season, two concussions, or the Brawl of the Century?

The only character I knew when the book began was Franklin, so I thought it was his story. But this story also belongs to Bart, and to Ricky, Doris, and Coach McInnis. And it belongs to Betsy, Harold, Coach Wittenburg and the myriad other characters who inhabit the tale.

**Q: Your biography indicates that you played football. How true-to-life are the football scenes in the book?**

**A:** They are as real as I could make them. Everything in the book either happened to me or to someone I know. Most of the things I did myself. I had a friend read the final draft of the book, this is someone who really knows football, and she was stunned by the violence of the football scenes.

Football is a great game for learning many lessons. It taught me (a weepy, chunky, clumsy, poet of a kid) to get up when life knocks you down. And it teaches teamwork in a way that most games can't. (Where else do eleven people have to do exactly what they are supposed to do, at exactly the same time, to have success?) But it is violent, and the potential for injury is very real. I especially worry about the potential for head injuries.

I played football seriously from 1965-1975, and sporadically up through 1981. Players are so much bigger now than they were when I played. I couldn't make a good 1-A high school team now, given the size I was in high school. And I was big enough to be a (lightly) recruited college prospect when I graduated in 1970.

**Q: Are you Franklin Gibson?**

**A:** No. Franklin and I have some things in common (write what you know, they say) but I am not Franklin Gibson.

244

**Q:** **Are any of the other characters based on real people?**

**A:** No. This is work of fiction. I have used names that occurred to me in the writing, and I actually know people with some of these names. But this is a work of fiction. In particular, there is not, nor has there ever been, a real-life version of Bart Wagram or of any of the people in Bart's nuclear or extended family.

**Q:** **Who is your favorite character and why?**

**A:** This is like asking a parent to choose a favorite child; it's not a fair question or one I can answer. I admire Bart's grit and envy his athleticism. Franklin reminds me of myself, a fat kid with a pretty good brain, but not much facility with sports. There is, I am sad to say, some of Doris Wagram in me and in most of us. Betsy Gibson is like many people in that she worries too much and catastrophizes to the point of madness. I have compassion for all of these people, and there is probably a bit of each of them in me.

**Q:** **What do you think Life on the Line is about? Did the focus of the book change as you wrote it?**

**A:** When I began the book, the first scene was about football. So I thought the book was going to be about football, and probably would be pitched to a middle-grade demographic. As the book grew, it also *grew up*. The theme expanded far beyond sports to encompass male adolescence and coming-of-age, family relation-ships, religion, and the pain that human beings experience and inflict on one another.

In the end, I think the book is about redemption, as I hope most of life is. And it seems to me that this book is appropriate for all adults and for students in late middle school or above.

**Q:** **Do you have other projects in the works?**

**A:** I came to writing first as a poet and continue to write and submit poetry occasionally (and with little success.) While writing *Life on the Line* there was a season when I was stuck and didn't know what to do next. During that time I began a second novel entitled *A Creeping Certainty*, which explores the deepening faith journey of two middle-aged men.

I like to write and will probably write, if only for myself, until they are shoveling dirt onto my coffin.

# About the Author

Frank McNair, author of *Life on the Line*, grew up and played football in small-town southeastern North Carolina. Frank studied at the Duke Writer's Workshop, and *Life on the Line* is his first novel. He is working on a second book, this one about the life of Christian faith, entitled *A Creeping Certainty*.

He graduated from the University of North Carolina, where he was a Morehead Scholar and an undistinguished student. After a brief stint in banking, Frank entered the MBA program at Wake Forest University, graduating in 1978. For a decade he held a range of sales and marketing positions in the corporate world. In 1988, Frank joined his wife, Laura, in her consulting and training business. They have been business partners in McNair & McNair for thirty years.

Frank has written two non-fiction books for business readers: *The Golden Rules for Managers* and *How You Make the Sale*. Both are available online and wherever books are sold.

Laura and Frank are active members of their church community where they teach, visit, and participate in mission trips. They live with their beloved chocolate lab, Buddy Brown, in a house overlooking the woods in Winston-Salem, NC.